# *Ill Met by Murder*

## Also by Elizabeth J. Duncan

**Shakespeare in the Catskills**

*Untimely Death*

**Penny Brannigan**

*Murder on the Hour*

*Slated for Death*

*Never Laugh as a Hearse Goes By*

*A Small Hill to Die On*

*A Killer's Christmas in Wales*

*A Brush with Death*

*The Cold Light of Mourning*

# Ill Met by Murder

## A Shakespeare in the Catskills Mystery

Elizabeth J. Duncan

NEW YORK

This is a work of fiction. All of the names, characters, organizations, places and events portrayed in this novel are either products of the author's imagination or are used fictitiously. Any resemblance to real or actual events, locales, or persons, living or dead, is entirely coincidental.



Published in the United States by Crooked Lane Books, an imprint of
The Quick Brown Fox & Company LLC.

Crooked Lane Books and its logo are trademarks of The Quick Brown Fox & Company LLC.

Library of Congress Catalog-in-Publication data available upon request.

ISBN (paperback): 978-1-68331-501-8
ISBN (hardcover): 978-1-62953-769-6
ISBN (ePub): 978-1-62953-792-4
ISBN (Kindle): 978-1-62953-793-1
ISBN (ePDF): 978-1-62953-794-8

Cover illustration by Stephen Gardner
Book design by Jennifer Canzone

Printed in the United States.

www.crookedlanebooks.com

Crooked Lane Books
34 West 27th St., 10th Floor
New York, NY 10001

Hardcover Edition: December 2016
Paperback Edition: October 2017

*To Fredrik, Luis, and Ryan*
Million Dollar Listing New York

# Chapter 1

It's not every day a gleaming, burgundy Rolls-Royce proceeds down the long driveway of Jacobs Grand Hotel. So it was with some interest that the woman walking a small dog on a beautiful May afternoon and her young male companion stood on the grassy edge of the roadway and watched the classic car go by.

Because the vehicle was being driven at such a slow, stately pace, they had plenty of time to examine the occupants. An elderly man wearing an old-fashioned peaked chauffeur's cap crouched behind the steering wheel, and in the back seat, a woman with dark hair pulled back in an immaculate chignon stared straight ahead, revealing a rather patrician profile.

"Who was that?" asked the young man when the vehicle had passed, allowing the threesome to move back into the middle of the gravel driveway to continue their approach to the hotel.

"That lady," replied Charlotte Fairfax, "was our patron and chief benefactor, Mrs. Paula Van Dusen."

"Huh. I wonder what she was doing here."

"Meeting with your uncle to discuss arrangements for this year's production up at her estate, I expect. She hosts an annual fundraiser for us. We do a one-time performance, and her rich friends pay heaps of money to come up from the city to sit on lawn chairs and watch."

"Why would this Van Dusen lady want to do that?"

"Because she fancies herself a patron of the arts; she's in a position to help because she knows all the right people with deep pockets, and because she has a soft spot for all things theatrical. Especially actors, or so I'm told."

"This play up at her estate. Sounds like fun."

"Fun." Charlotte turned the word over in her mind. "I suppose whether it's fun or not depends on your perspective, but all things considered, yes, it's fun. It's outdoors, on a lovely summer evening in the Catskills, and the audience members bring their own picnics. Hampers filled with smoked salmon and champagne." She grinned at the young man. "And it's fun for the actors because they get to do something special for just this one performance, once a year."

Aaron Jacobs raised an eyebrow and shot her a questioning look.

"The male actors play all the female parts, just like they did in Shakespeare's day."

"Isn't that a lot of work for just one performance? Memorizing all those lines?"

"Not as much work as you'd think. They're pretty familiar with all the lines from so many rehearsals and performances, and they perform a shortened version of the play, so there's not as much for them to remember. And to be honest, this production is pretty relaxed, so nobody really minds the odd flub or two. You won't want to miss it. And you won't miss it, because you'll be there with me, working."

They were approaching the front entrance to the hotel. Although it was nowhere near as grand as it used to be, the whitewashed, stuccoed main building, with its entrance portico, retained a certain vintage appeal. Built in the 1950s by the current owner's grandparents, the hotel had witnessed the glorious heyday of the Catskills as the summer holiday destination for Jewish families seeking refuge from the heat of New York City. But by the end of the 1970s, the Catskills had had their day, and one by one, most of the old hotels were abandoned to a slow, eerie decay or destroyed by fire. Jacobs Grand was one of only a handful to survive, mainly because the current owner's grandmother had launched a small Shakespeare festival one summer, attracting bard buffs from across the state. The festival grew into the Catskills Shakespeare Theater Company and was now the hotel's bread and butter. Shakespeare turned out to be an inspired choice. Summer stock theater with kirtles and partlets instead of boaters and parasols.

Charlotte and her companions—Aaron Jacobs, nephew of Harvey Jacobs, the hotel and theater company owner, and Rupert, her black, red, and white corgi—continued on past the front entrance and made their way around the side of the building to the staff entrance. This led to a maze of corridors that linked the kitchens, theater backstage area, rehearsal rooms, Charlotte's costume department, and eventually, by a circuitous, winding route, the front lobby.

At the sound of voices from the backstage area, they hesitated and then walked toward them. Two men seated on plastic chairs were deep in a lively conversation.

"Harvey, I hate abbreviated, simplified Shakespeare," said Simon Dyer, the theater company's resident director. "It just seems totally wrong. Plays should be performed the way the author intended them and in the language the author used, even if they are four hundred years old. It's what the audience expects. Especially our audience. They come to see real Shakespeare, not dumbed-down Shakespeare."

"But we do this every year," protested Harvey Jacobs. "I'm sorry, Simon, but this is the way it's got to be. Mrs. Van Dusen is our main patron, and she raises a lot of money for our company. Money that . . ." He hesitated as he caught sight of Charlotte and his nephew, Aaron, lurking in the wings and gestured toward them. "Money that is used for costumes, sets, and so on."

"Charlotte says it's actually quite fun," said Aaron, as he and Charlotte, holding Rupert's leash, came closer.

"Does she now?" Simon replied, throwing them a frosty glare.

"And it isn't just about the play," Harvey continued. "Most of the people who attend the performance stay for the weekend, and many of them book into our hotel, so it's good for business all around. In fact, we're already sold out that weekend, so we'll be taking on extra staff. Your high-minded, artistic principles are all very well, and I do understand what you're saying, but there's always the local economy to consider." He stood up. "Sorry, Simon, but this is the way it's got to be. Charlotte's worked on lots of these productions, and I'll leave her to tell you all about it. She'll be glad to fill you in, I'm sure." Charlotte gave Simon a sympathetic, encouraging smile. "Well, that's it for now, I guess," said Harvey.

He took a few steps toward the exit that would eventually bring him to the hotel lobby, then retraced his steps to rejoin the little group.

"Oh, I almost forgot. There's something else I should tell you. Mrs. Van Dusen's just told me that this year's performance is going to be a little different in that her daughter's getting married on the Saturday after our performance. Our play will be included in the wedding festivities. The wedding rehearsal will be on the Friday afternoon and then a bit of supper for the wedding party and then the play. She said dinner would be laid out for the cast and crew after the performance, as usual, along with her invited guests. Should be quite a party this year.

"And because the wedding will take place the next day, she asked if we'd keep the sets simple, so we can dismantle them after the performance or early the next morning to give the people who are working on the wedding enough time for setup. Apparently she hired a top florist from New

York, and there'll be bowers and arches covered in roses and God knows what else."

"Really?" said Simon, perking up. "Bowers and arches? That sounds perfect for us. I wonder if there's any chance they could be installed in time for the performance so we could use them, too."

"Possibly. Makes sense to me. You can at least ask," said Harvey. "Well, you know where I am if you need me."

Simon waited until Harvey was out of earshot before speaking.

"I'm really not looking forward to reworking a Shakespeare play. It just seems very wrong to me. But if we have to do it, do you suppose there's already an abbreviated script somewhere?"

"I think there's an abbreviated copy of every play in the archives," said Charlotte. "Really, it won't be so bad. The shorter scripts leave out minor characters, so there are fewer actors for you to deal with."

"Speaking of actors, does he know about the other thing?" Aaron asked. "You know. The men."

"Ah," said Charlotte. "Right. The men. That's the other thing. All roles are performed by men in this performance—an original practices production—so you'll have to think about how you want to cast it and schedule a couple of rehearsals."

"Christ almighty!" said Simon. "I don't remember signing up for this!"

"It's a lot of fun, though," Aaron helpfully reminded him. "At least Charlotte says it is."

"It is, Simon," she said. "Really, just keep an open mind."

"And what about costumes?" he said. "That's your bailiwick. Will all the men have to be fitted with dresses?"

"Of course," said Charlotte. "And that's why we've got Aaron."

"What?"

Charlotte laughed. "Don't look so worried. We've got about a dozen big skirts and bodices that they wear. We don't worry too much about a good fit for this performance. The costumes just to have to look right to someone who's had a glass or two of Veuve Clicquot."

"I forgot to ask the most important question," said Simon. "What play are we doing? Or am I supposed to sort that out, too?"

"It's always a play taken from the ones currently in production," said Charlotte. "And Mrs. Van Dusen gets to choose which one."

"And which one did she choose?"

Charlotte looked blank. "We forgot to ask Harvey! I expect she told him at their meeting." She thought for a moment. "My money's on *Romeo and Juliet*. Everybody loves that one. But let's find out."

She tipped her head at Aaron, who pulled out his phone. A moment later, he pressed the red button to end the call.

"Well?" said Simon.

"*A Midsummer Night's Dream*."

# Chapter 2

Paula Van Dusen's family had lived in the Catskills since their old money was new. Or more precisely, her late husband's family had. Peter Cornelius Van Dusen III had departed this life many years ago at a tragically young age, the victim of a late-night car crash on his way home from dinner at the country club. In one of those life-changing decisions, his wife had chosen at the last minute to stay home that evening because their young daughter was ill; had Mrs. Van Dusen accompanied him, the outcome would have been very different. Peter Van Dusen always refused to be driven by the family chauffeur. Paula, on the other hand, had never driven herself anywhere and refused to let Peter drive her. Had she been with her husband that night, he would not have been driving, and certainly not drunk.

Her Rolls-Royce turned off the main road and stopped in front of black wrought-iron gates with a graceful bell-curve arch and finials. The gates were mounted on two gray, stone pillars, and a granite sign affixed to one pillar read "Oakland." After the gates had swung smoothly and silently open, the car proceeded up the driveway, driven at the same stately pace as when it had left Jacobs Grand Hotel twenty minutes earlier, giving Paula time to admire the bright pinks and deep purples of the rhododendron bushes that lined one side of the route. With a bit of luck, she thought, they should be able to keep up their lovely show until after the wedding.

"Thank you, Barnes," she said to her driver as he opened the car door for her at the porte cochere of the Oakland mansion. "I won't need you anymore today."

"Very good, madam."

Her footsteps crunched across the gravel as she made her way to the steps that led to the front door. The three-story building, built in an exuberant late-Victorian style from locally quarried gray stone, featured an interesting and varied roof line with peaks, chimneys, and gables. Two large, round towers anchored each corner of the front facade.

Paula Van Dusen walked through the grand hallway, with its black-and-white marble floor and polished paneling, and turned down a corridor leading to the ground-floor tower room. This had once been her mother-in-law's morning room, but it now served as her office.

She sent a brief text. She couldn't imagine what her mother-in-law would have made of that. In old Mrs. Van Dusen's day, if she'd wanted to speak to someone in the house, she'd have rung a bell to summon a servant, and that servant would have been dispatched to bring the person she wanted to see to her. But for Paula, the way to summon her daughter was to send a text.

Before the renovation, this room had been paneled in dark wood and filled with heavy mahogany furniture. Now it was a light, airy space in which Paula and her part-time secretary managed the estate and took care of all her interests, including charity work.

"Hey, Mom." Belinda Van Dusen greeted her mother from the doorway, then entered the room. "You wanted to see me?"

Paula, who was seeing her daughter for the first time that day, sighed. Belinda was wearing a pair of black skinny jeans and a black cashmere sweater with white shirttails hanging out from under it.

Paula pointed at them. "What's with that look?" she asked. "Do women not tuck in their blouses anymore? Or can't the sweaters be made longer?"

Belinda shrugged. "It's just the style, I guess. Everyone dresses like this. And it's a shirt, not a blouse."

"Well, I think it looks unkempt and sloppy. But never mind that now. We've got to discuss wedding details. I met with Harvey Jacobs this afternoon to settle the arrangements for the play. The theater company will perform *A Midsummer Night's Dream* on Friday night, after the wedding rehearsal. You need to make sure that the whole wedding party is here for that. We've assigned some rooms here at Oakland for the wedding party, and I've booked—let me see . . ." She put on her reading glasses and flipped through a Moleskine notebook. "Thirteen rooms at Jacobs Grand. Harvey promises they'll all be painted and freshened up for our guests. New beds, new bedding, new towels—all at my expense, of course. This wedding is a godsend to him. It's costing me a fortune."

Belinda glared at her mother.

"If you liked the man I'm marrying, Mother, you wouldn't be complaining about the cost of the wedding."

"Darling, it's not so much that I don't like him; it's more that I'm not sure he's really right for you. I mean, can you trust him? What do you really know about him?"

"I know that he's one of the top real estate agents in Manhattan, he earns a lot of money, he's just bought us a beautiful apartment in Chelsea, and I'm in love with him."

"I just don't want to see you hurt, that's all."

"I'm thirty-two years old, and it's my life. I can handle it. Besides, this whole big wedding thing was your idea. Adrian and I would have been just as happy to have a simple ceremony at the Plaza with a few of our friends."

Paula laughed. "Simple? At the Plaza? Oh, please." She shook her head. "Belinda, you don't seem to realize there are appearances to be kept up. Ours is one of the oldest families in the whole of New York State. And besides, I've been to so many society weddings in the last few years that I have to invite the people who invited me to their children's weddings to yours. That's just the way it works."

"Well, if you're looking to save some money, maybe we don't need the play."

"Of course we need it. Including a live theater performance as part of your wedding celebrations is very special. How many other families do that? It's what the aristocracy used to do. And this isn't just any old theater group. Do I need to remind you it's the highly respected Catskills Shakespeare Theater Company? People pay good money to attend their performances.

"And the great thing is, I'm not paying for it! I'd be hosting the annual fundraiser here anyway, so combining the two events—the fundraiser and your wedding rehearsal party—is pure genius, if I do say so myself. Of course, it'll be a lot of work, but really, since we're holding the two events anyway, it just makes sense to combine them."

"Whatever. Are you finished with me? I thought I'd drive into town tonight and have dinner with Adrian."

"No, I'm not quite finished with you. There's still the matter of who's going to give you away."

"Mom, nobody calls it that anymore. It's called 'walking me down the aisle.' I thought you could do it."

"Certainly not. That would look ridiculous. We have to get an older man. Now, I thought perhaps your grandfather could do it, but he's in California with your Aunt Margaret, and she's not coming, so unfortunately, neither is he. He couldn't possibly make the journey on his own. And come to think of it, I doubt he'd be well enough or steady enough for the job, anyway. You want someone you can lean on, if you have to. Someone distinguished, hopefully, who will look good in the photographs."

"Well, I'm sure you'll think of someone." Belinda stood up and rearranged her long blonde hair on her shoulders. "*A Midsummer Night's Dream*. Isn't that the one with the fairies? Oh, what was his name?"

"Puck?"

"That's it. Anyway, I'm off. And don't worry. All this wedding stuff—it'll all get done. You've got Phyllis to help you."

"But we haven't talked about the bridesmaids' dresses," her mother protested.

"Not now. I'm going up to pack, and then I'm leaving for town. Adrian and I'll be back for the weekend, probably on Friday night. He wants to look at a couple of properties. He's got a client interested in a country place, and he sees this as a good opportunity to expand."

"Of course he does."

Belinda sighed. "I know you always wanted me to marry Hugh, but it's not going to happen. Ever. You've just got to accept that."

Belinda brushed past her mother and out the door, leaving in her wake a light trace of expensive scent.

When she had gone, Paula remained seated on the butterscotch-colored leather love seat, reflecting on her daughter's words. "It'll all get done." *Of course, it'll all get done because I'll have to do it.*

How she longed for a cigarette, but it had been fifty-eight days since she'd lit up, and she told herself she mustn't give in to temptation. She rubbed her hands together. Belinda was right about one thing, though. She'd always hoped that her daughter and Hugh Hedley would get together. The two families had been friends for years, and why shouldn't the children marry? Now that would have been what people used to call a good match. Two fine young people from similar backgrounds. Made for each other! It would have been so right somehow, but apparently it was not to be. Unless Belinda could somehow be made to see sense. Of course there'd be a bit of scandal if the wedding was called off at this late date, but that would blow over quickly, and in the end, Belinda married to Hugh Hedley would be so much better than this Adrian Archer.

The Hedley name, after all, was almost as old and respected in these parts as Van Dusen. Hugh's great-grandfather had established the Hedley brewery, his grandfather had been a United States senator, his stepfather served as an associate judge on New York State's Court of Appeals, and Hugh himself had a law degree from Yale and the Ivy League looks to go along with it. Yes, he certainly came from old stock and carried himself with the quiet confidence that speaks of generations of wealth and privilege. His name was beginning to be whispered in high places. With the right handling, he could easily be elected state governor, and after that, who knew? The White House? Why not? It had happened before with governors from New York, and look how well the Roosevelts had turned out. No doubt about it, her daughter couldn't do better than Hugh. Maybe there was still time to make that possible.

As the gray clouds that hung over her aspirations for her daughter parted to let in the tiniest ray of hope, she checked her watch. Not too early.

She strode into the large living room on the other side of the corridor, where a drinks table had been set up beside French doors that opened onto the extensive lawn and gardens. She lifted the lid of the ice bucket and peered in. Good. Phyllis had filled it. She fixed herself a gin and tonic, then opened the French doors and walked out onto the terrace. She chose a comfortable chair and eased into it, crossing her legs as she set her drink on the table.

Although she had a wide circle of friends, which included any number of men who would be happy to walk her daughter down the aisle, her thoughts turned to the handsome actor she'd met earlier that afternoon at the theater. He was just leaving Harvey's office, and they'd exchanged a few words. Such a beautiful voice. Deep, resonant, and completely seductive. And the British accent was so charming.

She laughed. What was that ridiculous expression that had been so popular a few years ago? He had me at "hello"! Well, maybe he had. Of course, there was that little scandal he'd been caught up in a few months back, but that was nothing to do with him, really. Then her thoughts turned to the bridesmaids' dresses, and she had another idea.

She took a sip of her lemony, crisp drink that led to a delicious little shudder. Maybe a tiny bit too much gin, but oh, how she looked forward to that first drink of the day.

Still, she was very strict and limited herself to two. Any more and you run the risk of putting on weight—and as everyone knows, you cannot be too thin or too rich.

Paula Van Dusen was both. Enviably thin and very, very rich.

# Chapter 3

Charlotte Fairfax had been the one and only member of the costume department of the Catskills Shakespeare Theater Company for the past ten years. But in early spring, just in time to help her prepare for this season of summer plays, Harvey Jacobs had assigned his nephew, Aaron, as her intern. At first, she'd felt resentful and resistant to having him, but she had quickly grown to like his youthful energy and to appreciate the contribution he made to her small department. He had been studying fashion design in Manhattan but had decided to change direction, and now, interested in a career as a costume designer, he was showing a lot of promise.

Charlotte had trained in classical theater with the Royal Shakespeare Company in Stratford-Upon-Avon and was delighted now, in her early forties, to be able to share her experience and insight with Aaron.

So over the past few months, despite the twenty-year age difference, they'd developed a relaxed, trusting relationship, and she'd come to see him as a much-needed breath of fresh air. And besides, he was just fun to have about the place.

This afternoon, the two of them were pulling the oversize skirts and bodices that the male actors would wear for their roles in *A Midsummer Night's Dream*.

Aaron held a skirt up to his waist and examined himself in the mirror.

"Have a go," Charlotte laughed. "You know you want to. Try it on!"

Aaron crumpled up. "I'd love to, but I'm afraid burgundy just isn't my color. It makes my complexion look sallow. Sallow. Is that even a word?"

"Oh, give it here." Charlotte took the garment from him and hung it on the rack. "We'll just check these to make sure the moths haven't got at them, and when Simon's had a chance to review the play and decide who's playing what part, we'll arrange fittings."

She stood back to examine them and lifted one by the hem.

"They're rather fun, aren't they?" she said. A somewhat more elaborate costume consisted of a pale-blue skirt with a matching bodice, worn beneath a voluminous dark-green velvet overdress, open at the front to reveal the blue from the skirt and bodice. A large, flouncy white collar was attached.

"The actor will wear a long string of pearls with this dress," said Charlotte. "And it comes with a little headpiece trimmed with pearls and a short veil."

"Will he wear a wig?"

"No, just his own hair brushed back and held in place by the band on the headpiece."

"How do the women in the company feel about being left out of the performance?" asked Aaron.

"Oh, they rather like having the evening off. Most of them come along to watch, and a few are really helpful with makeup and sometimes as dressers. The rest get to enjoy the performance like ordinary audience members."

Aaron's forehead wrinkled, and he ran a smoothing hand over the costume.

"Why weren't women allowed to act in the plays in Shakespeare's day? Weren't women allowed to work?"

"No doubt they worked really hard doing a lot of things, but acting was considered a trade, really, and the boys who played the women's parts were apprentices. And women weren't allowed to be apprentices."

She checked her watch. "Right. Well, let's organize a cup of tea, and then you'd best ask Simon if he wants you to do anything for this evening's performance. Oh, and we could do with a little tidying up around here." She pointed to a few bolts of cloth on the worktable.

Her costume department consisted of a large workroom with a large table in the center for measuring and cutting fabric. Deep, partitioned shelving along one wall was filled with bolts of cloth, ranging from heavy brocades to light silks for linings. There were even a few remnants of tartan, kept in reserve for the Scottish play.

Everything in her department was done on a minuscule budget. Recycled costumes were fitted for each actor, and only under exceptional circumstances was a new costume made. Such an exceptional circumstance had occurred earlier in the year when the actress playing Juliet had been murdered, and Mattie Lane, her replacement, asked that she not be required to try on or wear the costume that the deceased woman had worn. Actors have a lot of superstitions around their craft, and Charlotte was happy to accommodate Mattie's request, giving Aaron a fresh, creative challenge to design and make the costume.

Settling back in her chair, Charlotte sipped her tea, put on her reading glasses, and leafed through the latest issue of *The Costume Designer* while Aaron, who divided his time between the costume department and working as assistant to the director, tidied up and then headed off to the theater to speak to Simon. Charlotte had just become engrossed in an article on the top twenty film costumes of all time when her telephone rang.

Once the call was finished, she called Aaron back to the workroom, and when he arrived, she gestured him toward the chair beside her desk.

"I've just had an interesting phone call," she said. "Mrs. Paula Van Dusen would like to hire your services."

"My services? She asked for me? How does she know about me?"

"Well, she didn't ask for you specifically. She wanted to know if I could recommend someone to make the bridesmaids' dresses for her daughter's wedding, and I thought of you. The bridesmaids have decided they don't want off the rack, after all. They want couture, but they've left it a bit late."

"How many dresses?" asked Aaron cautiously.

"Just two."

"And do they want them both the same or different?"

"I don't know. That's something for you to discuss with your clients at your first consultation. As the designer, it would be your role to think about that and recommend something that they can all get excited about."

"What do you think?"

"I think it's a great opportunity for you, and you'd be crazy to turn it down."

"I guess that wasn't what I really meant. What I meant was"—he hesitated—"do you think I could do this?"

"Yes, you could take this on. Our season is well under way here. We're past our busy time."

"No, I didn't mean that, either. I meant, do you think I have enough experience? Maybe she really wanted you to do it."

Charlotte touched him lightly on the forearm. "We wouldn't be having this discussion if I didn't think you could do it. In fact, let me rephrase that. I know you can do this. Of course, it will stretch you, but you'll learn from it. And who knows? You might even have some fun. Would you like to give it a go?"

He didn't reply.

"If you get stuck or need some advice, I'll help you," she prompted.

Still no answer.

"Of course, you'd have to go shopping here in town at Uptown Silk Shop for fabric, and then if you don't see what you're looking for, you'll just have to go to Mood," she said. The very mention of Mood, the fabric supply emporium in Manhattan made famous on the television show *Project Runway*, did the trick.

"I'd love to do it."

"Good. I'll let Mrs. Van Dusen know. She'd like you to meet with the bride and bridesmaids on Saturday afternoon to discuss ideas. Just listen carefully to what they want, then come back here and sketch a few designs and think about what kind of fabric would work. And be sure to pin them down on color. Take a Pantone color chart with you."

"What about the bride's dress?"

"We don't have to worry about her."

"Don't tell me," said Aaron. "Kleinfeld."

"I don't know," said Charlotte, "but that sounds like a good guess. She's a girl about town in Manhattan, what used to be a called a 'socialite.' Maybe they still do call them that."

"How do you know that?"

"I read the newspaper." She smiled at him. "Oh, and one other thing. Be sure to tell Harvey about this. He's the boss, and bosses never like surprises. And besides, I think he'll be very pleased."

# Chapter 4

On Saturday morning, Aaron surveyed the bolts of fabric stored in the workroom. The selection, which Charlotte had picked up over the years on sale or by donation, ranged from deep, heavy damasks and brocades in deep greens, burgundies, and blues at one end to light, airy fabrics at the other. It was the latter group he focused on: soft, pale palettes of creams, ivories, blush pinks, and whispers of blue in silks, satins, and taffetas that could be used to make underdresses or to line garments. He'd known next to nothing about costume design when he started working here and had become increasingly drawn to it as Charlotte helped him explore the connection between Tudor and Jacobean history and Shakespearean costume design.

"You have to understand the time Shakespeare lived in," she'd explained. "An Elizabethan law designed to keep people in their place dictated what they could wear, according to their rank and class. And wealth, of course." And so it followed that characters onstage wore costumes that followed the same rules.

"So an actor playing a king, for example, would be dressed in rich velvets, furs, and silks and adorned with jewels, while characters of low status, such the workmen in *A Midsummer Night's Dream*, wear loosely woven, rough, shapeless garments made of wool or linen. And the interesting thing is that many of the costumes used to depict men and women of higher rank were real clothes worn by noblemen and titled ladies that had been donated to the acting companies."

"Oh, that's neat."

"Of course, it still happens today. Yesterday's clothes become today's costumes. Costume supply companies go to auctions and buy up wardrobes from the 1950s, say, and those clothes that people wore in their everyday lives become costumes."

Aaron cut swatches from a few pastel-colored fabrics, although he knew it was entirely possible that the women could request dresses in, say, midnight blue. However, for a June wedding, he expected them to choose summery fabrics in muted shades.

He'd never been to the Van Dusen estate, but of course he'd heard of it. Everybody in Walkers Ridge knew of the family that had lived for several generations in the big house overlooking the town, providing employment to local people.

As he drove to the consultation, he visualized the meeting and pondered what he should say. He'd watched a couple of episodes online of a popular reality show in which brides, accompanied by a group of bickering, disapproving relatives who can't agree on anything, shop for wedding dresses. He'd hoped this afternoon's session would go more smoothly.

He pulled over in front of the electronic gates, pressed the entry button, and told a disembodied voice his name and the purpose of his visit. The gates swung open and he proceeded up the driveway. Unlike Paula Van Dusen, however, he took no notice of the flowering rhododendrons. He was trying to remember everything Charlotte had told him to prepare for today. Be sure to bring a notebook to write down what they say. Listen carefully to what's being said and what's not being said. When you take the women's measurements, don't say a number out loud or let one woman see another woman's measurements. And finally, don't refer to breasts as boobs. The dressmaking term is "bust." Be professional at all times. And then she'd told him to have fun. As if.

The door was opened by a woman several years older than he. Her blonde hair hung casually and loosely around her shoulders, but even to Aaron's unsophisticated eye for such things, the color and cut looked expensive. Her pale-blue eyes, set in a narrow face, regarded him with a vague hint of amusement.

"Hello," she said. "I'm Belinda Van Dusen, the bride. Today you'll be meeting my two bridesmaids. Come on in."

Aaron tried not to stare at his surroundings as they crossed the vast black-and-white floor of the entrance hall.

Belinda led him down a corridor, past several closed doors, until they came to the last one. She threw it open, revealing an elegant sitting room with walls of a sophisticated beige with a surprising hint of pink. Two young women sat on a long, sandy-beige sofa decorated with colorful throw cushions. In front of them was a coffee table with several oversized hardcover books and a bouquet of white roses. The window alcove contained a love seat that matched the sofa; propped up on it, resting against the wall, was a guitar. Although it was early afternoon, table lamps had been turned on, bathing the room in a soft, warm glow.

The women on the sofa did not look up as Aaron and Belinda entered. One sat with a magazine on her lap; the other, her feet tucked under her, thumbed through her phone.

"Hey, guys, this is Aaron," said Belinda. "He's here about your bridesmaids' dresses." The brunette woman with the magazine looked up; the other's eyes remained fixed on her device.

Aaron smiled at them.

"This is Jessica," said Belinda, gesturing at the dark-haired woman. "She works at a local art gallery." Jessica adjusted the colorful scarf worn over one shoulder as she turned sideways to set her magazine on the coffee table and gave Aaron a bright, encouraging smile. "And that's Sophie." Sophie glanced up briefly, gave him a quick once-over, then returned to her phone. Her thin lips were tight and of the kind that in middle age would naturally droop, giving her the appearance of perpetually frowning.

Belinda waved her hand at a wingback chair at the end of the sofa, indicating that Aaron should sit in it. He did so, then pulled out a notebook from his bag.

"Ready?" Belinda asked as the three looked at him expectantly.

Aaron cleared his throat. "I wondered if you could tell me what you were thinking of for bridesmaids' dresses," he began. The three looked from one to the other and said nothing.

"Well, let's start with this," said Aaron, remembering what he'd seen on the bridal-dress show. "Where is the wedding to be held?"

"Here, at the house," said Belinda. While she explained the garden details to him, Sophie's eyes slid back to her phone.

"And were you thinking long or short?" Aaron asked.

"Long," said Jessica.

"Well, did you want them both the same, or different necklines, or . . ."

"I'd like mine strapless," said Sophie.

"Absolutely not," said Belinda. "Mine isn't strapless, and I don't want anyone else to be strapless."

"And as for color . . ." stammered an increasingly desperate Aaron.

The conversation continued for about twenty minutes, going nowhere, with Aaron trying to keep track of what everyone was telling him. Finally, Belinda stood up.

"I'm going for a diet soda. Anyone else want anything?"

"I'd love a glass of water, please," said Aaron.

"I'll have a vodka and cola," said Jessica.

"No, you won't," said Belinda. "I'm not mixing drinks. I'm just going to the fridge. You can have a cola." She turned to Sophie, who was back on her phone.

"Sophie!"

Keeping her eyes on her device, she turned her head slowly toward the sound of Belinda's voice. "What?"

"Drinks. Do you want anything to drink?"

"No, thanks. Oh, wait, yes, a coffee."

"Oh, you would? Now I'm going to need a tray. Don't make any decisions while I'm gone. Just keep talking to Aaron."

Aaron got out his fabric swatches and set them on the table.

"Maybe you could have a look at those and tell me if you like any of the colors. Or if you already know what color you want, please just tell me what you have in mind."

Jessica and Sophie picked up the fabric samples and started comparing them. And then, at the ping of an incoming text, Sophie turned her attention back to her phone, ignoring Aaron and his fabric samples.

"Hugh's just landed a big, new client," she announced.

"Anyone we know?" asked Jessica.

"Didn't say," replied Sophie.

"Do Adrian and Belinda know you've started seeing him?"

"I don't think so," replied Sophie. "At least, I didn't tell them. And I wouldn't call it 'seeing him.' We've met up for a couple of drinks, that's all."

"Well, are you planning on bringing him to the wedding? That could be awkward if Belinda doesn't want him here. And considering that you work with Adrian, and Hugh is Adrian's chief business rival, I doubt he'll want him here, either."

Sophie gave a dismissive shrug. "Not my problem. Her mother will probably invite him and his family, anyway."

"I think you should tell Belinda."

"Yeah. Maybe. Eventually. She's got enough on her plate right now." Aaron gently cleared his throat and, holding a square of oyster-colored silk, tried to catch Jessica's eye as Sophie sighed and looked up from her phone. "Look, let's just get through this. This wedding's taking up more of my time than I'd like. To be honest, I wish Belinda hadn't asked me. It's a bit awkward."

"How can you say that?" demanded Jessica. "If she hadn't asked you, you would have been really hurt."

At the sound of approaching voices in the hall, Jessica reached out to Aaron, accepted the silk, dangled it in front of Sophie, and asked, "What do you think of this one?"

"Too boring. We want something with a bit of drama," Sophie replied just as Paula Van Dusen, hair neatly coiffed, wearing a sleeveless sheath dress in a geometric design and a pair of beige court shoes, swept into the room, followed by Belinda and a tired-looking woman in a black skirt and white blouse expertly balancing a tray laden with drinks.

Aaron instinctively stood up.

"Hello, you must be Aaron," Paula Van Dusen said, then introduced herself. "I've just got back or I would have been here at the start of the consultation. Where are we? What have we decided?" Before Aaron could reply, she turned to the woman holding the tray and said, "Just set it down there, Phyllis, thanks. That'll be all for now, and if we need anything else, I'll call you." The woman set down the tray and slipped from the room, closing the door quietly behind her.

"We've just been discussing fabrics and colors, Mrs. Van Dusen," said Aaron. "I don't think anything's really been decided yet."

"Well, as for color, we'll want something that harmonizes with the garden," Mrs. Van Dusen said. "So something in a pale pink or mauve, perhaps."

Belinda groaned. "Mauve! Are you kidding me? That's for an eighty-year-old woman."

"Well, what would you suggest?" Paula demanded of her daughter.

"What about fuchsia?" Aaron broke the silence. "Vibrant. Dynamic. You have to be young to pull that off."

He showed them samples from his Pantone color cards, and they all leaned in for a closer look. And then, in what he later thought was an inspired observation, he added, "And of course in the photographs, you would want the wedding party to be the focus, the dresses complimented by colors of the garden in the background, not the other way around." At these words, the women suddenly came alive, zeroing in on the different shades of fuchsia to pick just the right one.

Aaron then discussed necklines and bodices, explaining the benefits and drawbacks depending on body type, and they all agreed on a softly draped off-the-shoulder style that left plenty of room for jewelry. Relieved that decisions had been made, and after promising to send over some sketches and fabric samples, Aaron pulled out a tape measure.

He took the women's measurements quickly and privately, jotting them down in his notebook. He needn't have worried about anyone trying to see anyone else's statistics—they were all too busy chatting to one another.

As he gathered up his supplies and prepared to leave, Paula Van Dusen approached him.

"Well, thank you, Aaron. Seems to have gone very well. The girls—women, I should say—seem very excited by your suggestions. When you're ready, I'll show you out myself."

She didn't speak on the long walk to the front door, but he was acutely aware of her presence beside him. He thanked her, got in his car, and drove off without looking back. When he reached the grounds of the hotel, he parked his uncle's car in its usual spot, but instead of entering the hotel, he walked a little way into the wooded parkland that made up part of the hotel grounds, leaned against a tree, and lit a joint. A satisfied smile lit up his face as he watched the smoke drift skyward and disappear into the treetops.

# Chapter 5

"All right, everybody, gather round, please." Simon Dyer, dressed in his usual casual outfit of khaki trousers with a sweater tied around his neck by its arms, clapped his hands to call the all-male cast together onstage. The female actors, seated in the audience, exchanged amused glances. Charlotte hurried in and took a seat in the front row, with a script on her lap to note costume changes.

"We start rehearsals today for the abbreviated version of *A Midsummer Night's Dream*," Simon began. "The one we'll be performing at the Van Dusen estate not only as a fundraiser but as part of the wedding program. We'll be doing this on the Friday evening before the wedding. One performance only, and then we resume regular show times Saturday back here at the theater." He checked the notes on his clipboard. "You all know what part you've been assigned and you've had time to review the script. Some of you will be playing several parts, so that'll mean quick costume changes backstage. No dressing rooms. The set will be kept very simple. You'll note that all the lines are Shakespeare's, it's just that some elements have been left out. This version runs about ninety minutes with one intermission.

"Now the fun thing for us is that this play is about two weddings, and we're actually putting on this performance as part of a wedding celebration, so there's a bit of life imitating art here.

"Right. Let's get started with act one, scene one. Aaron, cue the music, please." He stepped off the stage and made for a front-row seat with a small table in front of it, upon which Aaron had placed Simon's laptop, a binder, and a bottle of water.

The entrance music began, and Brian Prentice, the company's lead actor, who was playing the part of the Duke of Athens, led in a young man taking the part of Hippolyta. He was wearing a French hood—a wide, crescent-shaped band with a small veil at the back—and a floor-length skirt over his jeans, short enough to reveal a pair of tattered running shoes. When a few women in the audience behind him snickered, Simon kept his eyes on the stage but held up an admonishing hand to silence them, and then the action began. Brian spoke his opening lines, and the young actor playing Hippolyta responded:

*"Four days will quickly steep themselves in nights;*
*Four nights will quickly dream away the time;*
*And then the moon, like to a . . ."*

"Just hold it there a moment," said Simon. He approached the stage and beckoned to the actor. "Not in a falsetto. You'll find it too hard to sustain, and the audience will tire of it very quickly. Just speak in your normal voice, but soften it, just a little." He gave the actor a brief, encouraging smile. "Right, start over at 'Four days.'" He resumed his seat, and the rehearsal continued.

Charlotte scribbled and highlighted notes throughout her copy of the script, indicating when an actor would exit the stage and need a quick costume change before reappearing onstage as another character.

Then she made a note to ask Simon if he could free up Aaron from his deputy stage manager duties for this one performance, as she would need his help every minute with so many rapid costume changes. She suspected, though, that Aaron would end up having to juggle both roles.

The run-up to the wedding was going to be a busy time for everybody.

# Chapter 6

The delicate freshness of May foliage had given way to the deeper, robust greens of early June as Charlotte and Rupert strolled through the Jacobs Grand Hotel parkland. The morning sun warmed their way, and it was with some reluctance that they returned to the bungalow, Rupert to have his breakfast and Charlotte to get ready for work.

It was now just a week until the wedding, and two mannequins draped in white sheets greeted her when she unlocked the workroom door. A flash of fuchsia peeking out from beneath the protective covering told her what they were.

Aaron had worked secretively on the dresses, spending his evenings alone in the workroom, clearing away every scrap of fabric and keeping his works in progress covered up and hidden in a corner of the storage area. He'd approached Charlotte a couple of times for advice, and she'd asked him guided questions that had led him to find the answers for himself. "I won't do your thinking for you," she'd told him.

Now about to show her his creations, Aaron was proud of the work that she had let him design and execute on his own. He leaned against the worktable in anticipation of Charlotte's appraisal.

"So, Aaron," she said. "It's the morning of your bridesmaids' dress fitting. I'm dying to see what you've done. Let me just get rid of this." She strode to her desk and set down the mug of coffee she was carrying. She had strict workroom rules that kept food and beverages well away from tables and fabrics. "All it takes is one spill for hours of work to be ruined," she'd reminded Aaron several times.

"Right," she said as she approached the mannequin with her hands clasped in front of her. "Let's see what you've got. Show me!"

With a shy, expectant grin, Aaron carefully lifted the sheet covering the first dress, revealing an exquisite gown of soft georgette in a vibrant fuchsia. The dress was slit to the knee, revealing a lining of palest pink.

Charlotte fingered the fabric.

"I chose the georgette rather than chiffon because it's a bit less sheer. The saleslady at Mood recommended it for an outdoor, summer wedding," said Aaron.

"It's perfect," said Charlotte. "I can see even on the mannequin that it will flow beautifully when she walks." She beamed at him. "I think they're going to be thrilled."

Aaron pointed to the hemline. "I haven't done the hems yet. I want to pin it at the fitting so it will be perfect."

"Well, you did a fabulous job. I'm really proud of you. Would you like me to come to the fitting with you? I can pin one while you pin the other, if you like. I'd be delighted to act as your assistant."

"That would be great. I'll admit I'm a little nervous. They approved the sketches, and I gave them what they asked for, I think, but you know what clients can be like. When they see the finished garment, there's this big silence, and you just know they don't like it. Then they try to find something nice to say. 'Well, it's a nice color,' or something."

Charlotte nodded. "Your heart just sinks. It's an awful feeling. But I'm sure that won't happen here."

"I'll find a couple of garment bags for these while you finish your coffee, and then we can be on our way," he said.

Low-slung clouds skimmed the mountaintops, and a gentle midmorning mist rolled in over the fields as they drove to the Van Dusen estate.

"It'll be interesting to see how it goes today," Aaron remarked. "The first time I went there, as soon as Belinda left the room, they treated me like I was invisible." Before Charlotte could reply, they'd arrived at the Oakland gates.

Aaron recognized the woman who answered the door as the same woman who had brought in the tray of drinks on his first visit. She appeared to be in her late forties, her once-brown hair faded and flecked lightly with gray. With practiced politeness, she ushered them into the same sitting room where Aaron had conducted his first consultation.

Sophie and Jessica looked up expectantly as Charlotte and Aaron entered, Aaron with two garment bags draped over his arms. Charlotte lifted off the first one, checked the name written on a strip of masking tape, undid the zipper, and pulled out the dress.

"Jessica," she said, holding out the dress to her. Jessica smiled broadly as she took it.

"And Sophie," she said, presenting her with the other. Sophie frowned and reached for it.

"If you would just take the dresses into the room next door and put them on, please," said Aaron. "And as I mentioned last time, I hope you're wearing the undergarments and shoes that you plan to wear on the day so we can make sure the bodice fits right and get an accurate measurement for the hems, allowing for heel height."

The women trooped out of the room in silence. Aaron shot Charlotte a worried glance, and she shook her head slightly as a warning, then tipped it in the direction of the door to indicate someone might be listening. Aaron got the message and said nothing as they waited for the women to return.

But the women who came through the door were not the bridesmaids. In charged Paula Van Dusen, closely followed by her daughter, Belinda. Mrs. Van Dusen's mouth was clenched in a tight line and her brow was furrowed.

"I don't believe it!" she said, gesturing at her daughter. "Belinda's just told me she missed her appointment for the final fitting of her wedding dress."

"Mom, I just . . ."

Paula held up an imperious hand to silence her and turned to Charlotte. "I know it's a lot to ask, and I hate to be a bother, but I wondered if you'd be kind enough . . ."

"Of course we'll help if we can, Mrs. Van Dusen. And it's no bother." She smiled at Aaron. "Is it, Aaron?"

He looked a little uncertain but, taking his cue from Charlotte, replied, "No, of course not."

Mrs. Van Dusen looked from Charlotte to Aaron, her eyes narrowing slightly, and then back to Charlotte.

"Oh, but Charlotte, I really hoped that you would take care of this yourself. No offense, Aaron, it's just that, well, it is Belinda's wedding dress, and it's got to be perfect, and Charlotte has so much more experience."

"No worries, Mrs. Van Dusen. I've got the bridesmaids' dresses to fit and hem," said Aaron.

"Exactly! That's precisely what I was thinking."

"I'd be happy to have a look at Belinda's dress and see what needs doing," said Charlotte. "However, if it's a ball-gown style with several layers that need hemming, I will probably need Aaron's help. Now, is the dress here or still at the bridal salon? Once I've had a look at it, we can work out what's needed."

"It's here," said Belinda.

Before she could say any more, the bridesmaids entered, delicately pinching the skirts of their unhemmed dresses to lift them off the carpet.

"Well, what do you think?" Aaron asked them.

Jessica beamed; Sophie scowled.

"I love it," said Jessica. "It doesn't look like a bridesmaid's dress at all."

"It's okay, I guess," said Sophie. "I just don't think it's really me. I was hoping for something more . . . something with a bit more . . . oh, it's hard to describe." Aaron said nothing. Charlotte had warned him that the hardest part about this assignment would be the mind reading. Fortunately, Paula Van Dusen came to his rescue.

"How can Aaron be expected to give you what you want when you can't tell him what that is?" she demanded. "Did you explain to him at the consultation what you wanted? Did you give him something to go on? Were you perfectly clear?"

"This dress is exactly what we told Aaron we wanted," said Jessica. "Except for the lining. We didn't think of it, but I love it."

"The lining is pink, for God's sake," said Sophie. "I didn't want anything girly."

"It could have been navy blue," said Aaron, "but that's too wintery. Mrs. Van Dusen requested something that would harmonize with the garden, and the pale-pink contrast is the best choice for that. White would have been the second choice."

Charlotte gave him a mental thumbs-up for explaining his choice to the client in a moderate, measured tone, for bringing in Mrs. Van Dusen in a way that was bound to get her on his side, and for sticking up for himself.

"Well, I like it," said Mrs. Van Dusen, putting an end to the discussion. "The pale pink stays. And now," she continued, "while Aaron gets to work pinning the bridesmaids' dresses, Belinda, take Charlotte upstairs and show her your dress so she can see what's required."

As Charlotte and Belinda were about to leave, the same woman who had shown Charlotte and Aaron into the sitting room stuck her head around the door.

"You asked me to give you a fifteen-minute warning about your meeting with the event planner, Mrs. Van Dusen," she said. "And Adrian's here to see Belinda."

"Send him upstairs in a few minutes, Phyllis," Belinda said. "I'll talk to him while we're doing the fitting."

"Phyllis, you'll do no such thing," said Paula Van Dusen. "And before you start rolling your eyes, Belinda, it's bad luck for a groom to see his bride in her dress before the wedding day. I don't care about modern customs. He's not going to see you in the dress. As these theater people can tell you, it's never good to let the daylight in on the magic." She turned to her employee. "He can wait in my office or in the front hall, whichever suits him better. He'll spend the whole time on his phone, anyway, so I don't suppose it matters."

Belinda shrugged and gestured to Charlotte. "Come on," she said. "Let's get this over with."

Mrs. Van Dusen led the way into the corridor, and Phyllis, Charlotte, and Belinda followed her.

"Thank you, Phyllis," she said. "I don't know what we'd do without you." As Phyllis departed, Mrs. Van Dusen turned her attention to her daughter. "I hope you appreciate what Charlotte is doing for you. We mustn't take up any more of her time than is necessary."

Belinda led the way up the graceful, sweeping staircase to the second floor and along a wide, carpeted corridor with closed doors on both sides. About halfway down, she opened a door and stood to one side.

Charlotte found herself in a bedroom overlooking the garden at the rear of the house. The spacious, high-ceilinged room was painted a pale yellow and decorated with a light touch. It was feminine without being fussy.

"It's really good of you to do this," said Belinda.

"Glad to," said Charlotte. "Your mother raises a lot of money for our theater."

"Well, we'll make sure you get paid. Now, I'll just go put the dress on, shall I?"

Charlotte nodded. "I'll wait here while you undress. Call me when you're ready and I'll help you lift it over your head." Belinda disappeared into an adjoining room, and Charlotte stood by the window admiring the garden. A moment later, a man came into view, seeming to emerge from the back of the house. He was talking on a cell phone and gesturing widely with his free hand while he paced in a large circle.

"I'm ready now," called Belinda. "Here I come." She entered the bedroom with a white cloud of dress on top of her head.

Charlotte eased the dress over her body, took one look at her, and asked, "Does your mother know? Has she seen this dress?"

Belinda nodded. "Let's just say it wasn't really what she had in mind, but in the end she agreed it would be okay for a daytime wedding at home. She said it reminded her of a

Dior dress from the 1950s, and then she kind of started to warm up to it."

"It's not what I was expecting, I'll admit that," said Charlotte. "I thought you'd go for something slinky and minimal, but I like it very much. You have to be tall to carry it off, which you are. That style is very flattering to your figure. Good choice!"

The dress had a fitted bodice that showed off Belinda's small waist, capped sleeves, a plain bateau neckline, and a full tulle skirt that ended at midcalf.

Belinda rustled the skirt, plumping it up with her hands. The effect was youthfully endearing and certainly charming.

"The silhouette *is* like a Dior from the 1950s," agreed Charlotte. "Even a bit Audrey Hepburn–ish, you might say. A great choice for a summer wedding at home in upstate New York. And this length of dress has two great advantages that brides often overlook. One, it prevents tripping. And two, you can show off your shoes!"

Belinda laughed. "I've got a really fabulous pair. They're red! It's a subtle little surprise for Adrian. He's Canadian, you see, so red and white."

"Well, I'm sure he'll be touched."

Charlotte took a step back and ran a critical, practiced eye over the dress. "The length is fine, but then this length is forgiving. An inch either way doesn't make a difference, whereas with floor length . . . well, you have to be spot-on, although I always recommend an inch shorter rather than skimming the floor. The tripping thing again."

Charlotte placed her hands on Belinda's waist and gently swiveled her around, so she faced away from her.

"Let me look at the back. Oh, I see what they've done. The detail is in the buttons on the back. Very nice." She pinched two sides of the dress together at Belinda's waist.

"Even without the buttons done up, I think you've lost a bit of weight since your first fitting, as brides usually do," Charlotte said. "You should be all right, but you can't afford to lose another ounce. We'll know more once we've got it done up properly."

Her hands fumbled as she struggled to slip the delicate rouleau loops around the tiny fabric-covered buttons.

She reached for the glasses she needed for closeup work that usually hung on a black cord around her neck along with her tape measure.

"Damn," she said. "I'm wearing the wrong glasses. I'm sorry, Belinda, but I'm going to have to run downstairs and get my other pair. Oh, and I'll need to have a quick word now with Aaron. He needs to know the bridesmaids' dresses need to be short because yours is. I'll be back as soon as I can."

She dashed out of the room and down the corridor. As she flew toward the stairs, the strident tones of an agitated male voice drifted up from the hall below. She slowed down to listen.

"Money wants to go where money is?" He laughed. "Not in this case, Gino. Money wants to go where the money's going to be." He listened for a few moments and then, speaking slightly louder and in an impatient tone, said, "He's not even a good liar. If you're going to be a liar, at least be a good one. What an idiot. Even a monkey could put up a listing on MLS." He laughed and then continued. "Look, give me a day or two to think about it. I'll come up with something that'll ruin Hedley's day. Maybe even his week."

Charlotte continued down the stairs, and as she neared the bottom step, the tall young man wearing an impeccably tailored summer suit she'd observed from the bedroom window pressed the "end call" button on his phone and, head down, crossed the hall in long, impatient strides. Just as Charlotte stepped off the bottom stair, his head snapped in her direction. Seeing her, he frowned.

"Hello," she said lightly. "I'm just here helping with dress fittings."

He murmured an acknowledgement. "Oh, hi. I'm Adrian Archer."

"Ah, the bridegroom. Charlotte Fairfax. Nice to meet you."

She held out her hand, which he shook in a firm grasp. As he headed back outside, Charlotte made her way to the sitting room, where Aaron, kneeling on the floor and bent over the hem of Sophie's dress, was concentrating on his work. He looked up.

"Hey. How's it going?"

"I've just come to get my other glasses, but I need a word with you about the length of the dresses." She explained the issue with the bride wearing a tea-length gown. Jessica understood immediately and picked up her dress, knowing the hem measurement would have to be done over. Sophie, however, was another matter.

"I like it long," she said. "I want to keep mine long."

"No," said Charlotte firmly. "Sorry, but if the bride is wearing a tea-length gown, the bridesmaids have to wear theirs short, too."

"I don't see why," pouted Sophie.

"Because," explained Charlotte, "the bride sets the tone and style for everybody, and you do not upstage the bride."

"No," agreed a stern voice from the doorway. "You certainly do not."

Sophie melted under Paula Van Dusen's icy glare.

*

"Sophie wasn't happy when I told them their dresses would have to be short," Charlotte said as she tucked and pinned the waist of Belinda's wedding dress to sculpt it to her body.

"No, well, she's like that," said Belinda. "She's a stager in Manhattan, so she has very definite ideas on color and design. In fact, I met Adrian through her. She stages properties for him. He says she's very demanding, but she gets what she wants in the end, and the results are worth it." She laughed. "And I got what I wanted in the end, too, although my mother doesn't agree with my choice."

"Is any man ever good enough for a daughter?"

Belinda smiled. "She always hoped I'd marry Hugh Hedley. Our families have been friends for ages. Practically all our lives, I guess. He's a lovely man and all that, but he just wasn't my Mr. Right. Whereas Adrian . . ." She sighed, then twisted to the left and eyed the dress in the mirror over her shoulder.

"Stand still," Charlotte ordered. "We're almost finished." She inserted a few more pins and then stood back and studied the result. "I think that's it. Now I'll undo the buttons and help you out of this gorgeous dress so I can keep the pins away from your body. Don't want to prick you."

As Charlotte laid the dress carefully on the bed and Belinda disappeared into the dressing room, Paula Van Dusen entered the bedroom. Seeing the dress on the bed, she nodded at Charlotte and then called out to her daughter.

"Belinda, have you said anything to Hugh?"

"No, I haven't spoken to him in ages. Why? Should I have?" came the disembodied reply from the dressing room.

"Because he's just let Phyllis know that he isn't coming to the wedding. He says he'll still come to the theater fundraiser but not the wedding."

Belinda emerged dressed in her black pants and white shirt, carrying a pair of black ballet flats. She sat on the edge of the bed, slipped on her shoes, then picked up her hairbrush. Her eyes met her mother's.

"What do you want from me?" she said with more than a hint of annoyance.

"I want to know why he's changed his mind about coming to the wedding. Somebody must have said something to him."

"Not necessarily. Maybe he's feeling uncomfortable. Or maybe he's got something better to do." Belinda swiped the brush through her hair.

"I'm going to get to the bottom of this." Paula folded her arms. "Where's Adrian? I want to talk to him." And with that, she stormed out of the room with twice the determination as she'd entered it.

"Don't worry," Belinda said to Charlotte. "Adrian can stand up to her."

# Chapter 7

With the three dresses draped over his arms, Aaron and Charlotte walked to the car.

"I don't know whether to be relieved or insulted Mrs. Van Dusen didn't trust me to do the final fitting on the wedding dress," said Aaron as he laid the dresses on the back seat.

"It's not that she didn't trust you; she just wanted the organ grinder, not the monkey."

"What's that supposed to mean?"

"It's just an expression."

They drove in silence. Aaron slowed as they approached a stop sign, then signaled and pulled onto the main road that led to the hotel, located on the other side of Walkers Ridge. Charlotte watched the bright greens of trees in their early-summer finery flash by her window, then turned to Aaron.

"Did you think the atmosphere was pretty tense when Sophie said she wanted to wear a longer dress?"

"It sure was."

"There was just something about the way she said it that seemed so, I don't know . . . hostile? There's a lot of tension in that wedding party, which is too bad, because there's enough to worry about even when everybody gets along. I think there's something going on under the surface."

As they approached the hotel, they passed a large plot of land. Undeveloped and unloved, surrounded by an eyesore of a rusted chain-link fence, the land had been vacant as long as Charlotte could remember. Once a year, a man on a large mowing machine showed up to cut the tall weeds that were allowed to go to seed.

"Oh!" exclaimed Charlotte, twisting in her seat to look over her shoulder. "That's new. I haven't noticed that before."

"What's new?"

Charlotte shifted back to a front-facing position. "That sign on the chain-link fence beside the Middleton property. The land's been sitting there idle for donkey's years, and now there's a huge sign that says, 'Executive mid-rise condominiums.' That's all I could see as we drove past. I wonder when they'll break ground and get the project started. Maybe Rupert and I'll walk over later and take a closer look at it." After a moment she added, "I wonder if Harvey knows about that. And the Middleton place is starting to look really shabby."

The Middleton house was an imposing three-story structure that had been on the market for a few months and—unusually for the area, where most of the houses were wooden structures—was built of red brick. The elderly owner, a widow, had moved out, leaving the house empty, and what once would have been a lovely example of early twentieth-century architecture was now showing increasingly worsening signs of neglect. Dirty white paint peeled off rotten wooden frames that surrounded dull, expressionless windows, and the wraparound porch was beginning to sag.

A few minutes later, Aaron parked his uncle's car at the side of the Jacobs Grand Hotel, and they carefully lifted out the dresses they'd brought home for alterations.

"Do you want me to take the bride's dress to the workroom?" Aaron asked.

"No," said Charlotte. "I'll take it home and work on it there."

With Belinda's wedding dress draped across her outstretched arms and her purse slung over her shoulder, Charlotte set off on the short walk home. She and Rupert lived in one of three bungalows located on the hotel grounds. In the old days, these would have been occupied by holidaying families, but now they were assigned to staff. Charlotte rented one, artistic director Simon Dyer lived in the second, and the third was reserved for the season's visiting lead actor. This role was usually filled by a British actor or actress whose career had peaked but whose name still had just enough drawing power to fill seats, who had the right sort of accent to give American theatergoers a feel for authenticity, and who was willing to accept the job because they were realistic enough to recognize that their days of ego-fueled career choices were behind them. This year's star attraction, Brian Prentice, had gotten off to a rocky, alcoholic start, but he seemed to have got that under control, and he was performing well, garnering excellent reviews, and giving director Simon Dyer no cause for alarm.

Charlotte and Brian had history. They'd become involved at the start of their careers at the Royal Shakespeare Company and had come to New York together to work on a Broadway production. But when Brian told her he was breaking off their engagement to marry someone else, Charlotte had not returned home to Britain with the rest of the company. She instead stayed on in New York and, working through a broken heart, had carved out a different kind of career for herself. Although she worked primarily for the Catskills Shakespeare Theater Company, she also took on freelance costume design assignments for Broadway productions. Her life had been orderly and happy until Brian had arrived earlier this year, stirring up old memories, although not reviving old feelings. While they were not what could be called friends, they maintained a polite, professional relationship.

Balancing the bride's dress over one arm while she dug her keys out of her purse, she turned at the sound of footsteps on the path.

"Only me," boomed a familiar, deep voice.

"Oh, Brian, you startled me," said Charlotte. "Here, hold this while I open the door." Brian held out his hands and took the dress in its garment bag.

"Would this be a dress for the Van Dusen wedding by any chance?" he asked. "I heard Aaron was working on the bridesmaids' dresses."

"Yes, it is," said Charlotte, pushing open the door and entering her bungalow. She took the dress from Brian. "I'll be back in a minute." She laid the dress carefully on her bed and then returned to the steps, where he had remained standing.

"You can come in and close the door," she said. "I'm putting the kettle on. Fancy a cup of tea?"

"Oh, yes please. I could do with one."

The sound of running water filled the kitchen, and a moment later, Charlotte switched on the kettle. "I had a visit from Harvey this afternoon," said Brian. "We were rehearsing the truncated version of *A Midsummer Night's Dream* for the charity performance."

"Oh, yes. What did he want? Is everything all right?" She indicated a chair at the table.

"Everything's fine. It's just that he's had a call from Mrs. Van Dusen, and she wants me to walk her daughter down the aisle."

"Well, that's a lovely compliment." Brian frowned. "Isn't it?" Charlotte asked.

"I suppose so. It's just that I don't know her daughter. I've never even met her. It seems odd that she would ask me. They're meant to be a prominent family in these parts. They must know lots of chaps who could do this."

"Well, she asked you," said Charlotte. "She's after your star power, Brian! She probably thinks the theatrical sound of your voice will add to the occasion. You know, when the minister asks, 'Who gives this woman to be married to this man?' and you reply, 'I do.' Are you going to do it?"

"I don't see how I can say no," said Brian. "That would be rather churlish, don't you think?"

"It would be hard to get out of," agreed Charlotte. "She's our best patron and raises a lot of money for the theater, so Harvey would be very upset if you said no. We never want to disappoint Mrs. Van Dusen." She made the tea, set out cups and spoons on a tray, and brought everything to the table. "What's really bothering you about this, Brian?" she asked as she poured a cup and handed it to him. "You're an actor. This is nothing for you—it's a very small performance, compared to what you're used to."

"I think it's more the social aspects," he said.

"Ah," said Charlotte. "I see. You're afraid the temptation might be too much. The parties and all that alcohol on offer. Is that it?"

He nodded.

"Well, I'm sure there are ways to handle that. We'll help you. You know you have our support."

They sipped their tea in a quiet, almost companionable sort of way. Finally, Brian drained the last of his tea, then stood up, and Charlotte walked him to the door. Just as she opened it, a man in a dark-blue police officer's uniform approached. The two men nodded at each other, and as Brian disappeared up the path that led to his bungalow, Ray Nicholson, chief of police for Walkers Ridge, entered the bungalow. Tall, with dark, wavy hair and a fit body that shattered the stereotype of the overweight, out-of-shape, small-town policeman, Ray had met Charlotte about a year ago when she and Rupert brought a lost dog into the police station. They'd discovered a shared love of dogs, limited-release films at the local cinema, home-cooked meals on cozy nights in, occasional trips to New York City, and finally, each other.

He embraced Charlotte, then tipped his head in the direction Brian had taken.

"What did he want?"

"I'm not really sure. Either he's lonely and wanted a place to hang out for a bit, or he's afraid he's going to fall off the wagon at the Van Dusen wedding. He's been asked to walk the bride down the aisle."

"Are you going to the wedding?"

"Not really going. Working it. Aaron and I are doing the alterations on the bridal party's dresses, and I expect we'll be there the morning of to dress the wedding party. Aaron will give the men a hand."

"Speaking of the wedding party, I think one of them just passed me on the way here. Not a local guy, that's for sure."

"What makes you think that?"

"We've received complaints from several motorists about a crazy, reckless driver, so we ran a check on his license plates. Car belongs to an Adrian Archer with a Manhattan address. And to my knowledge, no one around here drives an orange Lamborghini. It sticks out like a sore thumb."

Charlotte laughed. "No, they drive tractors or Land Rovers, and that's the way we like it. And you're right. He is a member of the wedding party. The groom, in fact. Apparently not Paula Van Dusen's first choice for son-in-law. There's a strange dynamic in that wedding party, but I can't quite put my finger on it."

"Well," said Ray, "why don't you tell me about it over dinner. We've got time for a bite to eat in town before the movie."

"Good," said Charlotte. "It'll probably be my last night out before the wedding. We've got three dresses to hem and costumes for the play to fit. This next week's going to be really busy."

# Chapter 8

"I hope we don't get stopped by the police," said Brian Prentice.

As the members of the theater company riding in the small yellow school bus on the way to the Van Dusen estate howled with laughter, Ray Nicholson, who was driving, replied with a broad grin, "Well, if we do, better let me do the talking."

Brian, dressed in costume as Theseus, Duke of Athens, sat directly behind Ray, with director Simon Dyer beside him and Charlotte across the aisle with Aaron beside her in the window seat. The male actors on board, a few in women's costumes, were all in full stage makeup, with heavy foundation and dark slashes of eyeliner that gave a grossly exaggerated, sinister appearance up close but from a distance, under lights, looked natural and made their facial features easier for the audience to discern.

Aaron gazed out the window, watching the lush, dark-green trees that flanked the two-lane highway flash by. As an orange blur came alongside the bus, he called out, "Ray, watch it! Car passing and it's really moving."

Ray braked hard as the bus approached a sharp turn, and the orange car veered sharply in front of his vehicle, narrowly avoiding an oncoming truck.

"Christ!" exclaimed Ray, squinting into the late-afternoon sun. "Not that jackass Adrian Archer again! What I wouldn't give right now for a siren and flashing lights." But with the orange vehicle now in front of him, Ray could see that Adrian Archer wasn't in the driver's seat. The car was being driven by a blonde woman, her hair pulled back in a ponytail blowing in the breeze from the open windows. Archer was in the passenger seat turned toward her.

Keeping his eyes on the vehicle in front of him, Ray called out its license number to Charlotte, who wrote it down in the notebook she kept with her at all times. She also jotted down the details of the woman in the driver's seat. *Probably nothing*, she thought. *All kinds of legitimate reasons why Adrian would be out with Sophie. They could be running an errand for Belinda, say.*

Ray slowed as they approached the Van Dusen estate, and when the gates swung open, he drove up the drive and around the back of the house. The graveled parking area would eventually fill up with the cars of theatergoers, but for now, just a few cars were parked there, including the orange Lamborghini that had passed them a few minutes ago.

*

*A Midsummer Night's Dream*, with its elements of the natural and the supernatural, and much of it set in "a wood near Athens" and "another part of the wood," lends itself perfectly to an outdoor performance in a beautifully maintained garden with a wide expanse of lawn and beds filled with fragrant herbs and flowers.

The company responsible for the wedding's floral displays had agreed to Simon's request to install the white wooden arch a day early so the theater company could use it as Titania's bower. The head florist had donated baskets of red roses, pink carnations, white gerbera daisies, yellow lilies, and ferns that had reached their best-before date but had one more night left in them, and her enthusiastic staff had wired them to the arch. In the morning, those flowers would be removed and replaced with fresh, expensive white roses and orchids.

The theater company's carpenter and sound and lighting technicians had spent the afternoon preparing the stage for the evening performance, installing lighting and planting speakers around the stage, carefully hidden behind tubs of potted plants.

There was no real backstage area, just a painted curtain at the rear of the stage behind which actors would wait until they were needed onstage and Charlotte and Aaron could help them with quick costume changes. The props table had been set up to one side, along with another table filled with chilled water bottles for the cast during intermission.

When she had ticked the last of the costume items off her master list, satisfied that everything was in place for the performance, Charlotte wandered around to the front of the stage to watch the theatergoers arrive. She was always amazed by how quickly the audience for this production materialized; one moment, just a few early arrivals keen to get a good spot were staking out their places, and the next moment, there wasn't a spare inch left on which to unfold a lawn chair.

As the crowd unpacked their picnics, poured glasses of wine, and chatted with friends, Charlotte returned backstage, picked up a water bottle, and joined Ray at the prompt desk to one side of the stage. She set the bottle down near his copy of the script.

"Ready?"

"Ready. And so's he, by the looks of him." A man wearing a beige raincoat and fedora, with a camera slung around his neck and a notebook in his hand, beetled toward them.

"Oh, no," groaned Charlotte. "Not that awful Fletcher Macmillan. I wonder what he wants this time."

"Hello, Charlotte. Ray," said Fletcher Macmillan. "You've got a lovely evening for it." Macmillan, a dedicated anglophile, had perfected a pretentious, old-fashioned mid-Atlantic accent and manner of speech that reminded Charlotte of a character from a late-night black-and-white film.

"Still on the arts beat, are you Fletcher?" Ray asked.

"Well, that and other things. You know how it is when you work for a small newspaper like the *Hudson Valley Echo*. Bit of this, bit of that. I'm not here tonight for the play, though. I've already given that a glowing review. I'm covering Mrs. Van Dusen's annual fundraiser and hoping for an interview with the bride and groom. Have you seen them, by any chance?"

"No, sorry, I haven't," said Charlotte.

"Oh, well," said Macmillan. "The night is young. Lots of time. Must dash. Want to get some photographs of the crowd. See you at the after party."

As he wandered away, Charlotte remarked that she too must dash, as it was time for her to be getting backstage. Ray squeezed her hand in a parting gesture of encouragement and said, "See you at the intermission."

As the seconds ticked by until curtain up, the tension backstage rose. Simon gave the actors a few last-minute words of encouragement, and they stood in little groups, doing whatever they needed to do to reduce performance anxiety. One or two dangled their arms loosely at their sides while they shook out their hands. A couple exchanged quiet words, while others remained apart from the main group, eyes closed, taking deep breaths, focusing on whatever quiet ritual prepared them for the performance they were about to give. Charlotte had seen this many times and knew that their anxiety would evaporate the moment they stepped onstage.

The audience chatted quietly and then, although no announcement had been made, seemed to sense a change in atmosphere, a surge of creative energy. At a signal from Simon, Aaron told the actors to stand by and sent a message to the audio technician, and a moment later, Purcell's light, sprightly baroque music signaled the play was about to begin.

The audience hastily packed away the remains of their picnics, switched off their mobile phones, and settled back in their lawn chairs. Twenty seconds later, just after Aaron announced "Curtain up!," Brian Prentice reached out for the hand of the young actor playing Hippolyta, and with a swish of his skirts, the two swept onstage.

*"Now fair Hippolyta, our nuptial hour*
*Draws on apace; four happy days bring in*
*Another moon; but oh, methinks, how slow*
*This old moon wanes!"*

Brian intoned in his deep, mellow voice.

"And we're off!" Charlotte whispered to Aaron. The tenseness that had enveloped the players just before curtain up dissipated like morning fog and was replaced by a smooth confidence as the production got under way. Charlotte thought of it as an aircraft taking off through a tense climb until it reached cruising altitude, when passengers breathed a silent sigh of relief and relaxed back into their seats. The actors would soon hit their stride, as well as their marks. The novelty of male actors playing female characters wore off quickly as the audience not only got used to it and accepted it but began to enjoy it.

Behind the stage, Aaron rechecked a metal rack of costumes, arranging them in the order they'd be needed against a script with exit lines of dialogue highlighted to show which actors would need a costume change when they came offstage. A quick turnaround was needed in a couple of instances, as the actor returned almost immediately to the stage as another character. After satisfying himself that the costumes were in order for Charlotte and him to make the quick changes, he turned his attention to the props table. He touched each item as he checked it off against his list: donkey head, purple flower, scroll, lantern . . . Everything he'd unloaded from the bus was there, and as the deep shadows of the night began to gather along the edges of the garden and the players got the play up on its legs, he sat on a metal folding chair, unscrewed the cap of a water bottle, and relaxed, just a little, with one ear cocked to the action onstage. As the first scene ended, the actors dashed into the changing area, and Aaron and Charlotte removed the skirt of the actor playing Hermia and prepared him to appear onstage in the next scene as one of the tradesmen discussing the logistics of their play *Pyramus and Thisbe*, which they planned to perform at the wedding of the Duke of Athens.

The audience's laughter at the banter of the characters known as the "rude mechanicals"—Bottom, Quince, Starveling, Snout, Flute, and Snug—drifted up into a sky filling with the last pink blush of daylight. Slowly and almost imperceptibly, as the play unfolded, the warmth of a late-June evening gave way to the cool air of night. Sweaters and jackets were pulled out of bags and travel rugs draped over knees. The subtle fragrance of flowers that release their perfume at night crept over the scene. As the pale gray of twilight descended, floodlights suspended from trees came on, illuminating the stage and contrasting with the dimming light around it.

Aaron glanced up at the lights.

"If you think it looks good now," said Charlotte, "just wait a bit. It'll be completely dark soon, and when the moon starts to rise, everything will look absolutely magical. There's something about this play . . . is it a dream? Is it real? Perhaps the moon has something to do with that."

"Is it a full moon tonight?"

"Yes. This performance is always scheduled for the Friday night nearest the full moon. And we've certainly got a beautiful night for it tonight." She checked her watch, then tipped her head toward the stage, and they listened.

*"What thou seest when thou dost wake,*
*Do it for thy true love take . . ."*

"Okay. Oberon's just sprinkled the magic juice on Titania's eyelids, so the intermission's coming up in about ten minutes." She glanced at the clothes rack and Aaron's prop table. "Have you got everything ready to go for the third and fourth acts? Simon will be here in a few minutes to talk to the actors."

Aaron nodded. "Yeah, it's all good. I checked it."

"Right, we'll use the intermission to see the actors have everything they need, so I'm going to the loo now. Keep an eye on things here. I won't be long."

When she had disappeared into the house, Aaron waited a moment longer, then slipped away himself. A few moments later, puffs of marijuana smoke drifted down the garden, away from the audience, adding its distinctive odor to the fragrance permeating the night air.

# Chapter 9

Charlotte returned just as the second act was ending to enthusiastic applause.

The actors, charged and flushed, stepped off the few steps at the back of the stage and materialized in the grassy backstage area. Aaron's offer of bottles of cold water was accepted with grateful outstretched hands. A couple of actors reached into the depths of their costumes and pulled out phones, then walked off a little distance to check for messages. *Oh, Simon would be livid if he knew they had phones on them*, thought Charlotte. Bad enough when a cell phone in the audience rings, but can you imagine if a phone in an actor's pocket went off?

The intermission was scheduled to last twenty minutes, but based on previous shows, Charlotte expected it would run closer to thirty as audience members socialized, topped up champagne glasses, and checked their phones. Night had drawn in, and a cloak of darkness had settled over the garden. Charlotte and Aaron checked the actors' costumes and made sure they were prepared for the second half of the play. As the actors needed onstage for act three began to center themselves, Aaron let out an exclamation of dismay that brought Charlotte immediately to his side.

"What's the matter?"

He pointed at the items on the props table: the scroll, lantern, large purple flower, toy dog. "The donkey's head is missing! It was there when the play started. I know it was. I unloaded it off the bus. I put it on the table myself, and I checked the props one more time against the list just after the play started."

"Well, maybe the actor playing Bottom already has it. Let's find him."

They scrambled among the actors until they found the one they needed and exchanged a few anxious words.

"No, it's the last thing I put on," he said. "It's hot and heavy and it smells so bad I can barely breathe. I leave it until the very last moment and take it off the table just before I go back onstage." He shook his head, and the three of them set off to find Simon. In the usual course of stagecraft, the director's work is done at the end of the final rehearsal. Everything has been set, and it then becomes the stage manager's job to make sure every performance runs smoothly and as the director intended. As the stage manager for this show, with a vital prop missing, Aaron was in trouble, as was the performance.

They found Simon drinking champagne with Paula Van Dusen on the terrace. Charlotte interrupted them and led Simon to one side. His look of concern brought Paula over at once.

"What is it? What's happened?"

"It's the donkey's head," Charlotte said. "It seems to have disappeared."

"And that's not the sort of thing you'd have two of, I suppose," said Mrs. Van Dusen.

"No, it isn't," replied Charlotte, "and we've only got a minute or two to sort this out." She appealed to Paula. "Can we go into the house and see what we can find to improvise with?"

"Of course. Tell me what you need. And we'll have to find Phyllis. I'm pretty sure she was here just a few minutes ago. She's around here somewhere, and she's the one who knows where everything is."

"Have you got a fur hat?" Charlotte asked as they raced into the house. "The bigger the better."

"How did this happen?" Simon asked Aaron. "Weren't you backstage keeping an eye on things?"

Aaron nodded miserably.

"Did you see anybody hanging around backstage who shouldn't have been?"

Aaron shook his head.

"Some idiot probably took it for a joke," said Simon. "Well, let's hope Charlotte comes up with something in time." He gestured at the audience returning to their lawn chairs. "Tell the sound technician to play a bit of music. We can't start the third act without the donkey head."

To Aaron's great relief, Charlotte and Paula Van Dusen arrived a few minutes later carrying a small, brown bundle.

"It won't look too bad from the audience," Charlotte said, holding up a mink hat with a pair of black socks, sticking up like ears, pinned to the side. Aaron gingerly touched one of the socks. "Stuffed with wedding-gift tissue paper. Come on, you'd better get this backstage." She gave him a sharp look. "Let's get through this performance, and then we'll talk. Something happened here, and I want to know what."

As Aaron ran off, Paula exclaimed, "I'm just amazed I was able to find that hat so quickly! It'll look better on Bottom than it ever did on my mother-in-law. I'm going to really enjoy this."

"Thanks so much," said Charlotte. "I'd best get backstage now."

A change in the music announced the beginning of the second half of the performance, and once again, the audience, now happily lubricated and showing no signs of restlessness at the longer intermission, settled in their seats. The full moon had risen in a cloudless, starry sky, bathing the garden in an intense, cold white light that seemed to freeze everything it touched and heighten the audience's appreciation of the drama unfolding in front of them. The action began with the workmen, the rude mechanicals, meeting in the forest to rehearse their performance of *Pyramus and Thisbe*—the play within a play. The mischievous fairy, Puck, appears and then disappears offstage with the actor playing Bottom. Aaron fitted the improvised hat on him, and he returned onstage, then the business began of the fairy queen Titania, under a spell, awakening and falling in love with the first creature she sees—the weaver, Nick Bottom, whose head has been turned into that of a donkey.

Charlotte stood to one side, one hand over her mouth, watching the actor perform in Mrs. Van Dusen's mink hat. Judging by the audience's laughter, he seemed to be doing all right, and she gave Aaron a reassuring nod. Just as she stepped back to return to the clothes rail to prepare for the next costume change, a flash of white in a fleeting movement caught her attention, and out of the corner of her eye, she glimpsed a woman with a blonde ponytail running across the garden. *Is that Belinda?* she thought. *What's she up to?* But she couldn't spare any more time to think about it; an actor in front of her needed dressing.

The play gathered momentum in the final two acts until Puck stepped onstage to deliver his epilogue, suggesting to the audience that everything they had just seen had happened in a dream. The players took several bows to rapturous applause, and the audience, reluctant to accept that the play was really over, finally began to pack up their chairs and picnic supplies.

"I like the hat much better than that awful head," the actor playing Bottom told Charlotte as he stroked it. "I hope we can keep it. Do you think it would be okay if I wore it to the party?"

"Why not?" said Charlotte. "I think that would be fun." She grinned as he replaced it on his head and bounded off.

"We'll have to get all this lot to the bus," Charlotte said, surveying Aaron's pile of props as Ray appeared from the prompt table to help. "You'll never guess," Charlotte said to him. "Someone stole, or at least made off with, our donkey's head at some point when Aaron and I weren't looking."

"Really? What would anyone want with that?" he said. "It was a bit moth eaten, to say the least."

"Probably someone who'd had a bit too much to drink took it for a joke," suggested Charlotte. "You were at the prompt desk the whole time. Did you see anyone back here who didn't belong?"

"No, but my attention during the play is on the prompt book, and during the intermission, I just saw actors wandering around."

"Well, I wouldn't be surprised if it turns up in the morning," said Charlotte. "As you said, who'd want that old thing?"

"Maybe the actor hid it so he wouldn't have to wear it," suggested Aaron.

"I doubt that," said Charlotte. "But it could have been dumped somewhere on the grounds as a prank, so we'll have to make arrangements for you to be back here early tomorrow morning to look for it."

Aaron groaned. "It's going to be a late night, and I wanted the morning off before we have to dress the wedding party."

"That's exactly why we've got to look for it early. A wedding's going to be held in this garden tomorrow, and the place is going to get very busy with setting up. They'll have enough to do without us getting in the way looking for a donkey's head." Aaron folded his arms and looked at the ground.

"Well, the good news is I've decided to come with you and help you look for it," Charlotte continued. "Now, let's get ready for the after party. But we've got an early start in the morning, remember, so don't drink too much!"

# Chapter 10

Phyllis stood on the steps of the terrace, directing members of the wedding party, invited guests who had contributed generously to Paula Van Dusen's fundraising efforts, and the entire cast and crew of the Catskills Shakespeare Theater Company to a ground-floor room on the opposite end of the house from the room where Aaron had fitted the bridesmaids' dresses.

The room's double oak doors were closed and guarded by a middle-aged man in black tie who politely asked the guests to wait. "The doors will open at ten," he said, and promptly at ten, Phyllis excused her way through the waiting crowd of about fifty people. She took hold of one of the enormous bronze handles, the man in black tie seized the other, and together they pulled the doors open.

The guests at the front of the crowd gasped in delight as they filed into the spacious room.

Just inside, smiling young women dressed as fairies, in short white dresses with gossamer wings and crowns made of white roses, balanced silver trays, each holding six champagne flutes arranged in two perfect rows.

"Would you like a glass of champagne?" a young woman with cascades of tight blonde curls asked Charlotte, offering her tray.

"Lovely, that," Charlotte said to Aaron as they took in replica oak trees positioned in large tubs around the room with white fairy lights threaded through their branches. Tables with green cloths and centerpieces of white roses were placed around the walls. At the bar and buffet table, waiters dressed in workmen's clothes as the rude mechanicals stood ready to serve guests.

The lighting was atmospheric, transporting everyone to a magical forest on a midsummer evening.

"I wonder," Charlotte remarked to Aaron, "do you suppose the event planner who created all this"—she waved her hand—"might have spotted our donkey's head and 'borrowed' it? Take a good look around the room, especially under those fake oak trees, on the off chance. You never know."

Paula Van Dusen, having changed into a floor-length, loose-fitting gown that billowed as she walked and holding a glass of champagne, glided up to Aaron and Charlotte.

"Oh, Mrs. Van Dusen, you've been very clever here," laughed Charlotte. "Not only have you created a whole *Midsummer Night's Dream* décor—which is fabulous, by the way—but you've got the characters from the play, in costume, mingling with your guests."

"Well, of course, they'd all be more than welcome to use the bathrooms to change and remove their makeup, if they wish. Phyllis has stocked the bathrooms with all the supplies they'll need. And do call me Paula."

"Aaron will let them know. They'll appreciate that." Aaron gave her a quick nod and wandered off to speak to cast members. "Paula, I see Brian standing on his own over there, looking a little lost." She gestured toward one of the trees. "I think we should go over and see if he's okay."

"Why don't you leave him to me?" said Paula. "Belinda and Adrian will be making their entrance soon. My table is just there," she said, pointing about halfway down the room. "It's got a Reserved sign on it, so why don't you take a seat, and Brian and I'll join you in a few minutes."

"Sounds good." Charlotte signaled to Ray, who was talking to Simon, and the two walked across the room to her. "We're to sit at Paula's table," she said. "It's the one with the Reserved sign on it."

"Here it is," said Ray, pointing to an empty table. He pulled out a chair for Charlotte, then sat down beside her. A few minutes later, Paula and Phyllis arrived, with Brian just behind them.

Paula rattled off a list of instructions to Phyllis and then asked in a voice just loud enough to be heard over the crowd noise, "And Hugh? Is he here?"

"No, he's gone," Phyllis replied. "He said to give you his apologies, but he had to leave just before the play ended."

"Well, I suppose I can understand that. He probably finds watching Belinda with Adrian just too much. All right, Phyllis, thank you. I won't take up any more of your time. I know you've got lots to see to."

Paula Van Dusen turned to Charlotte. "I did have high hopes for those two, Belinda and Hugh, but sadly, it was not to be."

Just as she finished speaking, a recorded trumpet fanfare announced the imminent arrival of the evening's star couple. The bright beam of a spotlight illuminated the oak doors, and everyone's attention was riveted on them. Several more seconds passed to heighten the anticipation, then the doors swung open, revealing a smiling Belinda dressed as the queen of the fairies in a frothy, blush-colored ball gown with a tiara nestled in a complicated, upswept hairdo. Looking slightly sheepish, Adrian Archer stood at her side in a dark suit.

Holding hands, the couple made their entrance, pausing in the doorway to wave, then advancing into the room to enthusiastic applause led by Paula Van Dusen, who had risen to her feet, encouraging everyone else to do the same. The couple began to slowly circle the room, stopping to greet and chat with their guests.

"Can I get you something to drink?" Ray asked Charlotte.

"I'd love another glass of champagne. But first, I'd like to wash my hands. I haven't had a chance yet, after we handled the costumes and props. Won't be long." She took off her sweater, hung it over the back of her chair, and left the room.

She hesitated in the hallway, unsure whether to turn left or right, and hearing women's voices coming from her left, she turned in that direction. Approaching her, eyes down and deep in conversation, were Jessica, one of Belinda's bridesmaids, and another woman she didn't recognize. As she prepared for a friendly exchange of "hellos," they walked past her, their words drifting behind them.

"I think we should tell her," one of them said. "I'd want to know."

*Now that's intriguing*, thought Charlotte. *Tell who, what? Tell her she needs to lose ten pounds? Tell her she has bad breath?*

She returned to the ballroom to find the party in full swing. People were lined up at the bar and buffet, and the crowd din was at a much higher volume.

She slid into the chair beside Ray and tucked her arm through his.

He tilted his head toward her and asked, "You okay? What's wrong?"

She shook her head. "Nothing. It's just . . . you know when you overhear a snippet of conversation and wish you'd heard more or knew what they were talking about? How tantalizing that is?" He nodded. "Well, it's like that."

"What did you hear?"

She glanced at Paula, engrossed in conversation with Brian, who appeared a little more comfortable. His shoulders had relaxed, and he was smiling.

"I'll tell you later," Charlotte told Ray as she caught sight of Belinda threading her way between the tables toward them.

"Mom, have you seen Adrian?" she asked her mother. Paula lowered her head to hear her daughter better against the background of noisy guests. "I can't find him anywhere."

"He's probably outside having a cigarette," Paula said. She pushed her chair back slightly in a motion that indicated she was about to stand up. "I'm tempted to have one myself, actually, but I mustn't. Shall I help you look for him?"

"No, that's okay." Belinda, who had had to step back to dodge her mother's chair, bent over slightly and rested a light but restraining hand on Paula's shoulder. "You stay here. I'll find him."

Sighing heavily, Paula pulled her chair in toward the table just as Belinda turned to go, catching the hem of her dress.

Belinda grabbed at her skirt and was about to give it a tug to release it when Charlotte jumped up. "Don't, Belinda!" she said. "You'll . . ." Before she could finish came the sickening sound of tearing fabric. "Okay," said Charlotte. "Let's not make this any worse. Brian, you stand up and pull your chair out from the table to give us a bit more room." As he followed instructions, Charlotte indicated that Paula should slide over in Brian's direction, and when she had done so, Charlotte lifted Paula's chair off Belinda's dress, then dropped to her knees to examine the damage.

She held up a long piece of fabric, barely attached to the dress, and shook her head.

"You can't wear this dress, Belinda. It's a tripping hazard. If we had more time, I could repair it, but I think the best thing would be to go upstairs and change. Have you got something else you could wear?"

"She's got a closetful of beautiful dresses," said Paula. "I'll come up with you."

"No, Mom," said Belinda. "We can't both leave the party at the same time. You stay here and look after everybody. If Charlotte doesn't mind, I'd rather she came with me. She knows all about quick changes."

Charlotte gathered up the skirt and handed Belinda the torn strip of fabric. "You'll have to hold onto this so you don't trip over it," she said, and then with a glance at the table, she added, "We'll be back in no time."

As they entered Belinda's bedroom, Charlotte asked, "Shall I have a look in your closet while you take off that dress?"

"Yeah, that'll be good," said Belinda. Charlotte entered the walk-in closet, with its orderly shelving for shoes and bags on one side and drawers for sweaters and hangers for dresses and longer garments on the other. She ran several beautiful dresses along the rail, pulled a couple, and then returned to the bedroom.

Still in her torn dress, Belinda sat on the edge of her bed, furiously tapping her phone. Charlotte waited, a dress in each hand, until she finished.

"Sorry," said Belinda. "Just sending Adrian a text telling him to meet me downstairs." She set her phone down and stood up. "Right. What have you got?"

Charlotte held up the two dresses for her consideration. Belinda nodded at one, and Charlotte helped her out of the extravagant dress and into the simpler one she had indicated she wanted to wear.

"What about your hair?" Charlotte asked as she hung the discarded dress on a padded hanger. "Do you want to keep it up?"

Belinda studied herself in the mirror and, taking in the shorter dress she was now wearing, shook her head.

"No, the tiara looks silly with this. Let's take it off."

"If you sit down, I'll fix your hair for you," said Charlotte. "Working in the theater, you pick up a few hair and makeup tricks, too." She gently eased the tiara off and then the pins that held Belinda's hair up, along with a few extensions that had been clipped in for fullness.

A few minutes later, dressed in a vivid cobalt-blue dress, Belinda was ready, with her shoulder-length hair in place and an application of fresh lipstick. She glanced at the dress on the bed.

"I won't be wearing that again," she said. "If you'd like it, you're welcome to it. Maybe you can cut it up or something and use it for one of your costumes."

"Thank you," said Charlotte. "People would be surprised by how we can create costumes out of contemporary fabric. I'll leave it here for now, though, and collect it later, if that's all right."

"Fine with me," said Belinda. "How do I look?"

"You look great," Charlotte assured her. "Let's get you back to the party."

"It's almost over," Belinda said.

As they closed the bedroom door behind them, Jessica turned the corner and hurried down the hallway toward them.

"Belinda," she panted, "your mother said I'd find you up here. I need to talk to you. It's about Adrian, he's . . ." She stopped speaking, glanced at Charlotte, frowned, and waited.

Charlotte got the message. "Right, well, I'd better get back to the party," she said. "See you soon."

"Okay, thanks." Belinda opened the door to her bedroom, and as the two women ducked inside, Charlotte could just make out Jessica saying, "I didn't know if I should tell you this, but . . ." as the door closed behind them.

"Everything all right?" Ray asked when she rejoined the table a few minutes later. She nodded, then looked at Paula Van Dusen, who took a sip of wine, set her glass on the table, and leaned over to Charlotte with an inquiring look.

"She's fine," Charlotte said. "Should be down in a minute."

"Well, that's good. The fireworks are about to start."

*Yes*, thought Charlotte, *I think they are*.

As guests moved to the terrace and garden for the pyrotechnic display that would end the after party, Charlotte caught sight of Fletcher Macmillan scuttling toward the parking lot. She pointed him out to Ray. "Rushing off to write his front-page story for tomorrow's edition of the paper," he commented.

The crowd exclaimed in delight as shooting shells whistled high into the clear, still night sky, then exploded, scattering their payload of bright pink and silver stars across a velvety-black universe.

Arms folded, Paula Van Dusen watched from the terrace balustrade. She glanced every now and then toward the door, as if expecting someone.

"That's odd," Charlotte said to Ray, with a small gesture in Paula's direction. "I would have thought Belinda and Adrian would be out here with her."

"Maybe they're watching from somewhere else," he said, keeping his eyes upward. "Oh, look at that!" he exclaimed, as a burning streak of hot, white light illuminated the sky.

"I'm a bit chilly," Charlotte said.

Without lowering his eyes from the fireworks display, Ray stretched out his arm to put around her. When he felt her bare shoulder, he looked at her upturned face.

"Where's your sweater?"

"I must have left it inside. I'll go get it now."

"No, stay and watch the rest of the show." He draped his jacket over her shoulders and pulled her into him.

When a lingering sulfur smell and smoky trails were all that remained of the brilliant formations, the guests thanked their hosts, said their good-byes, and drifted toward their vehicles.

"While you're loading the actors and crew into the bus, I'll just run in and get my sweater," Charlotte said to him, handing him back his jacket. "Thanks for this."

She threaded her way through the departing crowd and entered the ballroom by the garden entrance. The food and beverage tables had been cleared, and workers were taking down the fairy lights and moving the potted oak trees to one side of the room. Phyllis was working her way around the tables, piling dirty plates and glasses onto trays and removing tablecloths. Charlotte approached her and asked if she'd seen her sweater.

"It's black and white, with diagonal stripes."

"Yes, it's over in the corner with the other things we found," said Phyllis. "I'll show you. I'm going that way with this tray, anyway." She led the way to a table covered with trays of dirty dishes and, beside it, a wicker box with a blue-and-white gingham lining. The box contained several small items, including a silver clutch purse, a Chanel lipstick, two pairs of reading glasses, a disposable cigarette lighter, and Charlotte's sweater.

"Speaking of lost and found," said Charlotte as she retrieved her sweater, "we lost rather an unusual item during the performance this evening."

"Oh, yes. What would that be?" Phyllis slid a tray loaded with dirty dishes into the trolley beside the table, then reached for another one.

"A donkey's head," Charlotte replied as Phyllis straightened up. "It's a prop we use in the play. It seems to have gone missing sometime before or during the intermission. Anyway, we'd like to come back early tomorrow to search the grounds. We won't get in the way of the setup for the wedding."

Phyllis's hand trembled slightly as she placed a few stray glasses on a tray.

She rubbed her hands together lightly and then shook them out. "Touch of arthritis," she said in an apologetic tone. "It comes on especially when I'm tired."

"You must be exhausted," said Charlotte. "And all this still to do?" She looked around the room. "You could do with more help."

"It's been a long day," agreed Phyllis. "But we'll be done here soon enough. We can leave some of it for the morning. Just got to get the dishes ready for the caterers to pick up." Her voice was flat, and her eyes were dull and lifeless. If she'd been wearing lipstick earlier, it was now gone, giving her a washed-out, drained look. She sighed. "Yes, I suppose it'll be all right if you come back in the morning to look for whatever it is you've lost, as long as you don't get in the way of the people setting up for the wedding. I'll let Mrs. Van Dusen know if I see her. I expect she's gone up for the night."

"Right. Well, it was a lovely party. Thank you. I mustn't keep you. We'll probably see you in the morning."

As she walked toward the door that would lead back to the garden, Phyllis stopped her.

"Ned will have locked the garden door by now. You'll have to use this door." She pointed to another exit. "Go down the corridor to the entrance hall and then go out the front door. It's the last one I lock at night."

Charlotte thanked her again and set off toward the main entrance. When she reached the entrance hall, the sound of raised voices made her pause. She entered the hall, but instead of turning right to reach the door, drawn to the voices, she crossed the hall, stepping lightly across the black-and-white marble floor, and entered the corridor that led to the sitting room where she and Aaron had fitted the bridesmaids' dresses.

She looked over her shoulder but saw no one, so continued down the hallway. The voices got louder as she approached the sitting room. The door was closed, and while she couldn't quite make out the words, she could tell that a man and a woman were having a heated exchange.

She backed away and, suddenly aware of the time, hurried down the hallway and out the front door.

Ray was standing beside the bus, watching for her.

"What took you so long?" he asked. "We were about to send a search party."

"Sorry, I had a word with Phyllis, then had to go the long way round to get out because the garden door's been locked."

Ray swung into the driver's seat, and soon the bus, filled with quiet, tired actors, many of whom were more than a little drunk, trundled down the drive and headed for home.

# Chapter 11

Ned Endicott, head gardener for twenty years at Oakland, let out a resigned sigh as he set his wheelbarrow down and surveyed the litter covering the lawn. It was the same every year. He wondered how supposedly well-brought-up people could leave so much trash behind. The grass was littered with it: empty champagne bottles, some upright, some lying on their sides, corks, turned-over chairs, napkins, paper plates—all of it just discarded and left for someone else to pick up. *What is the matter with people?* he asked himself. *Why couldn't they put their trash in the bins or take it home with them?*

And every last bit of it would have to be gone by the time Mrs. Van Dusen came down to breakfast, but fortunately the sun rose early now, so he should have enough time. He checked his watch. Almost seven. His grandson should be here any minute to give him a hand. Ned lifted the packet of green garbage bags and a pair of gardening gloves out of the wheelbarrow and set them on the bottom step of the terrace stairs. His grandson could pick up thc garbage and recycling, and Ned would make a start on the bigger debris, like picnic baskets and lawn chairs that might be of use to someone. He shook his head. Did these people have so much to spend that they could afford to just discard and abandon all this stuff that cost good money?

He picked up the handles of the wheelbarrow, and as he set off down the garden, a woman with dark hair in a blunt-cut bob leading a small dog and a young man carrying a takeaway cup of coffee came around the corner of the house. *Probably here about the wedding*, he thought, setting down the wheelbarrow.

"Morning," said the woman. "I'm Charlotte Fairfax, and this is Aaron Jacobs. We're from the theater company that performed here last night."

"Oh, yes?" said Ned. The stage from last night was still in place, but he'd been reassured that the theater people would be here first thing to dismantle it. "Here about the stage are you? I would have thought there'd be more of you to deal with that."

"No, not here about the stage. The thing is, one of our props went missing last night, and we're here to search the grounds in case someone made off with it and then dumped it, oh, I don't know, in some bushes, maybe."

"Not in my prize floribunda roses, I hope," said a startled Ned.

"I hope not, too," said Charlotte. She surveyed the litter on the lawn. "I'm sorry you've got all that to pick up.

It surprises me that this audience would leave that kind of rubbish behind. What's wrong with people?"

"That's exactly what I ask myself every year," said Ned, with the trace of a thawing smile.

"Right, well, we'd best leave you to it and get on with our search," said Charlotte. "It's a donkey's head we're looking for, in case you find it and wonder what it is." At his understandably puzzled look, she continued, "It's something we use in the play, so if it's here, which we hope it is, it shouldn't be too hard to find. Oh, and I'm sure the theater crew will be along very soon to dismantle the stage so you can get everything set up for the wedding this afternoon."

"I hope so," said Ned. "You can let your dog off his leash, if you like," he added. "The little fellow won't come to any harm here."

"Oh, that would be lovely for him," said Charlotte. "He'll enjoy that."

She unclipped Rupert's lead, and with a cheery wave to Ned, she and Aaron set off across the garden, headed for the border of hydrangea and roses that edged the lawn. The early-morning air was cool but held the promise of a lovely June day. Rupert ran on ahead, pausing every now and then to look behind him to make sure Charlotte was following and then charging off again.

They reached a well-maintained flower bed that stretched the length of the garden and started working their way along it, peering into the plants and occasionally pushing branches aside to make sure the donkey's head was not hidden in the foliage. "Ned keeps everything well trimmed and weeded," said Charlotte, "so if it's in here somewhere, we shouldn't have too much trouble spotting it."

"What's that?" asked Aaron, pointing a little way down the lawn.

"Where? What? I don't see anything."

Aaron strode on, then bent over and picked up something black and held it up for Charlotte to see. When she got a little closer, she recognized a man's dress shoe.

"I suppose someone could have lost it last night," she said slowly, taking it from him and examining the label on the insole. "But the crowd wasn't down this far during the performance. Still, who knows what people were getting up to out here during the party?" But even as she spoke, she felt a sinking in her stomach accompanied by a rise of swelling anxiety that something was very wrong. Realistically, how could someone lose a shoe, then hobble back to the house? It didn't make any sense. And where's the other shoe?

At that moment, Aaron let out an alarmed cry, then stumbled from the edge of the flower bed, falling backward, arms outstretched behind him, onto the grass. He landed in an awkward, sprawling position, then, panting heavily, righted himself.

With Rupert slightly ahead of her, Charlotte hurried toward Aaron and, following the line of his outstretched arm, saw a black-clad figure lying facedown in the flower bed. His arms and legs were spread out, and his head was turned to one side. Except it wasn't his head Charlotte saw; it was the brown, shaggy head of a donkey, its glass eye pointing to the sky and its mouth open in a mocking leer, revealing large yellow teeth. Rupert sniffed at the head, then turned his attention to the body.

"Rupert, off!" commanded Charlotte.

"What the hell is it?" exclaimed Aaron. "Who is it?"

Charlotte, reaching for her phone, just said, "Calling Ray. He'll know what to do." She explained the situation, listened carefully, then pressed the red button.

"Right. If you feel up to it, you're to go at once and tell Paula Van Dusen what we found. Police will be here in a few minutes, and she needs to know what's going on before they arrive. I'm to wait here so I can show them where it is."

Aaron scrambled to his feet and, relieved to have something to do that would get him out of there, loped off toward the house as Charlotte clipped Rupert's leash to his harness. Thinking it would be best if she stayed out of the flower bed in case there might be a footprint or some other clue, she stood on the grass at the edge of the bed and peered at the body. And then, as much as she didn't want to touch the body, she wondered if she should try to remove the head, in case by some miracle the man was still alive. But the police always warned people not to touch the body or disturb the scene, so she took a few steps back and sat down on the grass to wait.

She put her arm around Rupert and gently caressed his fur while her mind worked furiously. She looked back in the direction of the stage and thought about the woman with the blonde ponytail she'd seen running last night.

Could she have come from this direction? And who was it? Belinda? Possibly. Or maybe Sophie the bridesmaid?

In the distance, the whooping of sirens let her know help was on the way. She checked her watch. Not even eight am. She glanced over her shoulder at the diminishing figure of Aaron hurrying toward the house and then turned her attention back to the body. If it was who she thought it was, there'd be no wedding here today or any other day.

# Chapter 12

Wearing a dark-green silk dressing gown emblazoned with a large red-and-yellow fire-breathing dragon, Paula Van Dusen entered her daughter's room without knocking, as she always did. She took in the lump of bedclothes in the center of the queen-sized bed, then crossed to the other side of the room and pulled the cord to open the curtains. Sunlight poured in through the east-facing mullioned windows, casting a pattern of bright diamond shapes across the carpet. Paula glanced down the long drive and then turned her attention to the untidy mountain of rumpled bedding, which seemed to be groaning in protest.

"Up you get, Belinda darling," she said. "In case you've forgotten, it's your wedding day." The bedclothes shifted, and the sleep-swollen face of her daughter emerged. Belinda rubbed her eyes and squinted at her mother. She swallowed a couple of times, then licked her dry lips and reached for the glass of water on her bedside table. Her mother stood there, arms folded, and waited.

Belinda yawned. "What time is it?"

"Almost seven thirty."

Belinda let out a long, slow breath, picked at the bedclothes, and then met her mother's eyes.

"What is it, Belinda? What's the matter?" her mother asked.

"Promise you won't be mad, but I don't think there's going to be a wedding. We had a huge fight last night, and I told him I wouldn't marry him . . ."

"If he were the last man on earth," finished her mother. "Yes, well, people say things like that, don't they? But they don't mean it."

Belinda threw back the bedclothes, lifted her long legs over the side of the bed, and stood up. "Well, I meant it. I'm not going to marry him, and that's all there is to it."

She took a few steps in the direction of her bathroom as her mother called out after her. "Something must have happened to make you change your mind. You were so happy last night. I'm trying hard here not to be judgmental, Belinda. We'll discuss this when you come out."

"There's nothing to discuss," said Belinda. "I don't want to talk about it. I told him it was over and that I'm calling off the wedding, and that's all there is to it."

"That is not all there is to it," her mother shouted to the closed bathroom door. "He must have done or said something, and when you come out of there, you're going to tell me what's going on." The only response: the toilet flushing, followed a moment later by the distinctive sound of running water. Belinda's message from the shower was perfectly clear; for now, at least, the conversation was at an end.

At that moment, someone knocked twice on the bedroom door, and without waiting for a response, a young woman in gray slacks with a bright-pink T-shirt stuck her head around the door.

"What is it, Alex?" demanded Paula.

"Mrs. Van Dusen, I was sent to tell you that the police are on their way, and there's a young man downstairs who wants to speak to you. Says it's urgent."

With a backward glance in the direction of the bathroom, Paula left the room, closing the door behind her. She followed the young woman downstairs to the great hall, where Aaron stood just inside the front door.

"Sorry to bother you," he began.

"Yes, yes, what is it? What's happening?"

"Charlotte sent me to tell you that while we were looking for the donkey head that went missing last night, we found a, well, I'm not sure how to say this, but we found a dead body in your garden."

"You found a what?"

Before he could reply, the sound of footsteps behind him signaled the arrival of the police.

"It's all right, Aaron," said Ray, entering the hall. "Mrs. Van Dusen, we've been called out because a body's been found in your garden. We're on our way out there now, but I must ask you not to leave the house, and please don't let anyone else leave, either."

"But who is it?" demanded Paula.

"We don't know yet, but as soon as we have more information, we'll be back to talk with you."

Mrs. Van Dusen watched him leave and then turned to Aaron.

"Did you see the body? Do you know who it is? What can you tell me? I need to know."

Aaron shook his head. "I'm sorry, Mrs. Van Dusen. I don't know who it is. He was wearing . . ."

"So it is a man, then?"

"Yes, sorry, it's a man."

"And you were saying that he was wearing . . . what? What was he wearing?"

Aaron decided it wasn't up to him to tell her about the donkey's head and racked his brain for something else.

"Well, he might have been wearing Gucci loafers. We found one nearby. Black. You know, just the classic loafer." The color drained from Mrs. Van Dusen's face as she opened her mouth to say something, but nothing came out.

"Are you okay?" Aaron asked.

"Yes, yes, I'm fine. I . . ." She turned toward the stairs, glanced upstairs, then turned her attention back to Aaron.

"Look, you wait here, and I'll ring for someone to bring you some coffee. And for Charlotte, too, if she's coming in. Is she coming in? And breakfast if you want it. Are you hungry? There's plenty of food."

She turned to the young woman who hovered nearby.

"Alex, show this young gentleman into the sitting room, and then organize some coffee and breakfast for him. No, wait, for everybody. I must go and speak to my daughter."

It wasn't until she was halfway up the stairs that she realized she was still in her dressing gown. Pulling it a little tighter around her body, she bounded up the remaining steps and hurried down the hall to Belinda's room.

The door was open slightly, and Belinda was seated in her window seat, wrapped in a white terry cloth bathrobe with her legs tucked under her, checking her phone. She looked up with a puzzled look on her face when her mother entered. She was about to say something when her mother held up a hand, and reading the look on her face, Belinda stood up.

"You look awful, Mom," she said. "What's happened?"

"Belinda, have you spoken to Adrian this morning?"

"No. I've been trying to reach him to see what he wants to do about today. If he wants to go ahead with the wedding or not."

"But I thought you'd decided there isn't going to be a wedding."

"Oh, I don't know what I want," she moaned.

"Well, listen to me. Something bad's happened. Very bad. The best thing would be if we each got dressed and went downstairs. The police are here, and they're going to want to talk to us."

"The police? Here? What do they want? Has there been an accident?"

"I'm sorry, my darling. Apparently a body's been found in the garden. A man's body. Nobody's told me for sure, but you should prepare yourself for some bad news. It could be Adrian."

"Adrian? Dead? In our garden? Are you kidding me? What happened?"

"I don't know. Look, just get dressed, come downstairs, and we'll have some coffee and wait for the police to tell us what happened. The only detail I've been told is that he—whoever he is, was—had on Gucci loafers."

Belinda let out a long, low wail.

"That's not exactly the kind of reaction I would have expected. I thought you'd decided not to marry him."

"Well, yes, but just because I don't want to marry him doesn't mean I wanted him dead."

"No, of course it doesn't. Well, the thing is we mustn't jump to conclusions. We'd better wait to see what the police tell us. After all, we don't know for sure. It might not be him." She took a step toward the door and then, her hand resting on the knob, said, "About the wedding. I'd better get Phyllis to start making calls."

Her daughter gave her an uncomprehending look.

"Phone calls," said Paula. "We've got to let people know the wedding's off. If that is Adrian out there"—she paused until the howling died down—"the wedding's definitely off. But if it isn't Adrian, it'll be impossible to have a wedding in the garden with the police out there. We could move it indoors, I suppose, if you did want to go ahead with it. What do you think? Do you know what you want?"

"I don't know," whined Belinda. "I don't know what to do. What do you think I should do?"

"Well, if you're not sure you want to marry him, we'd better call it off, for today at least. You don't want to marry someone you're not sure about. Let's see. We'll donate as much as we can to charity. The flowers can go to hospitals and seniors' homes. The catering to the county soup kitchens. God knows what will happen to the cake."

Belinda let out another howl.

"Maybe the acting company would like the cake. On second thought, we could ask the cake design lady if she knows another bride who might like to have it. Some poor girl who couldn't begin to afford a cake that cost over a thousand dollars."

"Mom! How can you talk about the cake when Adrian could be lying out there dead?"

"Sorry, darling, you're right. I was being completely insensitive. It's just that my mind is racing, and I'm trying to work out what to do."

*

Aaron and Charlotte sat silently in the same sitting room where Aaron had conducted the bridesmaids' consultation just a few weeks before. With Rupert curled up at her feet, Charlotte flipped idly through a magazine while Aaron thumbed through his phone.

"Well, what now?" Aaron asked.

Charlotte shrugged. "I don't know. I guess we wait for someone to come and tell us what's going to happen. I have no idea what this will mean for the wedding. But I don't really feel like leaving. I want to stick around and see what happens. Don't you?"

Aaron shrugged. "Not really." He yawned. "We'll hear all about it soon enough. To be honest, I'm not feeling great. Finding that body kind of shook me up. If we're not needed here, I'd like to go home."

He perked up as Phyllis entered bearing a large tray, which she set down on the table, indicating that Charlotte and Aaron should help themselves to coffee, freshly baked carrot muffins, and sliced strawberries.

"Have you heard anything?" Charlotte asked her. "Is there any news about . . ."

"The last I heard, the police said everyone is to stay put for now." Aaron got up and helped himself to a muffin, then held up the coffeepot and shot Charlotte an inquiring look. She nodded, and he poured two cups as Phyllis made a point of frowning at Rupert.

"What about the bridesmaids?" he asked Phyllis, holding out a cup of coffee to Charlotte. "I was supposed to help them with their dresses."

"Well, I don't know anything about that," she said. "At this point, it looks like Mrs. Van Dusen's cancelled the wedding. We're trying to reach everyone to let them know, and that's really all I've been told," said Phyllis. Once again, she cast a disapproving look in Rupert's direction. He returned her gaze with expressive brown eyes and wiggled his bottom. "I'm not sure what Mrs. Van Dusen will think about that dog in here." She turned her attention back to Charlotte. "I guess it's best if you wait in here. I have to get back upstairs. Nobody's really sure what's happening. This is all uncharted water for us, as you can imagine."

"Yes, I certainly can," said Charlotte.

At the sound of approaching footsteps, Phyllis took a step backward out of the room and glanced down the hallway.

"Oh, Belinda, it's you. I'll bring another cup."

"Don't bother." Dressed in her simple uniform of black trousers and a crisp white shirt with pearl stud earrings, Belinda swept into the room, followed by her mother, just as the doorbell rang.

Phyllis rushed off to answer it, and a moment later she ushered in Ray Nicholson. He glanced at Charlotte and then cleared his throat and addressed Belinda.

"Miss Van Dusen, I'm afraid we might have some bad news for you. A body was discovered on the property this morning that we have reason to believe could be your fiancé. The medical examiner has arrived, but it would be helpful if you could help us establish the identity of the deceased."

Belinda threw her head back and let out a long "Ooh." She then glared at Ray. "I seriously hope you're not asking me to go out there and . . . no way!"

"Absolutely not!" said Paula. "What are you thinking?"

"No, no," said Ray. "I'm sorry. I didn't explain myself very well. I know this has been a most unpleasant shock for you. We could start by your telling me what your fiancé was wearing the last time you saw him. But the medical examiner's office will need someone to formally identify the body. We wondered if you have his parents' contact details, because we need to notify them, and perhaps someone from his family—his father, maybe—would be willing to do the identification."

"Well, yes, of course. Except they don't exactly live nearby. They live in Toronto. They weren't able to attend the wedding, unfortunately, because his grandmother is very ill and not expected to live. They wanted to come, of course, but they couldn't leave her."

"I see. Well, the team of detectives from Albany will be here soon to take over, so we'll leave the details up to them, and they'll decide next steps." He glanced at the table. "Is there any coffee left?"

"I'll send for more," said Paula. She pulled out her phone and typed a few lines. Then, just as she was about to slip her phone back in her pocket, she caught sight of a figure standing in the hallway and sank into the nearest chair.

"What's going on?" asked the tall man framed in the doorway.

Paula Van Dusen's eyes widened, and she raised a hand to cover her mouth.

Belinda let out a little shriek.

"Adrian! Oh, Adrian!" She ran across the room, threw her arms around him, and sobbed into his chest. "Oh, my God! We thought you were dead!"

# Chapter 13

Ray took a step forward. "Sir, just for the record, can you confirm that you are Adrian Archer?"

"I am. Why? Who are you?"

Ray introduced himself, then explained the situation and continued. "I have a few questions for you. What time did you leave here last night, and where did you spend the night?"

"Well, Belinda and I had a bit of a disagreement, and because I'd had too much to drink, I got someone to drive me into the city."

"So you spent the night in New York?"

"Yes, I went home. Then, this morning, when I'd sobered up and realized what had happened, I thought I'd better get back here so Belinda and I could talk things over. We're supposed to be getting married today." He looked from Ray to Belinda. "Is it still on?"

"What a mess," muttered Mrs. Van Dusen, then addressing Adrian directly and loudly, "No, it is not still on. When we thought you were dead in my rosebushes, we called off the wedding. Can you blame us?"

Adrian laughed easily. "Well, no, I can't say I do. But we can reschedule." He looked at Belinda. "Can't we?"

"I don't think so," said Mrs. Van Dusen. "At least not here you can't. That's it, as far I'm concerned. You two had your chance. I'm done."

"But Mom," protested Belinda. "It's not our fault someone's dead. The wedding would have to be rescheduled anyway. We couldn't possibly get married here today with all that going on." She lifted a hand in the vague direction of the garden. "The place is crawling with police."

"Well, you told me you'd decided not to marry him," Paula replied. "And I thought you'd finally come to your senses."

"Come on, Belinda," said Adrian. "I think we've got a few things to discuss, and this isn't the place." He glanced around the room with a look that bordered on a glare. "I don't even know these people."

"If I could just have a word in private, Mr. Archer, please?" said Ray, taking him to one side of the room. "I didn't want to mention this in front of everybody, but the Albany detectives are going to need to hear your full story. That includes who you were with."

"Who says I was with anybody?"

"You said that someone drove you. We're going to need that person's name."

"Why? Am I a suspect?"

"We'd like to be able to eliminate you from our inquiry," Ray replied smoothly.

Adrian scowled and charged out of the room with Belinda on his heels.

Ray turned his attention to Charlotte and Aaron. "There's really no reason for you two to stay any longer. We can take your statements later. Right now, the focus is determining the identity of the body in the garden. So why don't you two go on home, and I'll see you later?"

Charlotte gathered up Rupert, and as they prepared to leave, Phyllis reappeared in the doorway.

"Mrs. Van Dusen, there's a man here from the *Hudson Valley Echo*. He'd like to talk to you."

Fletcher Macmillan squeezed past her and entered the room. He briefly acknowledged Ray, then turned to speak to Paula Van Dusen. Charlotte groaned inwardly. *Oh, here we go,* she thought.

"Mrs. Van Dusen," he said, opening his notebook and folding back a few pages, "I heard on the police scanner that a body's been discovered on your property and—"

"Mr. Macmillan, I've got nothing to say to you at this time," Paula said. "Any information on this matter will have to come from the police. And now, if you don't mind, we're very busy this morning, so Phyllis here will show you out."

"I'll be glad to show Mr. Macmillan out," Ray said, stepping forward. "Come on, Fletcher. I'll give you the name of the guy from the state police you should be talking to."

"Is the wedding going ahead?" Fletcher asked Paula over his shoulder as Ray steered him out of the room. "Will it take place here, or has it been moved to another venue?"

As Charlotte and Aaron crunched their way across the graveled parking area, Charlotte remarked, "You know, it's odd that we didn't see the bridesmaids this morning. In my experience, bridal parties stick pretty close together, and I haven't seen either bridesmaid this morning. And come to think of it, I saw Jessica a couple of times last night, but I don't remember seeing the other one at all. The blonde one."

"Sophie," said Aaron.

"Right. Sophie. Did you see her?"

"I don't remember, but I don't think so. I'm not thinking too clearly right now."

They rounded the corner of the house and paused to look over the garden. White tenting—the police kind, not the wedding kind—guarded by a couple of uniformed officers, had been erected over the spot where the body had been discovered. Forensic experts to process the scene and homicide detectives from Albany were expected within the hour.

"Yes, Sophie," repeated Charlotte. "I saw a blonde woman running across the lawn last night, and she could have come from that direction." She pointed to the tent. "At the time I thought it might be Belinda, but now I'm not so sure. It was just after the intermission, but Belinda's hair and makeup were so elaborate, she must have been in her room getting ready for the after party. Her hair alone would have taken at least an hour. So now I'm wondering if the woman I saw could have been Sophie. I only caught a glimpse of her out of the corner of my eye."

"Could be," said Aaron. "If you only saw her for a moment and it was dark, it would be hard to tell." He unlocked the car doors.

"And if Sophie is the person who drove Adrian back to the city last night, that could explain why she isn't here this morning," Charlotte mused. "And we know she can drive that car because we saw her. They're big, powerful cars, those Lamborghinis. Tricky to handle. You don't just get in one and drive it to Manhattan in the dark like it's a rental car you picked up at the airport."

"She could have driven him home in his car, then he drove it back this morning," Aaron said as he put the car in reverse. "And look," he said, pointing out his window, "the Lamborghini's here now, and it wasn't when we arrived earlier. With that ridiculous orange, we'd have noticed it."

"True."

They rolled down the driveway in silence, and then Aaron spoke. "I wonder whose body it is out there. I've never seen anything like it. It really gets to you, something like that."

"Could be someone who attended the play, I suppose," said Charlotte. "Maybe it's not a member of the wedding party. The performance was a fundraiser, after all, and the audience was made up of friends and contacts of Paula Van Dusen. But of course the question is, why did that person, whoever it is, turn up dead here? And why now?"

As they turned onto the main road, Charlotte remarked, "We're going to need a new donkey's head. The police will keep that one as evidence."

"And anyway," said Aaron, as the car picked up speed, "who'd want to wear that thing after it's been stuck on a dead guy's head?"

Charlotte laughed. "You have such a way with words. But I'm glad for the chance to replace the moth-eaten old thing. We're long overdue for a new one. It was hot and heavy for the actor, almost impossible to talk through, and I really like the one we created with Paula Van Dusen's hat. I'll ask her if we can keep it. She won't miss it. Nobody wears fur anymore. And if we can't have it, then we can at least use the concept to create a new one. Something more modern. The actor said he loved wearing it."

"It was quite creative of you coming up with that on the spur of the moment," said Aaron.

"That's what you have to do sometimes."

She gazed out the window, and when they reached the main street, she asked Aaron to pull over at the convenience store. "I'm just going to run in and get a paper. Won't be a tick."

They continued the journey home, and as they passed the sign announcing the coming condominium development, Aaron glanced at it and then at Charlotte.

"Have you thought about buying one of those condos?"

"Not really. I'm happy where I am."

"Well, it could be a good investment for you. And it's close enough to the hotel that you could walk to work."

Charlotte thought for a moment.

"You know, I hadn't thought of that, but you might be on to something. According to recent newspaper stories, we're on the edge of a property boom here. And if I moved out of the bungalow, Harvey could get a much higher rent for it. Not a bad idea. If I could afford it, that is."

"Maybe you and Ray could go in together on one."

"Me and Ray? What? You mean live together? It seems a bit soon. I don't know that we're ready for that. We've certainly never discussed it."

"Well, maybe you ought to." He grinned. "Come on! You can't tell me you haven't thought about it. Of course you have."

"Well, maybe just a little. But you're right. Maybe I should think about this. There would definitely be advantages to the hotel if I did move out. And it would be really nice to live in my own place. A place I owned."

Aaron didn't respond.

"Oh, now I get it," said Charlotte. "You clever old thing. It's for you, isn't it? Come on! Don't tell me you haven't thought about it! You want to move into my bungalow!"

Aaron grinned sheepishly.

"Yeah, you're right. I do. I'm twenty-four years old, and living with my aunt and uncle is killing me. It's bad enough being here where there's so little to do, but my aunt treats me as if I'm twelve. 'Where are you going? When will you be back? Who were you talking to?' Honestly, it's driving me crazy. I've got to get my own place." He shook his head slightly as they turned onto the hotel property. "It's either that or go back to the city."

As they unloaded the car and prepared to go their separate ways, he to join his aunt and uncle in their apartment in the hotel and she to her bungalow, Aaron paused.

"About all the work I put into making those bridesmaids' dresses. Mrs. Van Dusen will pay me, won't she?"

"Of course she will. I'll mention it, if you like, when I speak to her about the hat."

"There's something else. Would it be all right if I came home with you so I could sleep for a while in your spare room?"

Charlotte smiled at him. "You've got a hangover and you don't want your aunt asking a lot of questions right now. Just want to get your head down for a bit."

He nodded. "Yeah, there's that. And discovering that body was awful. I think it's starting to get to me. I'm feeling a little shaky inside, to be honest, and I'd rather be here with you."

"Right. Come on then." They entered her bungalow, and Charlotte offered him a glass of water. "Drink this now, slowly, and then take a full glass with you to bed. If you wake up, have a sip or two before you go back to sleep. Hydration will help. And stay as long as you like."

She covered him with a light blanket and, when he was settled, returned to the sitting room. With Rupert on the sofa beside her, his head resting on her thigh, she unfolded the *Hudson Valley Echo*, glanced at the front-page photographs of last night's benefit performance of *A*

*Midsummer Night's Dream*, and began to read the accompanying text.

"Once again, the great and the good gathered at the sumptuous estate of Paula Van Dusen to enjoy our own Catskills version of Shakespeare in the Park," she read. Macmillan gushed on about the wedding, offering glowing, fawning descriptions of the beautiful bride and her handsome groom, but he saved his most lavish adjectives for Paula Van Dusen herself. Charlotte laughed and then turned back to the photographs.

The largest one showed Belinda and Adrian at the party. She gazed up at him, her face soft and adoring, but his eyes were elsewhere. Charlotte scanned the photo for background details to indicate where they were standing. The drinks table was behind them, and his body was turned slightly to the left, so he must be looking in the direction of Paula Van Dusen's table, where she and Ray had been seated. But why would he be looking at them?

He wasn't, she realized. He was looking at the table behind theirs, where the bridesmaids and ushers had been seated.

Setting the significance of that aside to ponder later, Charlotte turned to the next photo, a crowd scene, and if the strong lighting was anything to go by, it had been taken before the play started, as the audience members mingled and socialized.

The photo showed a black man in profile, arms folded, with a neutral expression, in conversation with a younger man holding a glass of champagne and grinning at the camera. The caption read, "Local lawyer Joseph Lamb, left, and Manhattan real estate mogul Hugh Hedley share a Midsummer Night's moment." *A Midsummer Night's moment*, thought Charlotte.

She returned to the image, holding the newspaper a little closer. Hugh Hedley was certainly handsome in that boyish, all-American way that never goes out of style. Brown hair with just a bit of curl flopping over his forehead and a broad, bright smile revealing expensive teeth. He was wearing a dark suit jacket that looked suspiciously like the one she had seen this morning on the body in the rosebushes. But then a closer inspection revealed a couple of men in the background wearing similar suits. Between the two men, with her back to the camera, was a woman with a blonde ponytail.

# Chapter 14

Nothing commands and holds your attention like murder. Throughout the endless Saturday afternoon, unable to stay focused on a small, routine task for very long and with everything feeling like a distraction, Charlotte tidied up her already tidy bungalow, cleaned the bathroom, and did a load of laundry.

Finally, in response to Rupert's gentle, pleading look and realizing it was the best thing she could do for him and for herself, she gave in to his request for a walk. After checking to make sure Aaron was still asleep, she clipped Rupert's leash to his harness, and the two set off.

As they strolled down the long drive to the main road that led in one direction toward town and rolled away in the other past forests and woodland until it reached the next town, she mulled over the morning's events and what must have led up to them. *Let's see*, she thought. *What do we know for sure?* At some time last night, a man was killed either during the performance of *A Midsummer Night's Dream* or during the after party. Aaron checked the props table just as the play started, and everything was present and correct. He discovered the donkey's head was missing during the intermission. The donkey's head was found on the victim's body. So does it follow that the man was killed sometime between when the play started and the intermission? Not necessarily. The man could have been killed anytime, and the donkey's head put on him later. And we can't even say for sure that the killer took the donkey's head. Someone could have taken it just for fun, dropped it somewhere, and the killer came along later, picked it up, and for some reason, put it on the victim's head before dumping him in the rosebushes. *That's getting complicated*, she thought.

What was that theory she'd recently seen being discussed on television? *Something sharp. Razor. Occam's razor, that's it.* Something about the simplest reasoning is usually correct. So the simplest way this could have happened would be that the man was killed sometime between the beginning of the play and the end of the intermission; the killer, for an unknown reason, took the donkey's head during that time; and at some point the body, with the donkey's head on it, was placed in the garden.

She sighed, trying to recall everything that happened last night and where everybody was, especially during the times when the backstage area might have been unattended. But as far as she knew, someone from the theater company had been there the whole time. There was always someone coming or going—crew members, actors waiting to go onstage, actors coming offstage. She couldn't recall seeing anyone in the area who shouldn't have been there. But with all the backstage bustle, it would have been impossible to take note of everything.

They reached the road, and Rupert hesitated, looked in both directions, and then opted for the direction that led away from town. She followed his lead, and on they walked, keeping as close as they could to the ditch, well off the paved surface of the road. Rupert stopped every few minutes to examine something interesting, then, with a quick confirming glance in her direction, he continued on his way.

The nearest property to the hotel, on the same side of the road, was the Middleton house. A broken concrete path with small weeds filling in the cracks led from the road to the front door. The path was flanked by two stone lions, and as he always did when they passed them, Rupert gave the first one a couple of short, sharp barks.

But instead of walking on past the other lion, Rupert turned up the path toward the front door, where a man and a woman were waiting. They stood a few feet apart, looking about in that loose, restless way of people who are waiting for someone or something. The man appeared to check his watch and then said something to the woman, who shook her head.

As she and Rupert got closer, Charlotte recognized the woman as Lynda Flegg, the real estate agent whose photograph was on the For Sale sign at the edge of the property. Charlotte had seen her signs dotted around town for years but had never met her. She wore a coral-colored, two-piece suit with a large brooch in the shape of a pink rose pinned on her left shoulder and bore only a passing resemblance to the woman in the photo on the sign. That woman was well groomed, with an even, polished smile revealing white teeth. The Lynda Flegg standing in front of Charlotte wore her blonde hair parted in the center, revealing gray roots. It was of uneven length and was crying out for a trim and a professional color and condition. The wrinkles around her eyes deepened as she gave Charlotte a professional smile.

"Hello," she said, holding out her hand. "I don't think we've officially met, but I've seen you walking your dog around town many times. I'm Lynda Flegg." She handed Charlotte a business card. Charlotte glanced at it before tucking it in the pocket of her jeans.

Charlotte introduced herself and Rupert with a return smile. "Yes, I've seen you around town quite a bit, too," she said, gesturing at the For Sale sign. Lynda laughed good-naturedly and then waved a vague hand in the direction of her companion: a tall, slim black man with a white streak running through his dark hair. Charlotte recognized him immediately as the man in the photograph on the front page of this morning's *Hudson Valley Echo*.

He wore an old-fashioned wool suit and seemed over-dressed, both for the warmth of the day and for a Saturday afternoon in a small town.

"This is Joseph Lamb," Lynda said. "He's Mrs. Middleton's lawyer. We're supposed to be meeting a realtor here today, but he's late."

Lamb spoke for the first time. "Twenty-five minutes late. I refuse to wait any longer. My time is valuable. What is it about these real estate people that they can't show up on time for an appointment? God knows they wear expensive enough watches, most of them." With a curt nod in the general direction of both women, he tucked his leather document case under his arm and strode off.

"Well," said Lynda, "I guess since Joe's gone, there's no point in me hanging around." She glanced at the door of the Middleton house. "Even if this guy did show up now, I couldn't show him the property, as I don't have a key. That's what Joe was doing here."

"I thought real estate agents had keys to properties they're showing," said Charlotte.

"Usually there's a lockbox with a key in it," agreed Lynda. "But old Mrs. Middleton wouldn't allow that. She's in a nursing home and insists that her lawyer takes care of everything. Doesn't trust anybody."

"I wonder . . ." said Charlotte. "I might be interested in the condos going up next door. Do you know anything about them?"

Lynda groaned. "We're having trouble getting any information on them, and it's not helping my cause, I can tell you. I've had a couple of people asking about them, and I'd like to be able to give them some answers."

"Oh, that's very strange, surely." Sensing they were about to get under way, Rupert stood up, and as Lynda and Charlotte walked down the path, he fell into step between them.

"I wonder if this real estate guy you were supposed to meet here . . ." Charlotte began.

"He's not a local real estate agent," said Lynda as they walked across a patch of grass in definite need of an appointment with a mower. "He's from the city. I've never met him. It used to be we in Walkers Ridge just sold our properties to each other, but now the area is becoming hot and we're seeing a lot more people from the city. Young people, with money. They have a shoebox apartment in Manhattan above a flashing sign and want something bigger and better for the weekend." She shrugged. "So apparently he wanted to view the property to see if would suit a couple of his city clients. Of course the place hasn't been touched since at least the late 1970s and is probably a teardown. Everybody wants open concept nowadays, and God forbid there's only one sink in the bathroom." They reached the gravel driveway that ran along the side of the house. "My car's parked around the back," Lynda said. "Do you need a ride anywhere?"

"No, thanks just the same," said Charlotte. "We're just out for a walk. We live at the hotel."

"Oh, Jacobs Grand? Wonderful, really, how it just keeps going."

"It is," Charlotte agreed. "We do our best."

"We?"

"I'm with the theater company."

"Oh, how interesting. I've been to several productions there over the years. Last night was your annual outdoor show, wasn't it? Like Shakespeare in the Park, only, well, not in the park. We used to take our best clients to that. The tickets are expensive, but of course, it's a fundraiser, so all for a good cause."

Charlotte glanced up at the peeling white paint on the second-story shutters as they crunched their way along the gravel. "Bedrooms upstairs, I guess," she said. "How many are there, by the way?"

"Seven. But only two bathrooms. That's what I mean when I say it would need a complete renovation. No one these days would have a seven-bedroom house with just two bathrooms. But the other agent told me his clients might be willing to do that. He said they were a gay couple from Brooklyn looking to open a bed-and-breakfast in the area." She let out a weary sigh as she reached into her purse for her car keys. "What a shame he never showed up. This place has been on the market for so long, and we don't get many showings. Eventually, of course, all properties do sell, but not necessarily at the price the sellers were hoping for. People are always so emotionally attached to their houses; they think they're worth much more than they are. 'But we raised our children here and have so many happy memories.' Well, guess what? The new owners aren't buying your memories, and they don't care." She opened the car door. "Sorry, I'm sure I sound very jaded, but it's a bit of a pet peeve with me. Trying to help sellers see the reality of their situation."

Lynda tossed her document case onto the front seat. "I doubt I'll be working with Hugh Hedley again. Not unless hell freezes over, that is. It's so unprofessional not to notify the other agent if you're delayed or can't make it." She waited for Charlotte and Rupert to step back before putting the car in reverse, and then, with a friendly little wave, she was gone.

*Hugh Hedley?* Charlotte thought.

She pulled Lynda's business card out of her pocket, examined it, and after flicking it back and forth, pulled out her cell phone.

"Come on, then, Rupert," she said a few moments later. "We haven't gone very far, so let's walk on for a bit before we head home. Ray'll be there soon, and we've got something important to tell him. At least it might be. We'll see."

They passed the fenced-in vacant lot with the sign announcing the condominium development. Now a large, white foam-board banner with "Coming Soon!" spelled out in giant, red letters had been fastened to the chain-link fence just above the sign.

She paused for a moment, then took out her phone and photographed the sign so she could record the name of the developer. It wouldn't hurt to call and get some more information. She'd managed to save a bit of money over the years, and if she and Ray pooled their resources . . . She forced herself to stop thinking along that line. Mustn't get ahead of herself. She scanned the property, or what she could see of it through the fence. The weeds were well established now, with splotches of purple and yellow flowers here and there. She couldn't see as far as the river, but she knew it was there.

Rupert signaled it was time to move on. They continued in the same direction until they came to the gas station, which was as far as this walk took them, and then turned around and headed home.

# Chapter 15

When Charlotte returned, Aaron had gone, leaving a scribbled thank-you note on the kitchen table. She peered into the refrigerator to see what she had on hand in case Ray arrived hungry, as he usually did. Not much. A few eggs and a bit of cheddar cheese. But there was a bottle of wine. Maybe he'd settle for scrambled eggs, or if not, they'd have to go out.

But then Ray appeared a few minutes later with the problem solved.

"I brought some takeaway. We haven't had Thai for a while, so I hope that's okay."

She gave him a big smile and reached out to hug him. "Perfect! I'll set the table, and you can pour the wine. And then I want to hear all about it. Or at least, as much as you can tell me."

She unwrapped the cartons and set them on the table. They helped themselves to spring rolls and pad thai, and when their plates were heaping, she took a sip of the wine he had poured for her and gestured at the bottle with a raised eyebrow. He shook his head. "Better not. I might get called back. Hope not, though. I'm exhausted."

"So tell me," said Charlotte. "Any progress on identifying the body?"

Ray shook his head.

"Well, I might have something for you. Rupert and I saw a man and woman standing outside the Middleton place, looking as if they were waiting for someone. Turns out the man was the Middleton's lawyer, and the woman a local real estate agent. Lynda Flegg. You know who I mean. If you haven't met her, you'll have seen her For Sale signs all over town. Anyway, they were waiting for a real estate agent from New York who wanted to view the property in case it might be suitable for a client of his. But the real estate agent never showed. Lynda said his name was Hugh Hedley."

Ray raised an eyebrow.

"Now, here's the thing. While I was doing the dress fitting for Belinda, Mrs. Van Dusen came charging in, all in a flap because Hugh Hedley had decided not to attend the wedding, even though he would still be at the play, presumably out of respect for Mrs. Van Dusen. And since he was at the play, and didn't show up for the appointment, I wondered if your man in Mrs. Van Dusen's rosebushes could be Hugh Hedley."

"It's possible, that's for sure," Ray replied slowly, "although it does seem a bit of a stretch."

"Why is it a bit of a stretch? Here, look at this." She set the newspaper in front of him and pointed to the front-page photo. “There. See? That’s Hugh Hedley, and he’s wearing a suit like the one on the victim. Of course, by the time we saw it, it was very dirty from being in the garden. And I’m sure your Albany detectives will have thought of this, but I was close enough to tell that the fabric is expensive. I think you’ll find that the suit is custom made and the tailor’s label may help. They’ll probably be able to tell you the name of the man they made it for. And then you can check that against your victim’s measurements. It could help.”

“Let me make a quick call. I’ll pass that along to the Albany detectives,” he said, reaching for his phone. “It’s Walkers Ridge Police Chief Ray Nicholson here,” he said, “about the body found this morning up at the Van Dusen residence. Got a strong lead on the identity of the body. It might be a Hugh Hedley.” He spelled the last name and, keeping his eyes fixed on Charlotte as he listened, nodded a couple of times, mentioned Charlotte’s lead about the tailor, and then wrapped up the call.

“He hasn’t been identified yet. He didn’t have any identification on him, and his fingerprints aren’t on file, but we wouldn’t have expected them to be. He doesn’t look like someone who would be known to the police in the usual way. They’re doing forensics on the clothes now.” He gave her a warm smile. “That was very observant of you.”

Charlotte speared a shrimp with her fork and paused with it in midair. “Well, there’s one thing we do know about him.”

“What’s that?”

"Somebody thought he was an ass. Why else would they put the donkey's head on him?"

Ray's eyes drifted toward the window and studied the river flowing by. He said nothing.

"Ray? What is it?"

"The medical examiner says he died from compressive asphyxiation."

"Compressive asphyxiation?"

"Yes, he was literally crushed to death." Ray placed his hands on his chest. "Until he couldn't breathe."

Charlotte considered the implications of what she'd just heard, made a little noise of disgust, and set her fork down. "Oh, God, I've just lost my appetite. That's really terrible. And then the donkey's head placed on him. There's just a really awful element of humiliation in that."

Ray nodded.

Charlotte pushed her plate away while Ray finished his meal in silence. When he was done, he glanced out the window and then smiled at Charlotte.

"Let's take Rupert for a walk. I sit too much on the job, and a little after-dinner stroll would be just the thing. Then maybe a cup of coffee when we come back."

On hearing his name, Rupert climbed out of his basket and walked to the door. He stood quietly while Charlotte slipped on his harness and clipped on his leash. Then he led them away from the bungalow and in the direction of the road.

The evening air was vaguely scented with flowers, but Charlotte couldn't have said which kind or where they came from. At moments like this, out of nowhere, she sometimes experienced a sudden, sharp longing for home—the familiar hedgerows of the Norfolk countryside, which at this time of year would be overgrown with wild honeysuckle, filling the air with a warm, diffused fragrance.

This evening's light, the kind favored by artists, was of that magic hour just before sunset, when it slanted and intensified, bathing everything it touched in a golden glow before fading and dying. They walked in appreciative, companionable silence down the drive that would bring them to the main road. Ray took her hand, and she moved a little closer to him.

As they approached the main road, a white police SUV pulled over and stopped. Letting go of Charlotte's hand, Ray walked up to the driver.

"What is it, Phil?" he asked his sergeant.

"Just had a call about some vandalism on the sign at the vacant property," he said. "Someone driving by called it in. Thought I'd check it out before I head home for dinner."

"Well, it was fine this afternoon when I saw it," Charlotte said. "I even took a photo of it, if you want to see it."

"We might," said Ray. Turning to Phil, he told him to pull up in front of the property, and they'd all have a look at it.

Phil drove slowly on ahead as Ray and Charlotte followed with Rupert.

The large foam-board sign announcing the condominium development now had the word "scum" written across it in bright-red paint and the name of the company partially painted over.

"Probably just kids," said Ray. "Who called it in?"

"Didn't say."

"Well, there's not much we can do until we hear from the owner," said Ray. "We'll wait and see if the owner of the property files a complaint."

Charlotte had been wondering if she should say something to Ray about the development, to try to get a sense of what his feelings might be about the two of them moving in together, but she wasn't sure how or when to broach the subject.

The light was slipping away, and she made a remark about returning home; so with Rupert leading the way, they retraced their steps. Ray was quiet as they walked up the drive, and she wondered what he was thinking.

"Do you like where you're living?" she blurted out.

"Like it?" Ray thought for a moment. "I don't really like it or dislike it. I needed a place to live when I took the job here, and there wasn't much to choose from at the time. Although I suppose if I'd put more effort into it, I could have found something better." He shrugged. "It's okay, I guess. I haven't spent much time there lately. I seem to spend more time here with you."

"Yes," said Charlotte. "And that's got me thinking . . ."

"I'm not wearing out my welcome, I hope," said Ray anxiously. "If I am, just say so."

She laughed lightly. "No, no, not at all. I want you here. I love having you here."

"Well, if it's okay with you, I'm going to drive over to my house and pick up a few things." He kissed her. "Won't be long."

As he drove through the quiet, orderly streets to the house he rented not far from the police station, he mulled over Charlotte's question about whether he liked where he lived. She had visited the house only a handful of times and refused to eat there or spend the night. He had rented it furnished, and she might be right when she said it looked as if it hadn't been updated since hippies lived in it in the 1960s.

He pulled a couple of flyers out of the mailbox and threw them in the recycling bin that sat on the wooden porch, unlocked the door, and let himself in. The hall smelled old and musty. He switched on the light in the living room. The sofa was such a nondescript gray that it was hard to tell if gray was its original color or the color it had acquired. A mousehole had been gnawed into the base, and it was anybody's guess if a family of mice were still living there.

He entered his bedroom, pulled a clean shirt out of the dresser drawer, added a few toiletries, and threw everything into a plastic bag. He'd moved to Walkers Ridge from Pennsylvania after his divorce and taken the first accommodation he could find. But now, he realized he didn't want to live like this anymore. He wanted better, and he wanted it with Charlotte. He thought about her in her cozy bungalow, the way she kept everything so clean and orderly, how homey it was. He wondered what she would think if he suggested they moved in together. Would she want that? Would she want to just live together, or would she want him to marry her? He wanted her to be part of his future, but no matter what happened, he realized it was long past time when he should have moved out of this place. Maybe he and Charlotte should check out those new condominiums. But first, maybe he should see about an engagement ring. But not here in Walkers Ridge. News that he was ring shopping would be all over town in no time. He could take a day off and go to New York. There was bound to be something beautiful in the jewelry district. But what about size? That could be tricky, and he wanted to get it right. The first time he'd been married, his wife had chosen the ring, and he hadn't had to think about it.

He threw the bag with his overnight things in the back of the patrol car and drove slowly through town, glancing out the window occasionally and gesturing to some teen boys on skateboards to get off the road. As he passed the police station, an idea came to him. Not so long ago, Charlotte had "borrowed" a ring that was in his custody for safekeeping, so why couldn't he "borrow" a ring of hers to get the sizing off it? She didn't wear a ring day to day, but surely every woman had a ring somewhere in her jewelry case, didn't she?

He turned off the main road onto the hotel's gravel driveway and parked outside Charlotte's bungalow. He was about to let himself in when the door opened, and there, framed in the doorway with the light behind her, stood Charlotte, holding out Rupert's lead. "Here, before you take your boots off, would you mind taking Rupert for his last walk?" Rupert grinned up at him and wiggled in excitement as she handed Ray a small bag and added, "Just in case you need one."

Ray took the bag and burst out laughing.

"What are you laughing at?" she asked.

"I was just about to ask you something romantic."

She raised an eyebrow.

"What you asked me earlier: 'Do I like where I'm living?' No, as a matter of fact, I hate it. I've just been there and decided I'm going to find a much nicer place and move. How about you? Do you like where you're living? Because I think it's time we talked about moving in together."

# Chapter 16

Charlotte and Ray talked long into the night, sharing for the first time their most intimate feelings and opening up about their hearts' desire for a future together. As the morning light filtered through the blinds, wrapped in the intense glow of deepening love, they lay wrapped in each other's arms, until the mood was shattered by Rupert standing beside the bed, softly woofing.

Charlotte eased herself out of bed, put on her walking clothes, and let herself quietly out of the house to take Rupert on his morning walk. Forty-five minutes later, she let herself into the bungalow to find Ray standing at the kitchen counter making coffee. Charlotte prepared Rupert's breakfast and set down his bowl, then she popped a couple of bagels in the toaster.

Ray touched her arm and gave her a look that she recognized as serious.

"What is it?" she asked.

"I just had a call. They've identified the body."

"And?"

"You were right. It is Hugh Hedley," he said. "Lives in Manhattan, but apparently he's got family in the area. His stepfather's something big in Albany."

"I guess you've got a busy day ahead of you."

"Probably. I'll check in with the Albany team and see what they need me to do."

As the police chief of a small New York town, Ray took care of misdemeanor crimes—vandalism, petty theft, simple assault, and trespassing. But for serious crimes requiring extensive investigation—felony crimes like money laundering, narcotics, computer crimes, kidnapping, and murder—New York State's Bureau of Criminal Investigation was called in.

"We'll provide local knowledge and support," Ray told Charlotte, "but as usual, the BCI guys will expect to take the lead."

He poured coffee and orange juice as Charlotte spread cream cheese on their bagels. They sat at the small table looking out over the river sparkling in the sunshine as a light haze drifted over the distant mountains under a brilliant-blue sky. Charlotte stirred her coffee and set the spoon on a saucer.

"It might be a good idea if you were the one to tell Mrs. Van Dusen that the body has been identified as Hugh Hedley's. You're her local chief of police, and she should hear this news from you, not a BCI detective she doesn't know."

He raised an eyebrow. "Go on."

"Belinda told me Mrs. Van Dusen had hopes that she'd marry Hugh—Belinda, that is, not Mrs. Van Dusen, if you see what I mean—so there's a strong emotional connection there. And Mrs. Van Dusen is so important in this community, very influential in a lot of areas, and she should certainly not hear this in the media. The body was found on her property, after all, so she is involved, and she does expect to be kept informed. I'm sure she'll be more likely to cooperate with the investigation if you keep her on your side."

Ray wrapped his hands around his mug and met her eyes. "I expect the BCI people will be informing the next of kin immediately. The family must be informed first. Probably on the way there now, and as soon as I hear they've done that, I'll speak to Mrs. Van Dusen. You're right, of course. I'll let the BCI team know that I'll inform Paula Van Dusen."

"Good," said Charlotte. "And I'm curious. Do you know how they identified him?"

"Well, technically, it's not official yet because someone from his family will need to formally identify the body, but once they had a name to work with, thanks to you, the rest was pretty easy. And the label on his jacket was helpful, just as you thought it would be."

"Still, I suppose if the killer could put a donkey's head on his victim, he could just as easily put a jacket on him."

Ray groaned. "Oh, God, I hope not."

"No, probably not. The jacket matched the trousers."

They finished their coffee in silence. Charlotte placed the empty cups in the sink and then pulled a file out of a black tote bag featuring an image of William Shakespeare that she used to carry documents back and forth to work.

"I have to get ready for a meeting with Simon," she said, "and then I'll be off."

"On a Sunday?"

"We've got a lot of things to go over."

She made a few more notes in the file, set it to one side, and then headed to the shower. When she came out, wearing a white bathrobe and a towel wrapped around her head, she sat on the sofa and dried her hair. A moment later, Rupert was beside her, his head resting against her leg, and she placed her arm around him and gently rubbed his chest and shoulder. Then, with a small sigh, she stood up and went to her bedroom to get dressed and, after saying goodbye to Ray, left for her meeting with Simon.

Ray stood at the open door watching her make her way down the small path that led to a hotel parking area and the staff entrance. Her walk was confident, and he admired the way she held herself with grace and poise. *Look back at me*, he thought. *Look back*.

She paused at the door of the hotel, and just before she opened it, she slowly turned around to see if he was still watching her. He waved, and in that moment, he knew.

He closed the door and returned to the kitchen. He put the breakfast dishes in the dishwasher, wiped off the counter, and turned off the light. He took a steadying breath and then entered her bedroom, mindful that it was hers, not theirs. He opened the top drawer of the dresser and withdrew a modest jewelry box. He sat on the edge of the bed and opened it. There wasn't much, really. A few pieces of costume jewelry, a couple of boxes that contained bracelets, and finally, a black box with gold writing that said "George Pragnell." He snapped it open. It contained a ring he thought must be white gold or even platinum, with a small solitaire diamond. Definitely an engagement ring. Given to her all those years ago by Brian Prentice? Probably. She'd told him they had been engaged many years ago, but he knew that she no longer felt anything for him.

He held the ring by the shank between his thumb and index finger for a moment, letting it catch and reflect the light. And then, feeling guilty about going through her possessions, he replaced the ring in the box and the jewelry case. It was there if he needed it, if and when he decided to make the trip into New York City. After putting the jewelry box back in the drawer and making the bed, he took one last look around the room and closed the door behind him.

A moment later, he reopened it, entered, and headed straight for the jewelry box. He looked at the ring again, wrestling with the idea of taking it. He was a police officer, for God's sake. Looking through her belongings was bad enough, but to take a precious item of jewelry? He could probably lose his badge for something like that.

On the other hand, to present her with a ring that fit perfectly when he asked her to marry him was just too tempting. He opened the drawer, removed the black box, and put it in his pocket just as his phone rang.

The state police had spoken to the victim's family, and a moment later, he, too, was out the door.

*

"Yes, what is it now?" snapped Paula Van Dusen. Her assistant, Phyllis, opened the door and popped her head into the sitting room. But before she could respond, Paula Van Dusen snapped a little more.

"For God's sake, Phyllis, will you please stop doing that? Either open the door and come into the room properly, or close the door and go away!"

The door swung open, and Phyllis entered.

"Good," said Mrs. Van Dusen. "Here you are. Now, what do you want?"

"I've come to tell you that there's a policeman here to see you."

"So early? I've barely finished my breakfast. What could he possibly want?"

"I don't know, but he said to tell you it's important that he speak to you, and that's what I'm doing. I'm only the messenger."

Paula Van Dusen rose to her feet, resting her fingers lightly on a table. "Of course, Phyllis. I'm sorry. Very well. Show him in." As Phyllis turned to go, she called after her, "And make sure he comes right into the room. I don't want any more of this halfway-in, halfway-out nonsense!"

Ray Nicholson entered, holding his hat by his side. He took in the soft lighting, the curtains partially drawn against the bright morning sunlight, and the glass in the hand of the woman he had come to see.

"Well?"

"I'm sorry to bother you, Mrs. Van Dusen. I know what a long and difficult day yesterday was for you." She did not reply but sank slowly into her chair and indicated that he should do the same.

"You asked to be kept informed, so I'm here to tell you that the body found in your garden yesterday has been identified, and we wanted to tell you before you heard about it on the media, as I understand this man is a friend of your family."

Mrs. Van Dusen slowly raised a hand to cover her mouth. "You don't mean . . ."

Thinking it best to get to the point quickly in case her thoughts were leading her in the wrong direction, Ray replied, "It's Hugh Hedley."

Mrs. Van Dusen gasped. "Oh, but that's terrible. We've known him since he was a little boy. He and Belinda were children together. I simply cannot believe this."

"I can see this news comes as a shock," said Ray. "Would you like me to get someone for you? That woman who showed me in—Phyllis, is it?—would you like me to get her?"

When he received no reply, he decided to fetch Phyllis, and when he opened the door, he didn't have far to look. She was retreating, just about to turn the corner that led to the main hall, which left him in no doubt that she'd been listening at the door. He called to her, and she stopped and began to walk toward him. He tipped his head in the direction of Mrs. Van Dusen's sitting room.

"She needs you," he said. "She's had a bit of a shock, and she's upset," he added as Phyllis got closer. "Stay with her. I'll see myself out."

He closed the front door quietly behind him, but instead of heading for his car, he turned toward the side of the house and then along the lawn that led to the garden. He chatted for a few moments with the uniformed state trooper who had been assigned to guard the scene. The garden was quiet and peaceful in the still morning air, making the sight of the forensic tent that remained even after the body had been removed all the more jarring. *That should have been a wedding marquee*, he thought. *What an awful way to ruin a young couple's big day.*

*

Charlotte and director Simon Dyer were starting a theater school in the fall, and they had a long way to go to prepare for it. She had to create a theoretical course in the history of costume design and a practical, hands-on course that would teach aspiring actors how to wear costumes and move in them, as well as the realities of costume fitting and dressing. Applications were starting to trickle in, and they were getting referrals from New York schools, so from the moment they accepted their first student, they had to be prepared to deliver the program. And there were so many grant applications to fill out. She wondered if Aaron might be able to help with that and made a note to speak to him about it the next time she saw him.

"Oh, Simon, there you are," said Charlotte. "I've looked all over for you."

"It's my office," he said with a slight smile. "Wouldn't this be as good a place as any to find me on a Sunday morning, drowning in paperwork?"

"Well, I checked backstage, just in case you were, I don't know . . ." Her voice trailed off.

"Backstage?" Simon supplied helpfully.

She raised her hands in a vague gesture. "Exactly. Anyway," she said, sliding into the chair that faced his desk, "I've had the most wonderful idea. At least I think it is, and I want to know what you think about it."

Simon listened while she explained what she had in mind. In his early fifties, he'd been through some hard, drug-addled times, but he had turned his life around and now commanded the respect of all his actors, especially the ones just starting out. He was patient with them, always challenging them to discover the meaning of the words, to experiment, to try different accents or inflections for different results. And when the newest, youngest cast member told them how hard it was to get into a New York theater school, he and Charlotte decided to pool their resources, experience, and training to start the Catskills Shakespeare Theater School.

The plan was to use the hotel for student housing, but then came the question of classroom and rehearsal space.

"The Middleton house!" said Simon when Charlotte had outlined her idea. "Of course. Why didn't we think of that sooner?"

"But anyway, we need to view it. And fortunately, I've got the number of the real estate agent right here." She held up Lynda Flegg's business card.

The idea of viewing the Middleton property had occurred to her yesterday when she'd met Lynda there. And after studying the photo of lawyer Joseph Lamb with Hugh Hedley, she wanted to know more about him. And then it came to her that showing interest in the Middleton house as a potential buyer might offer an opportunity to speak to him. Hadn't Lynda said that Mrs. Middleton wanted her lawyer to be present at all showings? And viewing the property with Simon would add a layer of credibility to her interest.

"But what about the money?" Simon asked. "I can't see how we could do this. To buy it and renovate it will cost a fortune. Way more money than we can put our hands on."

"True," said Charlotte, "but Paula Van Dusen might be able to help. She's a great patron of the arts, and when I mentioned our theater school venture to her at the after party, she seemed interested. I doubt she thought at the time that we might seek her out for funding, but it would be worth asking her. Wouldn't it?"

Simon thought about that for a moment. "We might be able to use Brian to our advantage here," he said. "Didn't you tell me that she likes him?"

"Yes," Charlotte said slowly, "but I'm not sure that he's ready for anything too emotionally demanding."

"Well, let's take it a step at a time. Let's talk to Lynda and see when we can view the property."

"Okay. I'll call her now."

# Chapter 17

Two hours later, Charlotte and Simon found themselves standing outside the Middleton property waiting for Lynda, just as Lynda and Joseph Lamb had waited for Hugh on Saturday afternoon. Charlotte had been disappointed when Lynda told her that Mr. Lamb couldn't be there but had given his permission for the viewing to go ahead. Charlotte, caught off guard, couldn't think of a reason quickly enough to back out and had done her best to sound enthusiastic.

Simon checked his watch more often than was necessary and, arms crossed, paced back and forth down the driveway.

"That won't get her here any faster," said Charlotte. "Look, I'll call her and see if she's on her way." She entered the number in her phone, but her call went to voice mail.

"She must be driving. Should be here any minute."

But she wasn't, and after a long half hour, it became obvious that Lynda wasn't coming.

"This doesn't feel right," said Charlotte. "If she's been held up or something's come up and she can't make it, she'd have called. I know she would have. That would be the professional thing to do, and that's the way Lynda would do business. Something must be wrong." She gave Simon an imploring look. "Look, you go. Enjoy the rest of the day. I'll get Aaron to drive me over to her office. I just want to check that everything's okay, and if she's still there, I'll talk to her about the asking price and see if the family or the lawyer or whoever's looking after this is willing to negotiate. After all, the place has been on the market for some time, and with a condominium development going up next door, hopefully they'll be willing to take less. It would be easier, of course, to make our case if we'd actually seen inside and had some idea of what kind of shape the place is in." She reached for her phone. "I'll see if Aaron's free now," she said as they fell into step and walked back to the hotel.

*

Aaron drove slowly along Helm Street and pulled over when Charlotte instructed him to. As she opened the car door, a large white poodle showing off a fancy cut that included turquoise bows on her ears emerged from the dog-grooming studio beside the real estate office and pranced down the street, owner in tow. The white cloud of curly hair on the dog's head fluffed and waved as she walked. Charlotte had to smile.

She pushed open the door of the real estate office, expecting to find someone at the reception desk, but it was empty. Well, it was Sunday, after all, so perhaps not. The four desks in the large room were empty, tidied up by their occupants on Friday afternoon and waiting for their return on Monday. But if the office was empty, why was the door unlocked?

They advanced further into the room and stopped. The room was silent except for the muted sound of traffic.

"Lynda?" Charlotte called. And then came a muffled groan.

"Where's that coming from?" Charlotte whispered.

"Over there, I think," said Aaron, pointing to a door with a large glass window.

"That'll be the conference room," said Charlotte. "Where they negotiate the deals and sign papers."

They approached it cautiously, then Charlotte called out, "Is there someone in there?"

The guttural moaning sound came again. Charlotte glanced through the window and, seeing nothing, opened the door. At the end of the room, in the corner so she could not be seen through the window, squirming against the tape that fastened each of her wrists to the arm of a chair, was Lynda Flegg. Her wild, wide eyes were filled with fear.

"Mph," she moaned through the tape that wound around her head and covered her mouth.

"You can't talk," said Charlotte, "so don't try." She turned to Aaron. "See if you can find a pair of scissors on someone's desk. We'll cut away as much of the tape as we can so we don't have to pull her hair. Lock the front door if you can. We don't want anyone else coming in here. And you'd better call the police."

"Mpgh," said Lynda, shaking her head violently. Charlotte knelt beside her and picked at the tape that bound her wrists to the chair. The base of the chair had been taped to the table to prevent movement.

Aaron returned, handed her a pair of scissors, and reached for his phone.

Lynda's eyes filled with tears as she shook her head. "Better hold off on the police for a moment, Aaron, until we hear what she has to say." Charlotte cut the tape from the chair but left it on Lynda's wrists. As Lynda rubbed her hands together, Charlotte gave Aaron some instructions. "Aaron, quick as you can, run to the drugstore and get a bag of ice and some baby oil."

As Aaron flew from the room, Charlotte turned back to Lynda. "Now comes the hard part. We can't just rip it off—it'll take your skin with it. The tape goes round the back of your head, but I'm not going to take that off. You're probably going to need to see your hairdresser, so let's not worry about that for the moment. I'm going to try to cut the tape here and here." She ran her fingers down Lynda's cheeks. "And then we'll see about getting it off your mouth. We'll start as soon as Aaron gets back. Just try to stay calm until he gets here."

He returned a few minutes later with a bag from the drugstore.

"Aaron, there's probably a room in the back where they make coffee." Lynda nodded. "Go in there and see if you can find a towel. Cloth is best, but bring some paper towels, too." When Aaron returned with towels, Charlotte placed a reassuring hand on Lynda's shoulder. "Now you'rc going to have to keep very still. Are you ready?"

Lynda closed her eyes and nodded.

"We're going to put some ice on the tape. This makes the adhesive less sticky. It's probably best if you hold it, so you can take it away if it gets too cold. Start over here, at this end." Charlotte placed a few ice cubes in the towel, handed it to Lynda, and guided her hand where she wanted her to start. "Aaron, set your timer for two minutes."

When his phone jangled that the two minutes were up, Lynda lowered her hand, and Charlotte began the delicate task of easing the tape off Lynda's cheek so she could slip the scissors underneath the tape and then cut it without hurting Lynda. When the tape came away at the top, she moistened a paper towel with oil and dropped some oil on Lynda's face under the tape. Gradually, with slow, painstaking work, the tape came gently away. Finally, it was off. Lynda touched her mouth and started to cry.

"Lynda what happened? Who did this to you?" Charlotte asked.

"I don't know who they were. Two men. Looked like thugs. They came in here just as I was leaving to get the key to the Middleton place from Joseph Lamb and manhandled me into this room. I don't know what they wanted. If tlicy were here to rob us, they were wasting their time. We don't keep money on the premises. Did they think people hand over thousands of dollars in cash for property deposits?"

"Did you tell these guys that you don't keep money here?"

"No, I didn't get a chance, and anyway, they didn't ask. They grabbed me by the arms and forced me in here. I honestly thought they were going to kill me. They tied me up, and I heard them going through the drawers. But they didn't have a lot of time. I think they were afraid someone might come in. And then one of them got a phone call, and they put the tape on my mouth and left."

"Were you able to get a look at them?"

"No, they were wearing those hooded jackets. But they seemed young. Their movements were quick."

"Well, we have to call the police," said Charlotte. "You've been assaulted, and the police need to know about this."

"No, please. They said if I told the police, they'd hurt Mandy."

"Who's Mandy? Is that your daughter?"

"No, she's my dog. She's next door getting her hair done. I was supposed to pick her up an hour ago. I was going to get her just before I met you. And I'm so sorry I wasn't able to call you. I thought about you waiting for me at the Middleton property and felt just awful."

"Oh, please, don't give that another thought. I knew something was wrong when you didn't ring me to let me know you'd been delayed."

Charlotte met Aaron's eyes, and she made a small motion with her head.

"Look, how about Aaron goes next door and collects Mandy for you? She'll be a comfort for you here, and I know you want her with you. But we've got to phone the police."

"I can't," wailed Lynda. "You have a dog, so you'll understand why I can't."

"But I have to," said Charlotte. "The police chief is my . . . well . . ."

"He's her boyfriend," said Aaron.

"Aaron, go and pick up Mandy," said Charlotte. He set off, and Charlotte continued. "Yes, he's my boyfriend, and I couldn't possibly keep something like this from him."

Lynda started to tremble, so Charlotte put an arm around her.

"You've been through an awful ordeal, Lynda, and I'm starting to think you should go to the hospital. Let me get you a glass of water." But before Charlotte could leave, Aaron returned, his face a confused mask of fear and anger.

Lynda looked at him and then at Charlotte. "Oh, no," she whimpered.

"I was too late," Aaron said, holding up his empty hands. "The woman said a man arrived a few minutes ago and told her Lynda had sent him to get Mandy. She handed her over to him. She feels awful."

Lynda let out a long, gasping kind of cry.

"Phone the police," Charlotte told Aaron, "and then let's get Lynda a glass of water."

"No police!" Lynda cried. "They'll hurt her if the police are involved."

"Lynda, love," said Charlotte, "let me tell you something. The only way you'll get Mandy back is if the police are involved." She didn't often use the English expression "love," because Americans found it confusing, but in times of stress, it sometimes just slipped out. She rested her hand on Lynda's shoulder. "Where's your phone? Is it in your handbag? You'll have some photos of Mandy on it, and the police will need those photos."

"I don't know where my purse is. Beside my desk or maybe they took it, but my phone's in my pocket." She pulled it out and thumbed through it. "Here she is. Here's my darling girl. Oh, she'll be so frightened." Her eyes filled with tears as she choked back sobs.

Charlotte looked at the photo and then showed it to Aaron.

The white poodle with the fluffy hair they had seen prancing down the street as they arrived sat in a dignified pose on a big, heart-shaped cushion, gazing serenely back at them.

"Calling the police," said Aaron.

# Chapter 18

"So I guess we're not going to get in to see the Middleton place today," said Aaron as they passed it and then turned into the Jacobs Grand Hotel driveway.

"I guess not," agreed Charlotte. "Were you supposed to see it today? I didn't remember that you were a member of the viewing party."

"Well, it didn't start out that way, but I'm here now, and I think it would be a good idea if I came along with you. I can point things out from a student's perspective. For example, had you thought about having a large room where students can just have a beer and chill? With lots of outlets for charging phones?"

"No," said Charlotte. "I must admit I hadn't thought of that. I was thinking more about classrooms and rehearsal space."

"Yeah, that's important, too," allowed Aaron.

He parked the car, and Charlotte opened the door and got out.

"Are you going to the office?" Aaron asked over the roof of the vehicle. She shook her head.

"No, it's Sunday, and anyway, I want to get home."

Aaron cleared his throat and looked at the ground.

"I don't love Rupert as much as you do, because he's not my dog, but well, I'd be devastated if someone took him. I can't imagine what poor Lynda's going through. She'll be missing her dog something awful."

"Yes, she will. Something awful."

"When the police arrived and Phil asked us about seeing the dog leave the groomers, I felt bad I couldn't tell them anything about the person who had her. I never even noticed if it was a man or a woman, never mind a description. I couldn't take my eyes off the dog with that crazy hairdo."

"That's the thing, isn't it? Whoever's taken her won't be able to walk her around town. That's a very distinctive dog. You don't see poodles these days the way you used to."

"I wish there was something we could do to help."

"There is," said Charlotte. "You can monitor Craigslist and any other sites you can find where people sell dogs. If you see anything that looks like it could be Mandy, let me know and I'll tell Ray." She checked her watch. "I've got to get home. I don't want to be away from Rupert one minute longer. Not after what's happened."

A few minutes later, she unlocked the door to her bungalow and stepped inside. Rupert did not come to greet her as he usually did, so she walked through the kitchen and peered into the living room. He wasn't asleep on the sofa or in his bed. Her heart pounding faster and her stomach starting to churn, she called his name. A moment later, she heard a faint scratching coming from behind the sofa, accompanied by a light whimpering. She rushed to it and pulled the sofa out from the wall. There, his furry bottom facing her, was Rupert. She pulled the sofa farther out and crouched down beside him, burying her face in the soft fur of his neck and wrapping her arms around him.

"Oh, my precious boy," she said, her eyes filling with tears. "Did you crawl in here and couldn't get back out? Let's get you out now."

She helped Rupert, and once he was safely in the middle of the room, she picked up the ball that he had gone behind the sofa to fetch and then pushed the sofa tight against the wall.

"Let's go for a walk, Rupert. I need to think."

Instead of walking toward the road, they stayed on the hotel grounds and headed off into the sheltered parkland where Rupert could be safely off leash. He ran ahead, his bottom wiggling as his short, stumpy legs propelled him forward. He paused every now and then to glance over his shoulder to make sure she was keeping up. She had always found that something about walking started her creative juices flowing, and whenever she had a problem to solve, she walked. Now her problem was trying to remember everything she could about what had happened from the moment Aaron parked the car in front of the real estate office. Of course the police would seek out surveillance cameras, but if the thugs were wearing hoodies, chances were good their faces were shielded. And those surveillance tapes, so grainy and gray, were almost worse than useless.

She walked on, trailing after Rupert. The parkland seemed to shimmer in the late-afternoon light as the sun slanted through the gently stirring leaves on the maple trees. *A beautiful summer's day*, she thought, *but not for Lynda, who must be desperate with worry.*

When they arrived home, she filled Rupert's water bowl, pulled the distinctive black Treats Happen bag from the cupboard, and gave him a dehydrated chew to work on. When he was gnawing contentedly in his basket, she asked, "Well, Rupert, if you wanted to hide a dog, where would you keep her? Where do you suppose Mandy is, and how do we find her? Got any ideas?"

Rupert's warm brown eyes scanned her face, and he resumed his gnawing. A moment later, a knock on the door had him charging out of his basket, barking and running across the kitchen.

Charlotte opened the door to find Aaron holding out a piece of paper.

"Thought I should walk this over. It's Paula Van Dusen. She left a message for you with Harvey. She wants you to phone her right away. Something about a dinner party."

# Chapter 19

Paula Van Dusen had an abiding belief in what she called the meal deal. She'd seen it in her grandfather's day, in her father's day, and now in her own time—business gets done when lubricated by the restrained manners of a social setting arranged by a thoughtful hostess who brings the right people to the table. And of course, the ambiance has to be just so: flowers, delicious food, and sometimes, after-dinner entertainment. Why else would the president of the United States go to the trouble of hosting a state dinner for visiting dignitaries?

"There's someone I think you should meet," she said to Charlotte on the phone. "Certainly not what I'd call a friend of mine, but an acquaintance who might be interested in investing in that little theater school of yours. I'm having them to dinner on Tuesday night, and I think you should come. And bring your business partner, of course. I'm sorry, I've forgotten his name. The director, I believe he is. Oh, and I'll also be inviting Brian."

Charlotte sighed. It wasn't the dinner party as much as what to wear. Because of what she did for a living, people always seemed to expect her to dress in some outrageously flamboyant style, wreathed in layers of billowing scarves, perhaps, whereas the reality was she preferred a simple, tailored look. A little black dress with one or two pieces of tasteful jewelry did her very nicely.

*

"Nervous?"

"A little," Charlotte replied as she and Simon approached the steps that led to Paula Van Dusen's front door, with Brian Prentice a few paces behind. "Yes, I do feel a little anxious. Not sure why."

"You'll be fine," said Brian, now standing beside them. Simon pressed the doorbell, setting the Westminster chimes echoing through the entrance hall. A moment later, Phyllis, dressed in a traditional uniform of a short-sleeved black dress detailed with a white collar and a white apron, opened the door and stood to one side to let them enter.

"They're just down the hall having drinks in the sitting room if you'd like to follow me," she said with the faintest hint of a smile. *She seems more rested tonight*, Charlotte thought. *Less anxious. Probably able to relax a bit now with all that wedding business behind them.*

As Charlotte entered the sitting room, Paula Van Dusen swept across the room toward her, a drink in her hand. "As soon as you've got your drinks, I'll introduce you," she said, handing Brian a glass of tonic water with a slice of lemon.

When Charlotte and Simon had received their drinks, she smiled at the couple standing by the window and led the three new arrivals over to them.

"I'd like you to meet Gino Bartucci and his wife, Carmella." Bartucci was short and stocky and appeared to be in his midfifties. His dark hair was obviously dyed, and the hand clutching a highball glass wore a heavy gold ring as a cumbersome setting for what Charlotte assumed to be a large diamond. His suit was well cut and looked expensive. Brioni? She smiled at him, and after shaking his hand—slightly damp, perhaps from the condensation on the glass—she turned her attention to his wife, who appeared younger than her husband by at least two decades. Tousled blonde hair, made fuller by extensions, fell below her shoulders. Her puffed, extravagant lips drew back in what passed for a smile, revealing her upper gums. She held out a limp hand, tipped with false nails done in a French manicure.

A skilled hostess, Paula Van Dusen finished the introductions and kept the conversation moving along smoothly.

Phyllis appeared a few minutes later with a tray and collected their empty glasses.

"Well, it looks as if dinner is ready," said Paula. "Shall we go in?"

They crossed the hall to the dining room, where the mahogany table had been set for six.

Paula took her place at one end and rested her hands on the back of her chair. She gestured to the place opposite her, at the other end of the table.

"Simon, if you'd like to sit there, and we'll have Brian here beside me," she waved a hand at the place on her right, "and Gino over here. And Charlotte beside him, and Carmella, you're on Brian's right."

They took their places, and Phyllis appeared with two bottles of white Chardonnay and made her way around the table, pouring it. Brian shook his head as he covered his glass with his hand, and she passed smoothly on. At each place was a radish-and-fennel salad with honey-pomegranate dressing in a small pitcher for passing. Carmella helped herself to the dressing, passed it to Simon, and after studying the forks at her disposal, selected one and started eating.

The conversation at the table started slowly, with Paula Van Dusen turning to Brian, leaving Charlotte to talk to Gino.

"Do you live locally?" Charlotte asked in that mildly inquiring way that launches a conversation until it can get a foothold.

"We live in Manhattan," he said, "but I have business interests in the area, so I'm spending more time here. So much time, in fact, that we're renting a place while we search for a property to buy."

"Oh," said Charlotte. "I hear there's a lot of that going on right now. People looking for second homes in the area."

"Unfortunately there is indeed a lot of that going on," said Gino. "It's a seller's market. Too bad. Driving up prices." He paused with a forkful of salad in midair. "Of course, if you are selling property, well . . ." He shrugged, leaving the unspoken words hanging in the air, and raised his fork the rest of the way to his mouth. "And you," he said, turning his head toward her but allowing his eyes to linger for a moment on his wife before giving Charlotte his full attention, "I understand you work for the Jacobs Grand Hotel."

"Not exactly," said Charlotte. "I'm with the Catskills Shakespeare Theater Company, and we're a separate entity. We're based at the hotel, but we're not really part of the hotel operation." Thinking this was the opening to begin the investment conversation, she added, "But we, that is, Simon and I—he's the artistic director, you see—we're working toward becoming more independent and well, you might say, setting up on our own. We're planning to open a theater school this fall. Drama schools in New York are full and hard to get into, and we have a lot of experience to offer. So the students would get wonderful training combined with the opportunity to perform with the company."

"That sounds very interesting," said Bartucci. "And Paula tells me you're looking for an investor. An angel, I believe you theater people call it."

"Well, angel, yes. In theater terms, that's someone who invests in a particular production, but in our eyes, that investor would certainly be an angel!"

She glanced at Simon on her left, who was doing his best to keep his eyes well away from Carmella Bartucci's enhanced breasts as he tried to carry on a normal conversation. Charlotte smiled to herself and turned her attention back to Bartucci.

"Do you like the theater, Mr. Bartucci? Do you go often?"

He made a sort of grunting noise and shook his head. "No, it's not what I like. But my wife, now, she likes the theater. Or she thinks she does." He shrugged. "How would she know? She doesn't go either."

"Oh." Charlotte made a deflated little noise. There didn't seem to be much hope here of any kind of investment.

"But she thinks she would like to get involved in some way," he went on. "She thinks doing something cultural would be good for her standing in her new community. It would help her meet people." He gestured vaguely with his fork and then set it on his plate as his eyes slid toward Paula Van Dusen. "The right people."

"How did you meet Mrs. Van Dusen? She's always helping out good causes," Charlotte asked.

"Yes, she is. I made a donation to one of her good causes, and she was so grateful. She mentioned your theater project to me, and we wanted to find out more, so she kindly arranged this little get-together."

"That was kind of her," agreed Charlotte.

"So you see, it is really up to your colleague there to convince my wife that this would be the right project for her. There are so many good causes, all deserving of our support. We can only do so much . . ." his voice trailed off wistfully, and his eyes flitted across the table to meet his wife's. "Of course, we would have to have assurances that all the legalities are in place before we could consider investing in your school. Just a formality, you understand. I have every confidence it will be very successful."

"Legalities?"

"Of course. You can't do anything these days without a contract. I don't think you need an entertainment lawyer for this matter. A business lawyer should do fine. At least to start with. I can recommend a lawyer here in town my firm uses, if you like."

"It wouldn't be Joseph Lamb, would it?"

He gave her a sharp look. "It would indeed. Handles all our transactions. He's busy and always pressed for time, which can make him seem a little gruff, but he gets the job done, and that's what counts."

"I saw him at the Middleton house. He's involved in that sale, I believe."

Bartucci took a sip of wine and then changed the subject.

"I heard your theater company put on a play here a few nights ago."

"We did. *A Midsummer Night's Dream*. Were you able to attend? We stage an outdoor performance here every June as a fundraiser, and everyone has a great time."

"Not quite everyone, if what I read in the papers is true," said Bartucci with a slight snigger. Charlotte did not reply, and at that moment Phyllis appeared to clear the table in preparation for the next course.

"No," Bartucci continued, sitting back stiffly, giving Phyllis room to remove his plate. "My wife and I were unfortunately unable to attend, as we chose to attend an event in Manhattan that evening."

"Well then," said Charlotte, "we'd love to have you and your wife attend our next performance. We're doing

*A Midsummer Night's Dream* again tomorrow evening at the hotel theater, if you'd like to come." Bartucci hesitated. "As our guests, of course. We'd be happy to give you a little backstage tour, and perhaps seeing our operation would help persuade your wife to support us."

"I'd have to discuss it with her, but I don't see why not," said Bartucci. "It might be rather fun. I don't know anything about Shakespeare."

Having cleared all the places, Phyllis returned, followed by a woman who appeared to be in her late twenties or early thirties, about the same age as the bridesmaids. Her skin was a pale-caramel color and her long hair of tight, springy blonde curls was tied back in a black bow.

Charlotte's eyes narrowed slightly as she tried to place her. Had she been a guest at the after party?

The two circled the table, each holding a white platter from which the diners helped themselves. Phyllis offered fillets of honey-mustard salmon, and the other woman's contained small new potatoes sprinkled with fresh dill and a medley of roasted vegetables.

When everyone had been served the main course, each woman approached one side of the table, this time with bottles of wine wrapped in white napkins.

"Would you like a glass of wine?" the younger woman asked Charlotte. Charlotte turned slightly and met the woman's eyes.

"I'm sorry?" Charlotte said.

"I said, 'would you like a glass of wine?'"

"Yes, I would. Thank you." Charlotte shifted an inch or two closer to Bartucci so the woman could reach around her to fill the wineglass.

"Thank you," Charlotte said, moving away from Bartucci and watching the young woman as she poured his wine. *"Would you like a glass of wine?" And now I know where I've seen you before*, she thought. *"Would you like a glass of champagne?" You were dressed as a fairy and serving champagne at the after party.*

Having finished serving and pouring, the two women retreated, closing the door quietly behind them.

"You've been looking at lots of properties, I hear," Paula said to Bartucci. "Have you seen anything you really liked?"

"We have our eye on one or two," he replied. "Nothing so grand as this, of course." He gestured with his left hand at the room.

"Oh, but this isn't a summer or weekend place," said Paula. "This is my late husband's family home. Van Dusens have lived here for generations."

"A family who has lived in the same home for generations! Such continuity. How I admire that kind of staying power," Bartucci beamed at her.

*How you admire old money*, Charlotte thought.

"Oh, Charlotte, before I forget," Paula said as they began the dessert course, "Belinda said she has one or two dresses for you. She said you'd know what she meant. If you could arrange to pick them up sometime this week or next?"

"Yes, of course," said Charlotte. "Thank you."

*

After coffee and liqueurs in the sitting room, the evening drew to a close. Paula walked with her guests to the front door, where Phyllis and the young woman were waiting in the hall, presumably to lock the door behind them.

"I was wondering about the young woman who was serving tonight," said Charlotte. "She's very pretty."

"Oh, that's Alex," said Paula. "She helps us out from time to time when we're holding an event."

"Oh, right. I thought I remembered her from the after party."

At the mention of the after party and its implied connection to the broken engagement, Paula frowned momentarily and then, after thanking her guests for coming, wished them good-night.

"Well, what do we think?" boomed Brian from the back seat as they drove out of the Van Dusen estate. "How did we do?"

"I think we did okay," said Simon. "Cautiously optimistic. I didn't realize at first that she's the investor, not him."

"Me too!" said Charlotte. "She's looking for an artsy cause to give her a bit of cachet in the community."

"Like Paula," said Brian. "Except Paula is a classy woman, whereas . . ."

"Mrs. Bartucci is prepared to be 'generous,'" said Simon, "whatever that means. But there would be one condition. She wants a room or something named after her grandfather."

"I don't think that would be a problem," said Charlotte, "but we'd have to look into it. Speaking of which, Mr. Bartucci did say something that got me thinking. He asked if we've looked into the legality of all this and recommended a lawyer who can handle it for us. The same lawyer, in fact, I met briefly outside the Middleton house. Joseph Lamb, his name is. I think the sooner we speak to him, the better."

As the car turned into the Jacobs Grand Hotel, Brian spoke.

"I wondered if the two of you would like to join me for what would have been a nightcap in the old days," he said. "Nowadays, of course, for me at least, it's a coffee."

"Not for me, thanks Brian," said Charlotte. "Ray's been looking after Rupert, and I'd like to get home."

"Some other time, Brian," said Simon. "But thanks just the same."

"On second thought," said Charlotte, "I think we should join Brian, if we're not too tired, that is. We need to discuss what we've learned tonight."

"Sorry, but my brain couldn't handle it," said Simon. "But tell you what, let's meet for coffee first thing in the morning and have a good chat."

He parked the car, and the three went their separate ways. As she walked up the little path to her bungalow, Charlotte was greeted by enthusiastic barking and Rupert rushing toward her. She bent down, put her arm around him, and rubbed her face in the ruff of fur around his neck. Ray held out a hand and pulled her to her feet.

"We heard you drive up," he said, "so I thought that would be a good time to let Rupert out." He gazed up at the sky. "It's a beautiful night. Should we take a little walk?"

"I don't think so," Charlotte replied. "I want to change out of these clothes."

"How did it go?" Ray asked as they walked toward the welcoming lights of Charlotte's bungalow.

"I don't know. Hard to tell. I don't know if they will invest, and I don't know if they're in it for the right reasons. I'm not sure if it matters what their motives are or if we should just take their money. The three of us are going to discuss it in the morning. But now that I'm getting to know Paula Van Dusen better, I like her."

"Is she in it for the right reasons? Whatever that means."

"Yes, I think she is." Charlotte opened the screen door and the three of them entered the kitchen. Ray locked the door behind them.

"Can I get you anything? Coffee? Glass of wine?"

"It's a bit too late for coffee. Wine?" She mulled that over for a moment. "No, I don't feel like that." She brightened. "I'll tell you what I do feel like. There's a bottle of brandy on the drinks table, and I'd love if you'd pour me a small one. I hope you'll join me."

"I'll get them while you get changed. I'll bring it in to you."

She turned away from him, and he pulled down the zipper of her dress, exposing her back. Then, with a quick look over her shoulder, she disappeared into her bedroom. She kicked off her shoes, then removed her dress and bra, setting them on the bed, and pulled on a pink T-shirt and a pair of cotton pajama bottoms with a pattern of dancing pink-and-purple sheep. She pulled off the clutch that secured one of her pierced stud earrings and dropped it into the little dish on her dresser, where it joined two or three other pairs. She pulled the earring from her ear and cradled it in her palm. A classic pearl earring with a round, brilliant diamond set in white gold just above the pearl. Not ostentatious or showy, but genuine and pretty.

Her mother had given her these earrings on her twenty-first birthday, and how she'd managed not to lose one in all the years since she didn't know. The last time she'd worn them, she'd left them in the little earring dish, but she thought now she should put them away properly. She opened her jewelry box and removed a red velvet case. She replaced the clutch that she had removed a few minutes earlier on the earring's post, did the same with the other, and set the red box lovingly back in the jewelry box. She closed the lid, turned away, and then, with a puzzled look on her face, reopened the box and examined the contents.

"Ray!"

"What is it?" He appeared at the door a moment later, wearing a lopsided smile and holding out a snifter of brandy. When he saw the look of dismay on her face and the opened drawer, he knew she'd discovered the contents of her jewelry box had been disturbed.

"Ray, I had a valuable ring and it's gone. I'm not sure what I'm supposed to do. Tell you to call the police, or do I just tell you, since you are the police?"

He set the drink down on a bedside table and advanced toward her.

"You don't need the police. The ring is safe. I've got it."

"You? You've got it? But why?"

"I borrowed it. I planned to take it to a jeweler so he can tell me what size you wear. I want to buy you a ring." He ran a hand through his hair and looked at the floor. "Oh, God, I've made such a mess of this." He bent awkwardly and made as if to kneel.

"No!" Charlotte said, covering her mouth with one hand. "Please don't."

He winced and swore gently under his breath.

"Oh, no, Ray," said Charlotte. "It isn't that. It's just your moment was ruined. Ask me again later when you can do it properly." He let out a huge sigh, let his head fall back for a moment, and then locked shining eyes on her.

"Come on, then," she said. "Give me that brandy. I need it."

They sat on the sofa, his arm around her as she nestled into him. She took a sip of brandy and then put the glass on the coffee table, and smiling, she lifted her face to him as he pulled her in closer.

# Chapter 20

The staff at the Jacobs Grand Hotel have a small cafeteria where they take their meals, meet friends, or simply read or work on their laptops over a cup of tea or coffee. It's never very busy, but it provides a comfortable, coffeehouse ambiance where members of the theater company can relax and mingle with the hotel service staff.

It was here at nine o'clock the next morning that Charlotte, Simon, and Brian met to discuss the potential funding for their theater school. The room was almost deserted. A couple of young actors were getting coffee but would probably take it back to their rooms. Theater people, recovering from evening performances, barely surface much before noon, cxcept on matinee days.

"It was good of you to join us, Brian," said Simon. "We know this is early for you."

"That's all right. I'm not sleeping much these days, so at least I can be doing something useful. Had a nice early-morning walk and here I am."

His face, formerly florid and jowly, was now a much better color and noticeably thinner since he'd quit drinking and started exercising. His abdomen, which had been distended, was now almost normal.

"Brian, the way you're going, you're not going to last the season in your current costumes. You've lost so much weight, I think you should come in and Aaron will do a refit. Are you feeling okay?" asked Charlotte.

Brian nodded. "I'm fine. In fact, probably better than I've been in a long time." He took a sip of coffee. "Right. Let's get on with it."

Simon began. "If the money were coming from Paula Van Dusen, I'd be very comfortable taking it, but I'm not sure about the Bartuccis. What do we actually know about them?"

Brian sat back in his chair, folded his arms, and looked from Simon to Charlotte.

"I think they, well, she has upward mobility pretensions, and being involved in the theater will help her with that. She's seen what supporting the arts does for women like Paula Van Dusen—and New York City is full of women like that who serve on boards and support art galleries, museums, theater companies—and she wants to join them. So if she's willing to invest in us, I say, let's take the money. Isn't her money as good as anyone else's?" asked Charlotte.

"Maybe," said Simon. "I'm not convinced. Something doesn't feel right."

"Well," said Brian, "if we go back to Shakespeare's day, he had patrons. Needed them, in fact, to operate his theater business. To see his plays into production, raise money to build the Globe Theatre, and all the rest of it. Of course, his patrons were titled—the Earl of Southampton springs to mind—but you could say there's a certain precedent here."

"Oh, it's not the idea of having a patron I object to," said Simon. "It's just who that patron might turn out to be."

"Well, let's do this," said Charlotte. "I've invited the Bartuccis to this evening's performance of *Midsummer*. We'll show them what our theater is all about, who we are, and what we do, and then, if they're interested, we'll do due diligence, including a thorough background check, just to know that everything's on the up-and-up. We would not want our school's reputation tarnished by an unfortunate association before we even get a reputation." She let out a little sigh. "On the other hand, she may not want to invest here. She might like to take her money somewhere else with a higher profile, maybe, and if that happens, Simon, I think you'll be singing a different tune when you see all that lovely money walking out the door to be sunk into some awful off-Broadway production that closes in three weeks, never to be seen again."

Simon allowed himself a nonchalant shrug.

"I'll put Aaron in charge of looking after them tonight," said Charlotte. "Should we sort out some champagne at the intermission?"

Simon shook his head. "Not the intermission. We're too busy and not enough time. Too rushed. After the performance, and not champagne. I'd say just a glass of wine."

"Right," said Charlotte. "I'm glad that's settled. See you this evening, and Brian, let me know when you're coming in for that fitting. It should be sooner rather than later. If we don't hear from you, Aaron will hunt you down."

As Brian placed his hands on the table and started to stand up, signaling he thought the meeting was over, Charlotte spoke again. "And just to make sure everything is legal and everyone's interests are protected, I suggest we see the lawyer as soon as possible."

Simon nodded. "I agree." He looked across the table. "Brian?"

"Yeah, of course. Fine with me, but I'll leave all that up to you two." Brian was on his feet. "I think I'll see if Aaron's available now," he said. "I don't like things hanging over me, so probably best if we get the costumes taken care of right away."

Charlotte gave him an encouraging smile as he departed, then turned her attention back to Simon.

"Is he all right? He seems, oh, I don't know, subdued," Simon said. "Do you know if there's anything going on?"

"He definitely seems a little low in himself. Has his performance level dropped off?"

Simon shook his head.

"No, he's giving everything he's got onstage."

"Well, let's give him a day or two, and if he doesn't pull out of it, you'll just have to speak to him."

"Me?"

"Of course you. He's your lead actor."

"Do you think we're doing the right thing, letting him into the partnership or whatever we are? After all, the school was our idea—well, your idea—and I don't really remember how he got to be part of it."

"Brian got to be part of it when he offered to invest two hundred thousand dollars," said Charlotte. "We needed his money." She corrected herself. "Need."

Simon thought for a moment.

"These Bartucci people. What do we really know about them? What business is he in? I'd like to know more about them."

"So would I," agreed Charlotte. "Well, I expect you have a busy morning ahead of you, so I'll leave you to it."

"What about you? What are you up to today?"

"I'm off to see a woman about a dog."

# Chapter 21

Charlotte debated whether she should take Rupert. Would the sight of him—happy, confident, trusting, and above all, safe in her loving care—be too upsetting for Lynda? Would his presence seem insensitive? Or would she find comfort and hope in the presence of another dog? Deciding that Lynda must surely have seen other dogs since Mandy had been taken, Charlotte fastened Rupert into his walking harness, closed the door behind them, and stepped into a perfect June morning.

Under a benign blue sky filled with gigantic, puffy white clouds, they walked into town, Rupert stopping to investigate smells of interest along the way, including poles with posters asking for help finding a missing white poodle. They reached the real estate office, and Charlotte pushed the door open.

The receptionist looked up from her computer as the two entered. She cast a vaguely disapproving look in Rupert's direction and then directed her full attention at Charlotte.

"I wonder if I could have a word with Lynda Flegg," Charlotte said.

"Is she expecting you?" the receptionist asked.

"Well, no. I'm just here on the off chance that she'd be . . ."

"She's out on an errand," the receptionist interrupted, "if you'd like to wait." She pointed at a few chairs against the wall.

"Thank you." Charlotte and Rupert sat down. Rupert looked around, and Charlotte checked her phone. A few minutes later, the door opened and Lynda bustled in. Charlotte stood up and took a step forward.

"Oh," said Lynda. "It's you. And Rupert." She bent down and gave him a friendly pat.

"Wondered if I could have a word," Charlotte said. "If it's not a good time, just say so and we'll be off."

"No, no, it's fine. We can talk in the boardroom."

"I just wanted to stop in and see how you're doing," Charlotte said when they were seated. "I've thought about you a lot. I hadn't heard that you've got Mandy back, so I just wanted to see how you're coping."

"Not well." Lynda's eyes filled with tears, and she scrabbled around in her purse for a tissue. "I think about her every minute. Is she okay? How is she getting along without me? It's awful. I can't eat, I can't sleep." She dabbed her eyes. "And then I get very angry with the grooming salon. None of this would have happened if they'd just phoned me to say, 'There's someone here to pick up your dog. Is that okay?' And then, when I didn't answer the phone, they should have refused to hand her over to them."

"I expect they've changed their policy," said Charlotte, adding, "not that that's any comfort for you."

"Exactly," said Lynda. "And the police have been totally useless. What do they care about a stolen dog when they've got parking tickets to issue?"

"Oh, but they do care," said Charlotte. "I can assure you of that. Ray Nicholson, the police chief, cares very much. It's just that it's hard to know where to start looking for her. So many places she could be."

"I've put up posters and registered her with missing dog sites online," said Lynda. "I don't know what more I can do."

"My assistant is monitoring websites that sell dogs," said Charlotte.

"Thank you," said Lynda. "That's very kind of you."

"Tell me, Lynda. Do you believe in coincidences?"

"Sometimes. Do you?"

"Yes, I do. I've seen coincidences that if you put them in a book, readers would scoff and say that couldn't possibly happen. But they did."

"Go on."

"Do you think it was just a coincidence that you were attacked and your dog was stolen, and Hugh Hedley, who you were supposed to meet at the Middleton house, was murdered? That's all I'm saying. Is there a connection? Can you think of anything?"

Lynda shook her head. "No," she said slowly, drawing the word out. "I can't think of any previous connection I had to Hugh Hedley, but I've just heard something about him that connects him to someone else."

Charlotte leaned forward. “What? Who?”

“Well, Hugh Hedley worked in high-end Manhattan real estate. It’s such a tangled world . . . clients—most of them foreign investors—other agents, brokers, stagers, mortgage lenders . . . and they all hate each other, it seems. They can be pretty ruthless in their business dealings. It’s a real snake pit.”

Charlotte nodded. “You can understand that, with so much money at stake. They’re selling properties worth, what, twenty, thirty million dollars?”

“That’s right. Very high stakes. Anyway, apparently as these Manhattan real estate guys go, Hugh was one of the nicer ones until recently, when he did something that almost seemed out of character.”

“Oh, what was that?”

“Well, the Manhattan real estate market is all about bigger and better apartments—the kind that foreign investors go for. So when a small apartment comes on the market, if a developer likes the location, they’ll buy it, then they’ll go after the apartment next door and the one beside that, until finally, they’ve bought the whole floor. Then they tear everything apart and renovate it to turn it into one or two huge apartments. And sometimes they’ll even do two floors, turning them into thirty-room apartments over two stories.”

Charlotte mulled that over.

“Oh, I think I see where this is going,” she said slowly. “Everything depends on—”

"That's right. The developer must get the whole floor for the plan to work. Has to. If there's one holdout, then the project can't move forward, and all that money's tied up, costing thousands every day in interest."

"So was Hugh Hedley involved in one of these schemes?" Charlotte asked.

"You bet. He was acting as the agent for the guy whose apartment they needed. The holdout. Interestingly, the guy who owned the apartment was in Argentina for almost a year and had no idea all the other units on his floor had been sold. So he comes home to find his tiny, little midtown apartment that he bought about twenty years ago is very much in demand. And Hugh managed to find him and offered to represent him. Because he wanted to go head-to-head with the other agent. The agent acting for the developer."

"Who was it?"

"None other than Adrian Archer, who was supposed to be getting married at the Van Dusen estate—where Hugh turned up dead. How do you like that for a coincidence?" Lynda said. "But there's more in this tangled web. The developer involved is a guy named Gino Bartucci, and I hear he's a friend of Paula Van Dusen's."

"No! Bartucci? Really? I just met him. He's considering investing in our theater company. So I guess it's his money that's all tied up in this deal."

"That's right."

"Hmm." Charlotte was silent for a moment, and then said, "But I'm not sure I'd call Bartucci a friend of Paula

Van Dusen's. I think he just donated to one of her causes, and that's how she knows him."

"Well, okay, fair enough," said Lynda.

"And after Hugh was killed, what happened then?" Charlotte held up a finger. "No, wait. Let me guess. Without Hugh Hedley urging his client to hold out so he can drive the price up, the guy from Argentina gives in and decides to sell his apartment. Adrian Archer, acting for the purchaser, makes a handsome commission, and Gino Bartucci can green-light his multi-million-dollar real estate development."

Lynda nodded. "That's exactly what's about to happen. So you see, with Hugh out of the way, Bartucci and Adrian get what they wanted."

Charlotte considered everything Lynda had just told her and then asked, "How do you know all this?"

"Oh," said Lynda, "one of the brokers here is friendly with someone in New York and heard all about it. It's a small world. News spreads fast when so much money is involved. Sometimes a rumor is all it takes for an agent to make a killing. He goes to an open house, hears that an apartment is about to come on the market, pounces, and . . ." She raised both hands in an open gesture. "A Manhattan apartment about to come on the market is pure gold to an agent who knows what he's doing."

"So developers working on these big, fancy deals get to know one or two agents they trust and they develop a kind of business partnership. Would I be right?"

"Oh, yes. The real estate agent gets to know what types of properties the developer's interested in and how much financing he's got to work with, so he keeps his ear to the ground, and in the best-case scenario, he can source properties before they come on the open market. A lot of top deals are done that way."

"And Bartucci works closely with Adrian Archer."

"Well, now he works with Adrian Archer. He used to work with Hugh Hedley. Until they had some kind of bust-up a little while ago. I don't know what happened . . . a deal in Manhattan went wrong, something like that."

"So there was bad blood among all of them," said Charlotte. "That reminds me of a conversation I overheard up at the Van Dusen house. I didn't think much about it at the time, but Adrian was talking to someone on his phone—now that I think about it, it might have been Gino—and he said something like, 'Leave it with me, and I'll think of something that'll ruin his week.' Words to that effect. He was definitely talking about Hugh Hedley. I'm sure of it."

"Wow, that doesn't sound good," said Lynda. "Was it a threat, do you think?"

"Sounded like it," said Charlotte. She stood up. "You've given me a lot to think about," she said as she made a mental note to try to remember all the details so she could tell Ray.

"I have?"

"In fact, so much to think about that I almost forgot the real reason I came here. You mentioned you haven't been to the theater for a while. Would you like to come tonight?

We're doing *A Midsummer Night's Dream*. It's fanciful, filled with magic and enchantment. It's fun, not heavy. If you've nothing else on, do come. As my guest. It might be a distraction for you, and I think you'll enjoy yourself. Starts at seven thirty, so come a bit before then."

When Lynda hesitated, Charlotte smiled at her and added, "Did I mention we've also invited the Bartucci couple?" Charlotte raised an eyebrow for emphasis. "I really hope you'll come. It should be interesting."

Lynda smiled back. "The Bartuccis, eh? You know, as you say, it's been much too long since I've been to the theater."

# Chapter 22

"Ladies and gentlemen of the Catskills Shakespeare Theater Company, final half!" At seven pm, assistant stage manager Aaron Jacobs roamed the backstage area of the theater at Jacobs Grand Hotel, knocking on dressing-room doors, calling out the thirty-minute warning to cast and crew. And because Brian Prentice liked an individual notice, Aaron knocked on the designated star dressing-room door. "Final half, Mr. Prentice. Final half!"

Brian sat at his dressing table and, holding an eyeliner pencil, gazed at his reflection in the mirror. His weight loss was now reflected in his face. Where once it had been full and relatively unlined, now every line, every furrow was pronounced and deep. He looked older than he was, and he felt older than he looked. His eyes drifted to the top drawer of his dressing table. Adjusting the robe on his right shoulder, he opened the drawer, and after moving aside an old theater program, he pulled out the whisky bottle underneath it.

*Just a drop to steady my nerves won't hurt*, he thought. *It's been so long, and I've been so good.* As he was about to twist off the cap, a knock on the door startled him. With a small sigh, he replaced the bottle in the drawer and closed it.

"Yes. Who is it?" he shouted.

"It's me. Charlotte. I've brought your trousers."

"You'd better come in then."

"Sorry to disturb you, Brian, but Aaron's sorted these out for you. The waistband will be a much better fit." She handed him a pair of gray trousers. "Even though your cloak mostly hides them, you've lost so much weight, I can't let you wear your old ones onstage tonight." She removed a pair of trousers from his costume rail. "You'll be better in the new ones. Aaron customized them to your new measurements." He said nothing, but indicated with a brief movement of his head that he'd been listening. "You all right, Brian? Is anything the matter?"

"I'm all right. Just tired, that's all. Not really up for it tonight. Got to psych myself up to get through this performance."

"Well, there's a lady here with just the thing to cheer you up." She stood aside and gestured to someone in the hall to come in, then disappeared into the hallway.

"Hello, Brian! Brought you these from my garden." Paula Van Dusen, carrying a huge vase of red-and-white roses, slipped into the room. She looked about for a place to set them, and Brian swept the contents of his dressing table to one side, clearing a space.

"I read somewhere that sending flowers to an actor before the curtain has fallen on the first performance is bad luck," said Paula, "but since you're well into your run, I thought these might brighten up your room."

"They're lovely, and I thank you," said Brian.

"Well, I mustn't keep you from your preparations," said Paula. "There's to be a little get-together after the play, and I hope you'll be joining us."

"Will you be there?" asked Brian.

"Oh, most definitely."

"Then so shall I." He stood up. "And now, dear lady, thank you for the lovely flowers, but if you'll excuse me, I must complete my preparations."

"Of course. Your audience awaits."

When the door had closed, Brian unfolded the trousers Charlotte had left. He pulled them on and was pleasantly surprised at how much better they felt. He hadn't realized how much weight he'd lost. Until this summer, he'd always had his own dresser to help him get ready for a performance: somebody who would make sure his costumes were clean and laid out for each performance; his makeup was smudge-free; his wig was on straight; and any accessory, like a ring, was on his hand and any accessory not needed, like a wristwatch, was left behind on his dressing table. But now, he had to fend for himself much of the time, although to be fair, Charlotte helped him when she could. And although Aaron was too busy during the performance with all his backstage tasks, he occasionally helped before or after a performance, too.

With a disgruntled sigh, he sat down once again in front of the mirror. His makeup was finished; it just needed a light dusting of power to fix it. He did this, washed his hands, and then began his articulations. "Red leather, yellow leather," he repeated over and over, as fast and as clear as he could. "Red leather, yellow leather, red leather, yellow leather." He started off softly but increased the volume each time he said it.

"A star," Noel Coward once said, "is someone with that little bit extra." And whatever he meant by "that little bit extra," Brian undoubtedly once had it. His onstage presence was commanding and magnetic; every member of the audience felt he was speaking directly to them. And even those seated in the gods, the last rows of the balcony, could hear every word he uttered, clearly and plainly. In his darkest moments, he realized that his star power was turning to dust, but to maintain the illusion onstage, he had to maintain the illusion that put him there.

"You've still got it, Brian, old son," he reassured himself, leaning into his face in the mirror. A pair of dark-brown eyes, heavy with eyeliner and mascara, stared back at him. He switched off the bright makeup lights that surrounded the mirror, throwing the room into a shadowy gloom.

He stood in front of the door, squared his shoulders, made a little exploding gesture with both hands, and whispered, "Show time!"

"This is your five-minute call. Five minutes, please. Stand by, technical staff." Aaron raced down the corridor.

A rapid pounding on the star dressing-room door. "Five minutes, Mr. Prentice. This is your five-minute call." The actors who would appear in act one, scene one, including Brian, prepared to take their places onstage while others emerged from the dressing rooms and gathered in the wings.

"Stand by, everyone," Aaron called, eyeing the red-and-green light system that provided timing cues visible to the actors and crew backstage but was invisible to the audience. The actors onstage stood motionless beside the small pool of flashing red light.

Tension rose as a recorded announcement warned the audience that the play was about to begin.

"Good evening, ladies and gentlemen, and welcome to this evening's performance of *A Midsummer Night's Dream* performed by the Catskills Shakespeare Theater Company. Please make sure your cell phones are switched off, as they can prove distracting to other members of the audience and the performers. Flash photography is also not permitted. We hope you enjoy the show!"

Aaron silently counted down the seconds, then pulled the lever to raise the curtain. When it had almost reached the top, he pressed the button to change the cue light from red to green. Brian reached out his hand to the actress playing Hippolyta, former Queen of the Amazons, to his Theseus, Duke of Athens, and the performance was under way.

When the scene ended, he exited the stage and hurried to his dressing room to change into his next character, Oberon, king of the fairies. Charlotte would be there in a few seconds to dress him. He pulled open the drawer in his dressing table and moved the theater program covering the bottle aside, but at the sound of approaching footsteps, he closed it again. He stepped back from the dressing table just as Charlotte rushed in. Wordlessly, he swung around and turned his back to her so she could pull off his robe, help him switch shirts, and drape another cloak over his shoulders. Each knew what they had to do, and the costume change was swift and efficient. He turned to face her, and she changed wigs and placed a crown on his head, centering it.

"Let me see you," she said, stepping back. "You look fine, but you seem very tense. Is the performance going all right?" A dark scowl crossed his face, and he clenched his fists.

"Fine," he muttered. "I'm fine. But I do wish people would stop asking me how I feel."

Charlotte opened the door. The voices of actors onstage drifted down the hallway, and she turned to Brian, signaling it was time for him to go and stepping to one side to let him pass.

*The vanity of actors*, she thought as he swept past her. *Something's got him wound up. Oh, well, it'll have to wait, and we can sort him out later*. She hung up the robe he'd just taken off and picked up the wig from the dressing table, placing it on its stand.

Her eye was drawn to the black-and-yellow corner of a theater program sticking out of the table drawer. She pulled out the drawer to close it properly, revealing a bottle of whisky half covered by the theater program. She picked up the bottle and, with some relief, noted it was unopened. She hesitated, not knowing what to do, and then realizing it was neither her business nor hers to take, she put the bottle back where she'd found it, covered it up with the program, closed the drawer firmly, and hurried toward the backstage area. She stood in the wings, watching, as act two began with an exchange between Puck and a fairy. A few moments later, Brian, as Oberon, entered from one side of the stage, and the actress playing Titania, queen of the fairies, entered from the other.

"Ill met by moonlight, proud Titania," said Brian. The actress playing Titania carried most of the dialogue at the beginning of the scene, but as it unfolded, Brian had more and more lines. Charlotte hoped he wouldn't forget them and moved closer to the prompt desk to warn Ray that Brian was on edge and might be headed for trouble. As she slid into the empty chair beside Ray, he glanced briefly at her, then returned his attention to the prompt book. Charlotte said nothing but, with rising apprehension, watched as the actress playing Titania and a couple of other actors left the stage.

"Well, go thy way; thou shalt not from this grove . . ." Brian was saying as a door at the rear of the theater opened, allowing a burst of bright light to flood in. Two dark figures, silhouetted in the smoky light beaming down on the stage, made their way down the aisle.

"Is this row four?" Gino Bartucci asked a seated audience member in his normal speaking voice.

"I think those are our seats right there." His wife pointed to two aisle seats, and they sat down. Gino took a sip from a water bottle just as Brian picked up his cue from the actor playing Puck.

> *"That very time I saw, but thou couldst not,*
> *Flying between the cold moon and the earth*
> *Cupid, all arm'd; a certain aim he took*
> *At a fair vestal, throned by the west,*
> *And loos'd his love-shaft smartly from his bow . . ."*

Bartucci leaned forward to say something to his wife just as the James Bond theme song alerted everyone in the theater that his cell phone was ringing. As the theatrical illusion was shattered, Brian Prentice stopped speaking, stepped to the edge of the stage, and raising an arm, pointed at Bartucci and bellowed, "Switch that bloody thing off!" After a moment of stunned silence, the audience burst into applause.

As Brian returned to his place on the stage, Bartucci stood up, and with his wife running along behind him trying to keep up, the two left the theater. When the door had closed behind them, Brian took a moment to refocus, then picked up where he'd left off, and the play resumed.

Charlotte covered her face with her hands, and Ray put his arm around her.

She lowered her hands and remarked, "Well, there goes our funding."

*

The curtain calls over, the clapping subsided and the audience members gathered up their belongings and began to file out. After sending Aaron along with Brian to help him change and saying good-bye to Ray, who had gone home to check on Rupert, Charlotte caught up with Lynda.

"Well, what did you think?" Charlotte asked. "Did you enjoy yourself?"

"I certainly did. It was terrific when that actor gave Bartucci what he deserved. What's that old saying? 'Money can't buy class'?"

"Well, I suppose anybody's cell phone can go off in the middle of a performance—it's certainly happened before and in better theaters than this. And if we had proper ushering staff at the main door, the Bartuccis never would have been allowed to enter in the middle of a scene. They'd have been made to wait until a suitable break in the play, maybe even until the next act. But the audience certainly supported Brian. He hasn't had an ovation like that in years."

"Well, I did enjoy the play. It's been too long since I've seen a performance here. When you live somewhere, you don't take as much advantage of what the area has to offer, as visitors do."

"Oh, I know what you mean. How many people who live in London have been to the Tower? And yet in the summer, you can't move because of tourists."

They'd reached the small backstage rehearsal room, where a couple of bottles of wine in ice buckets and light refreshments awaited them.

"Could I get you a glass of wine, Lynda?" Charlotte offered. "Red or white?"

"No, not for me, thanks. I don't drink anymore, but a mineral water would be just fine."

"Still or sparkling?"

"Still, please."

Charlotte poured her a glass and handed it to her. "I suppose if there'd been any news of Mandy, you'd have told me."

Lynda picked at a napkin.

"Yes, I would have. It's just awful. One of the worst things is, I've been so tempted to start drinking again." She gave the glass of water in her hand a slight tip. "Sometimes this just isn't enough."

Before Charlotte could reply, Aaron and Simon entered, discussing the night's performance.

Excusing herself, Charlotte joined them.

"Where's Brian?" she asked Aaron.

"In his dressing room. He said he didn't need me anymore and wanted a few minutes to gather himself. Said he'd be along in a few minutes."

She let out a small sigh and then pulled Simon aside. "I think Brian's about to start drinking again," she said in a low voice. "I found a bottle of whisky in his dressing table. I think you should check up on him right away, just in case."

Simon tilted his head to one side. "Not sure I'm comfortable with that. I'm not his nanny, and if Brian chooses to drink, well, that's his business, isn't it?"

Saving him the trouble of having to make a decision, Brian himself appeared in the doorway with Paula Van Dusen by his side.

"Good," said Simon. "There he is. Problem solved."

"Still, I hope everything's all right with him. Not just for the theater company, but for him. For Brian, personally," said Charlotte. "For health reasons. For his well-being."

"Yeah. Well, there's definitely something going on with him. And now I've got to deal with the fallout from what happened onstage tonight. When actors step out of character like that and break the fourth wall, it's a big deal. I'll speak to him tomorrow and see . . ." His voice trailed off as a slight commotion in the doorway drew everyone's attention. "Oh, God," said Simon. "Just what we need. Who let him in?"

Fletcher Macmillan took a moment to survey the room, and then, fixating on Simon and waving his reporter's notebook, made a beeline for him.

"Simon, old chap, how are you?" he said, reaching into his pocket for a pen. "Listen, I got a tip something happened in the theater tonight, so I hurried right over. Something involving Brian Prentice. What can you tell me about it?"

Simon said simply, "Here's your quote, Fletcher. 'A member of the audience's cell phone rang during the performance, causing Brian Prentice, in the role of Oberon, to lose concentration, so he asked the gentleman to switch it off.' How's that? Will that do you?"

"Well, it's a start, I suppose, but I suspect there was rather more to it than that. I see Brian over there, so I'd like to hear his side of the story. And this gentleman, the one with the cell phone, you wouldn't happen to know who it was, would you?"

"It's a theater, Fletcher," said Charlotte. "It's dark. You know how it is. It's difficult to see who's in the audience across the footlights."

Macmillan's eyes narrowed, and his head tipped downward and turned slightly to one side.

"Right. Well, I'm still going to talk to Brian and hear what he's got to say for himself." As Macmillan approached Brian, Paula left him to join Simon and Charlotte.

"How's Brian doing?" Charlotte asked her. "I haven't had a chance to talk to him since the performance ended."

"Well, I don't know him as well as you do, of course, but he doesn't really seem himself. I got to his dressing room just as Aaron was leaving, and he seemed a bit agitated. Jumpy. Could be a result of what happened during the performance, I suppose. And there's that Fletcher Macmillan snooping around."

"Won't be long until he finds out who Brian shouted at, and then he'll have a real story," Charlotte said.

"Bartucci that newsworthy, is he?" asked Simon.

"I'm sure he likes to think so, but I suspect only when he's in control of the content. I don't know what he'll do if this gets out. And I hope it won't affect Brian too badly."

"Well, maybe it won't get out. Let's just hope Brian isn't saying too much to Macmillan. Hopefully the theater was dark enough from his vantage point onstage and with the light in his eyes that he didn't recognize Bartucci from the dinner party."

"We shouldn't have left them alone together," said Charlotte. "Excuse me." She touched Paula Van Dusen lightly on the arm and left to join Brian and Fletcher Macmillan. Lynda Flegg, who had remained near the drinks table, hovered nearby, keeping a concerned eye on Brian.

"And that's the trouble with theatergoers today," Brian was saying. "It used to be that going to the theater was a proper night out. People dressed up for it. Now, people treat it much too casually instead of with the respect it deserves."

"Oh, you are so right, Sir Brian," said Macmillan. Although Brian Prentice had never been knighted, Macmillan had somehow got it into his head that he had, and liking the sound of his name with a title in front of it and fully believing himself overdue for a knighthood anyway, Brian had never bothered to correct him. He suspected, however, that Macmillan knew the truth, and calling him "sir" had become a little joke between them.

"Hello again, Fletcher. I wonder if I might have a word," Charlotte asked. "But before we do, I'd like to introduce Brian to Lynda Flegg. Lynda, would you be so kind as to fix Brian a drink? I'm sure he'd like what you're having."

"Sure." Understanding what Charlotte meant, Lynda smiled at Brian and picked up a glass.

"Fletcher," Charlotte said, turning back to him, "I'd be so grateful if you'd do something for us. That lady, Lynda Flegg, her dog was recently stolen from the groomers, and we're desperate to get her back. Could you please talk to Lynda and do a story on the theft? The kind of publicity only you can bring might be just what we need to find it. I don't know why we didn't think of contacting you sooner. The missing dog's a white poodle called Mandy."

"Sorry, no can do. We don't do stories about missing pets, or there'd be no room for real stories."

"Oh, that's too bad," said Charlotte. "Are you sure?"

"Well," said Fletcher, "unless you have something to offer me. A name perhaps? Now that you've had a few minutes to think about it, maybe something has occurred to you about that incident in the theater involving Brian?"

"Actually, Fletcher," said Charlotte, "I do have a name for you. Paula Van Dusen. She likes dogs, and I'm sure she'd be very grateful to you if you ran that story to help us find Lynda Flegg's lost dog."

Macmillan smiled. "You know, I think she would, too. I'll have to clear it with my editor, of course."

"Oh, I'm sure he'll go along with it. Would you like Paula to have a word with him?"

"That won't be necessary. Now I'd better ask Lynda for some photographs." Lynda's brown eyes glistened as Fletcher told her the local paper would run a story on her missing

Mandy and asked her to send him a few photographs. Her hand trembled as she reached for her phone.

"You don't have to do it right this minute, dear girl," he said. "Tomorrow will be fine. I'll ring you in the morning to get all the details of the abduction." And then, hugely satisfied that he had much bigger fish to fry with the Brian Prentice incident, he sauntered off.

"Brace yourself, Brian," said Charlotte. "He'll be off to call in your story to the *New York Times*."

"Oh, really? Too bad we don't have a video of it," he said. "It certainly gingered up my performance. I felt invincible after that. Haven't felt that on top of things in years."

"The audience loved it," said Lynda. "And they loved you."

"Do you really think so? How kind of you to say. Yes, they did seem to appreciate it, didn't they?" said Brian. "Well, it was lovely to meet you, Lynda, but all in all it was rather an exhausting performance, so I think I'll be off home. Must just say good night to everybody."

"Good night, Brian."

They watched as Brian spoke to a few people, including Paula Van Dusen, who placed a reassuring hand on his arm. Almost imperceptibly, he shrank back from her touch and continued on his way out the door.

"Brian's in danger of relapsing, I think," said Lynda, lowering her voice. "I recognized the signals from my own experience. He's headed for a dangerous place, if he's not already there. I gave him my card and told him to phone me if he feels like he's going to take a drink. Recovery is a long, hard road, and often at this point, people feel they've got it all under control and a drink or two won't hurt. They think they can handle it. But in a twelve-step program, we say, 'While you've been resting on your laurels, your disease is out on the front lawn doing push-ups.'"

"I hope he will call you," said Charlotte. "Would it be acceptable for you to call him in a day or two to see how he's doing, or is that . . ."

"As long as he doesn't feel I'm checking up on him or judging him in any way," said Lynda. "You hear about actors and musicians—creative people—having fragile egos, and I wouldn't want to upset him or say anything that could possibly tip him over the edge."

"Yes, you're right. We've been asking him if he's okay, and he's getting fed up with it. Wants us to leave him alone. It's hard to know what to do for the best."

"If he were just an ordinary guy, I'd offer to take him to an AA meeting, but he'd be uncomfortable going to one in Walkers Ridge. He'd be afraid of being recognized. We could find one somewhere further afield, though, where he could be anonymous."

"Simon and I really want him to be okay, for a lot of reasons."

"Because you're good people," smiled Lynda. "I'll do what I can. And Walkers Ridge is no different than any other place. All kinds of people here have the same problem. Paula Van Dusen's husband, for example, had a drinking problem, and so did Mr. Middleton, who owned the house you're interested in."

"I am interested in that house, and I'm also interested in Gino Bartucci. In fact, I'm sorry that unfortunate business with Brian meant they left. I was hoping to talk to them tonight, to learn more about them. And after what you told me about the Manhattan real estate world, I can't help wondering if there could be a real estate connection to Hugh Hedley's murder. What do you think?"

"Me? Haven't got a clue. It's possible, I guess. But I do understand now how ordinary people can be moved to kill someone."

"What makes you say that?"

"Because if I ever find out who took my Mandy, I'll be so tempted to kill them myself."

"Kill who?" asked Paula Van Dusen, who had joined them in time to catch the last of what Lynda was saying.

"The thugs who stole her dog from the groomer's," said Charlotte. "You must have heard about that."

"No, I haven't," said Paula. "Tell me what happened."

Lynda told her story, to Paula's dismay and indignation.

"So if you haven't heard about it," said Charlotte, "it's just as well that Fletcher Macmillan's agreed to do a story about it, so hopefully more people will be on the lookout for Mandy."

"Fletcher Macmillan! That awful man," said Paula as the three of them laughed lightly. "I've never been able to figure him out. Such a social climber. And a name-dropper."

"Well, speaking of namc-dropping," said Charlotte, "I'm afraid I just dropped yours to get Fletcher Macmillan to do the story on Lynda's missing dog. Hope that was okay."

"Absolutely!" agreed Paula. "If that's what it takes. And I'd be happy to offer a reward for Mandy's safe return, if that'll help."

"Oh, I'm sure it would," said Lynda. "Thank you."

"Right," said Paula. "I'll call Fletcher myself and tell him." She brightened. "I was happy to see during the performance that Bottom's still getting some use out of the mink hat."

"Oh, yes," said Charlotte. "I meant to ask you if we could keep it. Obviously we can't use the old donkey's head, and the actor really loves the lightness of the hat. We'd like to put better ears on it, if we can keep using it."

"Oh, by all means," agreed Paula. "I don't need it. Nobody's worn that old thing in years."

"Donkey's years!" said Charlotte. As everyone laughed, she added, "We were fortunate you were able to sort it out so quickly during the performance. There really wasn't much delay at all, not so the audience would have noticed, anyway."

"Yes, I'm surprised I was able to find it," Paula said. "I rely on Phyllis for that sort of thing because she knows where everything is kept, but she had so many things to attend to that night, including getting ready for the after party, she couldn't be in two places at once."

"Has she been with you long?" asked Charlotte.

"Oh, gosh, let me see. Must be about twenty-five years. She used to work for my mother-in-law, and I inherited her, you might say. I don't know what we'd do without her. Oh, and by the way, Charlotte, I'm still waiting for you to come and pick up that dress Belinda wants you to have. Phyllis will see to it for you."

# Chapter 23

Charlotte arrived at work the next morning to find Aaron seated at her desk stroking the mink hat on his lap.

"Have you thought about getting a cat?" Charlotte asked.

Aaron laughed. "I don't think my aunt would allow that. Of course, if I had my own place . . ."

"Well, just hang in there a little longer. It'll happen. Where there's a will, there's a way."

"I guess so," said Aaron. "If you say so. Anyway," he lifted the hat, "did you ask Mrs. Van Dusen if we could keep it? I thought I'd work on the ears today when there's no matinee, and it's *Romeo and Juliet* tonight, so the hat isn't needed."

"Good plan. Yes, we can keep it. What did you have in mind for the ears?"

Aaron unpinned the socks stuffed with tissue paper and set them aside. "I thought about using a faux fur, but now I think a dark-brown felt with a bit of pale pink for a lining.

I don't know. What do you think? I'm not really sure what a donkey's ears look like, but I think what I've got in mind will look good onstage."

"The main thing is that the audience gets the message that Bottom has been transformed into a donkey, so they should be fairly large." Aaron walked over to the shelving where the fabrics were stored and held up the hat to various bolts.

"If you don't see anything you like, talk to Mr. Grafstein at the Uptown Silk Shoppe," said Charlotte. "He's sure to have a remnant that will be perfect, and you won't need very much. He might even give it to you." She joined him in front of the fabrics, took the hat from him, and turned it around in her hands. "I've just had an idea," she said. "Before you make the ears, you could make a bendable frame out of something light, like florist wire. That way you could bend the tips if you wanted to, and you'd be sure they would stand up straight." She put the hat on her head. "How do I look?"

Aaron smiled at her. "You look pretty good, but I think it's too far back. It would look better sitting more forward"—he reached up to adjust it—"like this."

Charlotte checked herself in the mirror. "Yes, it does look better more straight on."

Charlotte took the hat off and smoothed her hair. "We haven't had a chance to talk about what happened the night of the play at the Van Dusen estate when the donkey's head went missing. Did you see anyone hanging around who shouldn't have been there?"

"There were people all over the place. Actors, crew, guests. How would I know who shouldn't have been there? I'm not sure I understand what you're getting at."

"It's just that at one point I thought I saw Belinda running across the lawn, but what you did just now when you adjusted the hat on my head reminded me of something. It couldn't have been Belinda I saw, because at the time, she would have been getting her hair done."

"Okay." He drew out the word.

"Are you with me?"

"No."

"You saw Belinda when she entered the ballroom. Her hairdo was elaborate and had a tiara set in it. That hairstyle would have taken at least an hour to do, plus, she had to get dressed. So she couldn't have been the one I saw running across the lawn."

"One of the bridesmaids, maybe? Sophie's blonde. Could have been her."

"Possibly. Or I thought when I saw Alex at the dinner party that it could have been her. We know she was at the play because she served drinks at the after party."

Aaron wrapped the hat in tissue paper and placed it in a bag. "Could be, I guess. Anyway, I'll be off now to see about some fabric. I thought I'd walk. Do you want me to take Rupert with me?"

"No. Although I find this impossible to understand, Mr. Grafstein isn't keen on him. And you certainly can't leave him tied up outside with dog thieves on the loose, so no, but thank you for offering. He'll stay here with me. Enjoy yourself, and I'll see you later."

"Well, if Rupert isn't coming with me, I'll drive and maybe do a couple of errands for my aunt while I'm out."

Aaron set off, and Charlotte busied herself tidying up the workspace. She was just starting to think about a cup of coffee when someone knocked on her open door. She turned around to see Fletcher Macmillan.

"Oh, Fletcher, it's you. Come in."

"Hope I'm not intruding. Won't take up much of your time, but I wondered if I could have a word. Been interviewing Simon about the new theater school. It's going to be big news in these parts. Need a quote from you."

"Oh, right. What would you like to know?"

They talked about the theater school for a few minutes, and Fletcher told her Simon had asked him to be a guest speaker every now and then to explain to the students how the media works and how to give an engaging interview.

"That sounds like a good idea," said Charlotte. "And speaking of how media works, how are you coming along with the story about Lynda Flegg's missing dog?"

"Oh, I'm working on it," said Fletcher. "I've been assigned this feature about your school, and I'm also working on the Hugh Hedley murder. The Albany police haven't been very forthcoming, I must say. I wondered if you'd heard anything new."

"Me? Why would they tell me anything?"

"Well, not the Albany police, but I thought you might have picked up something from your boyfriend."

"Absolutely not. He never tells me anything, and quite right, too. Operational, you know."

"It seems a shame, though, that Hedley should have been killed so soon after . . ." His voice trailed off. "But no, I mustn't keep you. I know how busy you are."

"So soon after what?"

When Fletcher did not reply, Charlotte pressed him. "You might as well tell me, Fletcher. All I've got to do is Google him."

"Well, his mother died in an accident not very long ago."

"Oh, that's terrible." She thought for a moment. "Did she live around here? What was her name?"

"She was from here but lived in Albany. Her name was Joanna . . . something. I can't recall. Not Hedley, though."

"Oh, so I guess Hedley must have been . . ."

"Her first husband. Hugh's father."

"Of course. And this accident. Was it a car crash?"

"No, it was a hiking accident up on Devil's Path. She lost her footing on a very steep section and fell, apparently."

"Devil's Path. I've heard of that. It's dangerous and recommended for experienced climbers only. Was she an experienced climber, I wonder?"

"Don't know. You'd assume so."

"Yes, you would do."

She looked at her watch. "Well, if you'll excuse me, Fletcher, I've got several things I must get done this morning, so best be getting on. And do, please, follow up with Lynda about her dog. Mrs. Van Dusen is offering a reward, so you might want to include that in your story."

When she was sure he was well out of earshot, she picked up her phone and called Lynda.

"I've just been speaking to that awful Fletcher Macmillan," she said. "I reminded him he needed to get in touch with you about Mandy's story, and if you don't hear from him today, then you should call him and you should keep calling him until he does it."

And Lynda had some news for Charlotte, too. She'd managed to arrange a private viewing of the Middleton property with Joseph Lamb.

*

An hour later, Charlotte walked up the sidewalk that led to the front door of the Middleton property, where Lynda Flegg and Joseph Lamb had just arrived.

"Good timing," said Lynda, after introducing Lamb to Charlotte. "Mr. Lamb has to check on something, so we can do a quick tour of the property, and then, if it interests you, we can arrange a second viewing, where you can take longer and bring your partners."

Joseph Lamb unlocked the door, and the three stepped into a small entranceway. An interior door with decorative glass panels opened into the hallway proper. Ahead of them lay a large, old-fashioned kitchen, and to their right, an oak stairway led to the second floor. On their left was a large living room with an adjoining dining room, with another door that opened to the kitchen.

As Lamb disappeared upstairs, Lynda directed Charlotte to the living room. The wooden floor creaked under their weight, and a smell of old furniture polish, books, dust, and candle wax mixed with a large swirl of abandonment greeted them. It was as if the house knew, somehow, that the woman who had called this empty place home for all her married life would never be coming back.

"I know," said Lynda. "Sad, isn't it? Lamb brings in someone to clean every few weeks, but you just can't get away from the emptiness. I wish the owner had let me clear out all the personal effects and do a bit of staging, but she wouldn't hear of it. What can you do? Still, here's my advice when looking at properties—don't let emotion get in the way. It's just about the structure. Don't think about the décor. You wouldn't believe how many times I've heard people tell me, 'I don't like the table.' They're not buying the table! And fixtures, paint, and wallpaper can all be changed. So ignore all that. Just think about the size of the rooms and whether the space will work for you. And walls can be knocked down and rooms made larger."

Charlotte nodded, although it was difficult to overlook the 1970s colonial furniture. A boxy, shapeless sofa in a brown-and-yellow pattern, worn, frayed, and dirty at one end where someone had sat eating and watching the floor-model television; a matching overstuffed armchair; and a coffee table with a couple of drawers filled much of the space. The dining room held a table that could probably be configured to seat eight, an oversized hutch filled with a dinner service in a popular rose pattern, and drawers that Charlotte expected would contain a set of silverware. A silver tea service sat on a side table.

At the sound of footsteps descending the stairs, Lynda whispered, "We'd better get upstairs for a quick look around. He'll be impatient to lock up." The two women brushed past the lawyer at the bottom of the stairs and hurried up to the second floor.

They peered in the bedrooms, some with peeling wallpaper and dirty windows, until they came to a large double room at the end of the corridor.

"Mrs. Middleton's room," said Lynda. "A good size. Could be a classroom, possibly." Charlotte stepped into the room and walked around the double bed, with its mattress sagging slightly in the middle, covered by a quilt, to the dresser under the window. She peered out the window to the garden below, but as she turned back to the room, the handbag over her shoulder caught the corner of a picture frame and tipped it over.

"Are you ladies ready to go?" called Joseph Lamb from the downstairs hallway. "I haven't got all day."

"We have to go, Charlotte," urged Lynda. "He doesn't like to be kept waiting."

"Right." She picked up the frame and set it back up, catching a glimpse of a photo of a seated woman with two little girls, one dark haired and the other fair.

The two women returned to the ground floor, where Joseph Lamb was waiting for them with the front door open.

"Thank you," Charlotte said. "Mr. Lamb, I hope you don't mind my asking, but I saw the photo in the paper of you talking to Hugh Hedley. Did you know him well?"

Lamb scowled at her and did not reply. As he locked the door behind them and pocketed the key, Charlotte continued: "I'd like to bring my partners back for a viewing as soon as it can be arranged. When do you think we could do that?"

"I'll check my diary and let Lynda know," he said. "She'll be in touch. Good-bye."

"Would you like to come back to my bungalow for an iced tea?" Charlotte asked Lynda when Lamb had reached his vehicle. "I'd like to talk about the property."

"Of course."

After Rupert had given them an exuberant greeting, they took their drinks to a little table set outside the bungalows facing the river.

"The Middleton house—is it structurally sound, do you know?" Charlotte asked when they had settled into a couple of Adirondack chairs. Rupert wandered restlessly around for a few minutes and finally settled at Charlotte's feet, his feathery back legs stretched out behind him in what corgi owners call a sploot.

"I believe so," said Lynda. "But it would need new heating and air conditioning and a new roof. And I imagine you would get an architect to draw up some designs. He'd come up with creative ideas to maximize the space."

"Possibly," said Charlotte. "It's funny, you know, how I must have driven and walked past that place hundreds of times without really giving it much thought. It's always just been . . ."

"There?" suggested Lynda.

"Exactly. But now I'm very curious about the lives that were lived in that house. It felt quite sad, somehow."

"Well, Mr. Middleton, who died a few years ago, was a lawyer in the same firm as Joseph Lamb, actually. They did general law, wills, real estate, some family stuff, like adoptions. Basic small-town legal stuff. No courtroom trials or anything like that. Which is probably why Mrs. Middleton wants a lawyer handling every aspect of the house sale."

"About that. The asking price seems way too high for the condition of the property, and if we make an offer, it will be much lower."

"That's fine. People selling houses have a price in mind, but what they don't realize is that the house is worth what somebody's willing to pay for it. And that's it. So you decide what you're willing to pay for it, and I'm obliged to present the offer, then she can decide what she wants to do about it."

"With Joseph Lamb looking after her interests, is she still capable of making decisions?"

"Oh, yes. Mentally there's nothing wrong with her. It's her heart that's failing."

"And she's in a nursing home?"

"Yes. Quite a nice one in Saugerties."

"The photo I saw in her bedroom. She had two daughters?"

"I didn't see the picture, so I'm not sure who they were, but I think Mrs. Middleton just had the one daughter. Sorry, I don't know all the family details. Although now that I come to think of it, her husband was a senator at one time, I believe." She drained the last of her iced tea. "Thanks for the tea. I'd better be going. As soon as I hear from Lamb about a second viewing appointment, I'll be in touch."

As she stood up, Brian Prentice came around the corner of the bungalow and greeted them.

"I was just on my way to the hotel and saw you here. Thought I'd say hello." He nodded at Charlotte and turned on his smile for Lynda. "How are you, Lynda?"

His face looked open and relaxed, the smile genuine, and Charlotte inwardly breathed a sigh of relief. It looked as if whatever had been bothering him had passed.

"I was just leaving, actually," said Lynda. "I'll walk along to the hotel with you, since you're going that way."

"Oh, splendid."

Charlotte picked up the empty glasses, and she and Rupert followed them to the path that led in one direction to the hotel, which Lynda and Brian took, and in the other to her bungalow.

She set the glasses in the sink and, when Rupert was settled in his basket, got out her laptop and Googled retirement and nursing homes in Saugerties. Ten minutes later, with a list of four prospects beside her phone, she dialed the first number.

"Hello," she said to the woman who answered the phone. "I wonder if you have a Mrs. Middleton living there." She listened and then replied, "No, sorry, I don't know her first name." She was then told, in any case, a Mrs. Middleton did not reside there. Charlotte thanked her and then sent Lynda a text asking for Mrs. Middleton's first name. A moment later, her phone pinged with the reply. June.

Charlotte continued with the calls, asking if a June Middleton lived there. Finally, on her fourth attempt, she heard what she'd been waiting for. Yes, June Middleton was one of their residents.

"Would it be all right if I came to visit her?" Charlotte asked. "I'm sort of a neighbor of hers, and since I'll be in Saugerties tomorrow or the next day, I wondered if I could pop in and say hello?" When told that would be fine, she hung up and wrote down the address.

She opened the fridge, took out the pitcher of iced tea, and poured herself another glass. With Rupert beside her, she went back outside to think about June Middleton and why she wanted to visit her. Because something about the photograph she'd seen in Mrs. Middleton's room puzzled her. And then she realized it wasn't the photograph that puzzled her; it was why it was there. She didn't have a lot of experience with seniors in nursing homes, but on the few occasions she'd visited one, the elderly people were surrounded by photographs of people they'd loved or who had loved them. Old black-and-white photos in silver frames, school photos showing a grinning child with a missing tooth, soldiers in uniform, a young bride and groom, a beloved dog . . . a memory that lasted a lifetime caught in the fleeting moment of a photograph. Such mementos were apparently important to those with failing memories, Charlotte had read, for people who couldn't remember yesterday or last year or the person who just left who had called her "mom." But they could remember fifty years ago and even the day the photo had been taken. So it seemed odd that June Middleton, whose heart was failing but whose mind was sound, hadn't taken the photo of the two little girls with her. If it had been precious or significant enough to sit on the dresser in her old Walkers Ridge home, why wouldn't she have taken it with her to the nursing home in Saugerties? Maybe she had other photos that were newer or meant more to her.

Charlotte's thoughts turned to her own mother, now over seventy, living on her own in England. When Charlotte had made the decision ten years ago to stay behind in New York and that decision, meant to last only a few weeks, turned into a life-changing one, she hadn't thought about her parents. But since she'd been living in America, her father had died, and with her mother approaching a new stage in her life, Charlotte now realized that the decision hadn't been hers alone to make. She should have involved her parents more, because living here had profoundly affected their lives, too.

And if she married Ray, she would probably never return to England to live. Her mother would grow old, alone, and

Charlotte wasn't sure she was prepared to carry that heavy emotional burden.

As she finished her drink, Aaron's car turned into the hotel driveway, so she and Rupert walked over to the parking lot to meet him, and they walked together to the costume room.

"I saw Brian in town," Aaron said. "He's looking better. More relaxed. He was with Lynda." He pulled the mink hat and some dark, felted material out of a bag and laid them on the worktable. "What do you think?" he asked Charlotte.

"Fine, good," she said. "I thought Brian looked better, too. More confident, somehow."

Aaron pulled out a piece of pattern paper and began sketching what he thought the hat should look like, then drew several shapes in different sizes that looked like leaves. "I'll cut these out," he explained, "so we can see what size works best."

"How do you feel about taking a little drive to Saugerties tomorrow?" Charlotte asked. He didn't look up from his work but shrugged an okay. "Good. I want to visit someone in a nursing home. We'll stop on the way for flowers. Well, I'll leave you to get on with your work. Would you like a coffee?"

"No, I'm fine, thanks."

"I think I'll make a cup of tea then." A room, barely larger than a closet off the main workroom, housed a tiny kitchenette—a kettle, sink, microwave, and bar fridge. Charlotte plugged in the kettle, and as she waited for it to boil, her phone rang. She checked the name: Ray. He was calling to tell her he wouldn't be home for dinner. Did she want him to spend the night at his own place, or would she mind if he arrived late?

"What's happening with the investigation?" she asked.

When he told her, she said he should come to her as soon as he could.

She liked her tea made properly. She swished some hot water from the kettle around in a small, brown pot to warm it, tipped the water into the sink, then added loose tea to the pot, covered it with hot water, and left it to steep.

"There's been a development in the Hugh Hedley case," she said, walking into the workroom.

Aaron stopped snipping and, scissors poised, looked at her.

"They've made an arrest?"

"Not quite. The police have gone into Manhattan to interview Adrian Archer, and Gino Bartucci's been picked up here in Walkers Ridge and brought in for questioning. The police are unhappy about their business dealings with Hugh and are taking a closer look at their alibis."

"I always thought that Bartucci was a weasel."

"When did you meet him?"

"Well, I didn't really, but I saw him in action in the theater when he arrived late and disturbed everybody."

"Oh, right. Well, at least you didn't have to sit beside him at dinner."

"Do you think he did it? Killed Hugh Hedley, I mean."

Charlotte shrugged. "I don't know what to think. It's starting to look as if several people had a reason to want Hugh Hedley dead."

They turned their attention back to the hat. "So you've got one ear pinned on here. Put the hat on and let me see if it's in the right place. Oh, and the hat's just reminded me that I need to go to Oakland and pick up a dress. Maybe we could do that this afternoon. If you've got nothing better to do, I'll make the arrangements."

# Chapter 24

"Oh, hello, Jessica," said Charlotte to the dark-haired woman who answered the door. "I haven't seen you since the night of the play."

"Come in," said Jessica. "Belinda and her mother are out for the afternoon, and they asked me to take you up and get the dress for you." She led the way upstairs and down the hall, then opened the door to Belinda's bedroom. Two large boxes, one from Saks Fifth Avenue and the other from Barney's, both tied with wide ribbons, were displayed on the bed. Jessica gestured at them. "There's another one there that Belinda wondered if you might like."

"Oh, thank you," said Charlotte. She walked toward the bed and raised her arms to pick them up. But before she could do so, Jessica placed a restraining hand on the top box. Charlotte turned to look at her.

"There's something I wanted to ask you," Jessica said, releasing her hand to free the box. "Something's been bothering me, and I'm not sure what to do. I heard that your boyfriend is the chief of police. I think I should go to the police, but . . ." Her voice trailed off. Charlotte gave her time to speak, but when she didn't, Charlotte prompted her.

"You think you should go to the police, but you don't want to betray a confidence. Is that it?"

Jessica nodded. "If it's nothing, I'd hate to go to the police, and if Belinda finds out, I'd lose her friendship over nothing."

"Well, why don't we sit down, and you can tell me what's bothering you, and maybe once we've talked it through, you'll have a clearer idea what to do," Charlotte said. They moved to an attractive seating arrangement at the far end of the room, beside windows that overlooked the front drive.

"It's about Hugh's murder," Jessica began. "And Sophie. She was dating Hugh. She said they'd just met up a couple of times for drinks, but I think there was more to it than that. And then she started seeing someone else." She bowed her head and looked at her hands, lost in misery.

"And that someone else was Adrian?"

Jessica nodded. "She made me promise not to tell Belinda, but I hated keeping that secret and thought she'd want to know. I know I would have. I would have hated for Belinda to marry him, and then for it all to turn out very badly, and then later for Belinda to say to me, 'If only you'd told me, I'd never have married him.' I just didn't want that responsibility."

"Fair enough," said Charlotte. "So you told Belinda during the after party. When you came to her room just as she and I were going to rejoin the party after she'd changed out of her ripped dress."

"Yes. And then Belinda and Adrian had a big fight, and the wedding was called off."

"And Sophie drove him in the Lamborghini to New York that night," Charlotte said.

"Yes, and they spent the night together, but Adrian woke up appalled at what he'd done and came back here in the morning to try to make up with Belinda."

"Okay, so how does Hugh come into all this?"

"He knew Sophie was having a fling or whatever you want to call it with Adrian, and he confronted Adrian and threatened to tell Belinda. But I don't think he would have. He wouldn't have wanted to hurt her. It was Adrian he was after. He hated Adrian because of some business deal that went bad. Hugh made a lot of money working with Gino Bartucci, then something went sour, and Adrian became Bartucci's new agent. They made an awful lot of money together—money that Hugh thought should have been his."

"So, Jessica, what are you saying?"

"Oh, I don't know what I'm saying. It's all really confusing. But I know that Sophie was really angry with Hugh and just wanted him out of her life. And she really valued her friendship with Belinda—it gave her a lot of things she wouldn't otherwise have and opened a lot doors, socially and professionally. She was terrified Hugh would tell Belinda about her and Adrian."

"Sleeping with your friend's fiancé—that's a funny way of showing how much you value her friendship," Charlotte mused. She leaned back in the chair and gazed out the window. "So Sophie wanted Hugh out of her life, and now he is." Jessica remained silent. "Were you with Sophie during the first half of the play and the intermission?" she asked.

"No, I wasn't," Jessica said in a soft voice. "That's the thing that worries me. I think she and Adrian were together for some of it, but I don't know what they were doing. But everyone was wandering all over the place, so it's hard to keep track of everything."

"What about Hugh?" Charlotte asked. "Did you see him at all?"

"I saw him soon after he arrived. He talked to Paula for a few minutes, and then he wandered off, and the next time I saw him, he was talking to someone. A black man I didn't recognize. And after that, sorry, I don't know."

"Have the police interviewed you yet?"

"No, not a proper interview. They just took a brief statement the morning after it happened. Sophie was in New York, and I came downstairs about ten o'clock to find police everywhere."

"I was wondering why I didn't see you that morning."

"Nobody woke me up, and I'm a bit of a sound sleeper."

"Right. Well, you should tell the police what you saw, but I think you knew I was going to say that. So why are you really telling me all this?"

"I don't know. Conflicted, I guess. I want to do the right thing, but I don't want to jeopardize my relationship with Belinda. She and I are still friends, but she doesn't have anything to do with Sophie anymore. You can't even mention her name, which is why I can't talk to her about all this."

"No surprise there," said Charlotte. "Look, you want to be loyal to Belinda, and that's fine, but a man has been killed, and if you can help the police find out who killed him, then you need to do the right thing and tell them what you know. And if things get stirred up and come to light that hurt or upset Belinda, well, unfortunately, that's just the way it is. She's a big girl and she can handle it. There's always collateral damage with murder. Things come out that people wish had stayed hidden. In fact, the things that come out are sometimes the reason for the murder."

A couple of loud knocks followed by the appearance of Phyllis's head poking around the door prevented Jessica from replying.

"Sorry to interrupt, but Mrs. Van Dusen and Belinda are back. I told them you were here, and Mrs. Van Dusen asked if Charlotte would please join her downstairs for a drink."

Thinking of Aaron in the car waiting for her, Charlotte was about to refuse, but something about the way the sentence was worded suggested it wasn't an invitation, but rather a polite summons.

"Yes, of course." As she walked toward the boxes on the bed, Phyllis continued: "Leave those. I'll see that they're brought downstairs. They'll be in the hall waiting for you when you're ready to leave."

"I'll just send a quick text before we go down, then," said Charlotte. "Someone's waiting for me, and I need to let him know I'll be a little longer."

They descended the stairs together, in silence.

Phyllis opened the door to the sitting room and stood aside as Charlotte entered. Paula Van Dusen, standing in front of the window, drink in hand, turned as Charlotte entered the room.

"Thank you, Phyllis," she said. "Charlotte, may I get you something to drink?"

"Just a mineral or tonic water, thanks," said Charlotte.

"You don't mind if I . . . ?" She held up her tumbler and shook it lightly so the ice cubes rattled.

"No, of course not."

When they were seated, Charlotte's eyes strayed to the door, which had been left slightly open.

"I owe you an apology," Paula said.

Charlotte's eyes widened in surprise. "Me? What for?"

"That Bartucci character. I try to keep an open mind about people. Just because someone's a little rough around the edges doesn't mean I shouldn't give him the benefit of the doubt. But I should have had Bartucci checked out before I introduced you to him. I hope you haven't got your hopes up about them investing in your theater, because they're not right for you, and if you take my advice, you'll steer clear of them."

Charlotte thought back to Simon's misgivings about the couple. Was Paula Van Dusen about to prove him right?

"Is he involved in illegal activities?" Charlotte asked.

"Not that I know of. But the thing is, investing large amounts of money in business ventures works both ways. The investor needs to know that the organization is above-board, and the organization needs to know that that money being invested and the investors themselves aren't tainted in any way. That the money is clean and there's no scandal or skeletons in the closet attached to the investor."

"What are you trying to tell me?"

"Just be careful, that's all. Don't rush into anything. My instincts are telling me something's not right, and I've learned to pay attention to that feeling."

Paula gave Charlotte a few moments to think about what she had just said, then shifted slightly in her chair and leaned forward.

"I've been thinking about Hugh's murder," Paula began. "I'm sure the police are doing their best to get to the bottom of it," she said, "but so far, I haven't really heard much from them." She took a sip and paused before continuing. "I've been going over everything in my mind, trying to work out what could have happened. Now something has occurred to me, and I wanted to run it by you. When you found the body, you found a black shoe. A Gucci. Adrian wears the same kind of shoes and the same kind of suits, and I thought it might be possible that the killer mistook Hugh for Adrian. As far as I know, Hugh had no enemies, but Adrian . . . well, the way Manhattan real estate business is conducted, it's a wonder someone isn't murdered every other day."

"So you think it could have been a case of mistaken identity?"

"Why not? It's dark, both men are wearing the same kind of clothes and are about the same build. And"—she raised her index finger—"I've been hearing Bartucci wasn't too happy with the way Adrian handled a deal that went south when Hugh orchestrated a holdout."

"The holdout from Argentina who almost caused the whole deal to go pear-shaped?" asked Charlotte.

Paula raised an eyebrow. "How did you hear about that?"

"Oh, you know. Word gets around."

"Well, he was very lucky it didn't collapse, if you ask me," said Paula. "But it certainly ended up costing him a lot of money. Anyway, I was wondering if you think I should go to the police with my theory."

"Yes," said Charlotte without hesitation. "I certainly do. In fact, I can ask Ray to call round to talk to you, if you wish."

"Yes, I think that would be a good idea," agreed Paula. "And now I want to ask you about something altogether more pleasant. I was hoping you'd have brought your little dog with you today. He seems very well behaved. What do you call him?"

"His name's Rupert."

"That's a charming name, but no, I meant, what kind of dog is he? I don't think I've ever seen one quite like him, although something about him seems familiar."

"He's a tricolor corgi. You may be thinking of the red-and-white ones. The queen's had them all her life, but she's only got one or two left now."

"Ah, the queen, yes. That must be where I've seen them. And nice little dogs, are they?"

"Delightful. The best."

*

Aaron was leaning against the car, checking his phone, when Charlotte approached.

"Sorry it took longer than I thought it would," she said as she fastened her seat belt. "But if you don't mind, I'd like to pop into the town hall on the way home," she added as they drove off. "I won't be long. At least I hope I won't be. On second thought, you can drop me off there, and I'll make my own way home. But when you get home, please check on Rupert. You could take him for a little walk around the grounds, but don't let him off the leash. There's a spare key to my bungalow in the top drawer of my desk. And while you're there, you can drop off the dress boxes."

"What dress boxes?"

"The boxes from Saks and Barney's with the dresses from Belinda."

"I don't remember seeing any dress boxes."

A few minutes later, Aaron stopped in front of the white brick town hall, next door to the police station. Charlotte peered into the empty back seat.

"We forgot the boxes!" she said to Aaron. "They'll think I'm a complete idiot. Never mind. We'll get them another time. You go on home, and I'll catch up with you later."

Charlotte entered the town hall, exchanged a few words with the receptionist, and followed her directions to the planning department. About half an hour later, she left the building and walked across the asphalt parking lot to the police station, where she was waved through the squad room and into the office of the chief of police, Ray Nicholson.

He looked up from his desk, grinned, then rose from his desk to embrace her as he gently closed the door behind them with his boot.

"What brings you here this afternoon?" he asked. "Everything all right?"

"I've just come from the town hall, and you'll never guess. Bartucci owns the vacant land next to the Middleton place. Where the sign is, saying the condos are going up."

"And?"

"He doesn't have planning permission in place, so the town has instructed him to take the sign down."

Ray's eyes widened slightly as he began to understand.

"Exactly. He's put up the condo development sign deliberately to drive down the price of the Middleton property or even drive potential buyers away. A lot of people would be discouraged from buying a single-family house beside a midrise condominium. Or with the condos going up, a buyer would certainly expect to get the Middleton property for a much lower price. We thought that ourselves."

"Oh, of course. The Middleton place at a knockdown price."

"Exactly. But of course it's the land the house sits on that he wants, not the house itself. He wants the land so he can make the condos bigger. Lynda Flegg said the Middleton house would probably be a teardown."

"So there is no condo."

"Nope. At least, not yet. And the planning officer doesn't know when or if approval will be granted. So Mr. Bartucci could be stuck with a white elephant."

"And who sold him this white elephant, I wonder?"

"I'm sure it won't take you long to find out," Charlotte said, placing her handbag on his desk and lowering herself into the visitor's chair. Ray returned to his desk, and after a quick phone call, he said, "What's your guess?"

"Hugh Hedley?"

Ray shook his head. "Adrian Archer."

# Chapter 25

"Adrian Archer! I hope you're not going to ask me if you should go to the police with that," Charlotte said.

"What?"

"Oh, I'll explain later. It's just the day I've had. I've got so much to tell you."

Ray picked up his hat. "Come on. First a word with Phil, and then let's go home." He closed the door behind them and strolled over to Phil's desk. "Any news on that condo sign near the hotel that was vandalized?"

"Just kids, it looks like. Nobody filed an official complaint," Phil said.

"Just going to check on it now and then I'll be at Charlotte's after that. Call me if you need me."

"Will do."

Charlotte and Ray climbed into the police car, and a few minutes later, Ray pulled into the Middleton house driveway and parked the car.

They got out and, hand in hand, walked the short distance to the Bartucci land. The condo sign was gone.

"Let's talk this through," said Charlotte, gesturing at the tall grass behind the chain-link fence. "Bartucci, a speculator and property developer, buys this property at the suggestion of his agent of record, Adrian Archer. He wants to build condos here. He puts up a sign here," she said, pointing at the fence, "hoping to drive down the value of the adjacent property." She gestured at the Middleton house. "The listing agent is Lynda Flegg, and Hugh Hedley is supposed to view it on behalf of a client. The lawyer Joseph Lamb, who acts for the vendor of that property," she said, making a chopping motion at the Middleton house, "is also acting as the lawyer for the owner of this property." She swept her arm toward the vacant property. They turned to each other. "So the common denominator here is Joseph Lamb."

"We'll have trouble getting any information out of him," said Ray. "Lawyers always cite attorney-client privilege and tell you nothing."

"I need to go and see him, though. About the theater school." She looked up at him. "I get the feeling he holds the key to Hugh Hedley's murder. I tried asking him if he knew Hugh very well, but he didn't answer. What do you think?"

"You might be right. Knowingly or unknowingly, he could be withholding the piece of information that will crack this case wide open."

He put his arm around her, and they walked back to the car. As they passed the Middleton house, Charlotte glanced up at the upper floor. She stopped and pointed. "I thought I saw a curtain move," she said. "And the house is supposed to be empty."

Ray's eyes followed her finger. "I'll ask Phil to check it out on his way home. Could be some kids have broken in." He pulled his car keys out of his pocket and unlocked the doors. "I hate vandalism."

*

Charlotte grated Parmesan cheese over some fresh pasta and tore up a few leaves of basil. She set the plates on the table, and as they ate, she summarized her conversations with Jessica and Paula.

"So, according to Jessica, Adrian and Sophie were having a fling, and they spent the night of the murder together in New York. And Paula has a theory that Hugh was killed by someone who mistook him for Adrian. That Adrian was the intended victim."

"Those are lines of inquiry to be investigated," said Ray. "In any murder inquiry, everything is looked at with a view to ruling people out, and those who can't be ruled out become suspects. But even if Sophie and Adrian did drive into Manhattan that night, we can't rule them out, because the murder could have been committed earlier. In fact, the Albany detectives haven't found anyone who saw Hugh during or after the second half of the play."

"Anyway, Paula would like to talk to you about it. I think she likes you. You play your cards right, and she might invite you to her annual Fourth of July barbecue."

# Chapter 26

"Won't this Mrs. Middleton lady find it a bit weird—you coming to see her out of the blue?" Aaron asked Charlotte the next morning as they drove to Saugerties. "And why are you going to see her, anyway?"

"She might think it strange," replied Charlotte, "but if she doesn't get many visitors, she might be glad to have one. I thought it would be nice to have a chat with Mrs. Middleton and explain that we're thinking of buying her house to convert into a learning center for the Catskills Shakespeare Theater School, and once she understands what we're trying to do, she may be agreeable to accepting a lower offer."

"Learning center!" Aaron snorted.

"What else would you call it? The living/dining room area will be a common room, with classrooms upstairs. It'll be all done up beautifully. And by the way, if you want a place in the school, you need to apply now because we're going to be sending out acceptances soon."

"I'm not sure. I thought I wanted a theater career, but designing those bridesmaids' dresses gave me a taste for that, and I wouldn't mind doing more of it."

"That's understandable. You're good at design, and in some ways, you're wasted here, but we would all be so sorry to lose you. But look, Aaron, do what you love, and if it's design, then maybe you should think seriously about going back to Parsons this fall."

They drove in silence along Route 212 for a few more minutes until Aaron pulled up in front of a well-kept cream-colored building with a sign in front that declared the building to be Pine Tree Lodge. As the car came to a halt, Charlotte asked, "You'll be all right to amuse yourself for half an hour or so?" Assured he would be, Charlotte gathered up the cellophane-wrapped bouquet she'd been holding on her lap, stepped out of the car, and walked to the entrance.

The lobby was bright and spacious, with clean, modern furniture in neutral, sophisticated tones. No expense had been spared in the decorating or furnishings.

The receptionist looked up as Charlotte approached, gave her a professional, welcoming smile, asked her to sign in, and pointed to a room at the rear of the building that opened onto a large garden.

Several residents were seated in comfortable armchairs, reading, talking quietly to one another, or simply watching what was going on around them. Unsure which one was June Middleton, Charlotte hesitated in the doorway.

"Who are you looking for, dear?" asked a bright-looking woman with tightly permed white hair seated at the entrance to the room.

"June Middleton."

"I think you'll find her in the garden. She likes to sit in the garden when the weather permits."

"Thank you."

Charlotte stepped through the French doors into a mature garden that reminded her of Paula Van Dusen's, only smaller in scale. Beds of roses in rich reds, deep pinks, and regal whites flanked a stone walkway that ran the length of the garden. Under a large maple tree, a cluster of wrought-iron chairs had been set up around a table. Seated in one of them, wearing a straw hat with a wide, dark-colored ribbon around it that ended in a bow at the back, was a solitary figure bent over a book. Charlotte advanced toward her.

"Mrs. Middleton?" she said.

The woman looked up. "Yes?" she said in a puzzled voice.

"Mrs. Middleton, hello, I'm Charlotte Fairfax. You don't know me, but I wondered if I could talk to you for a few minutes." Mrs. Middleton inserted a bookmark into her book and closed it. Charlotte held out the flowers. "I brought you these."

"Thank you. They're lovely." Charlotte set them on the table and, with some effort, lifted one of the heavy chairs closer to the woman she had come to see. June Middleton's hair had been carefully tinted a pale blonde, and her manicured nails were a light-coffee color. She wore a plain short-sleeved blouse with a Peter Pan collar and a navy-and-white polka-dot skirt.

"Mrs. Middleton, you don't know me," she repeated, "but we were actually neighbors at one time. I work for the theater company and live at the Jacobs Grand Hotel, next to your old home."

"Yes, I saw you walking by the house many times with your little dog. He likes to bark at my stone lions."

Charlotte smiled. "Yes, he does." She paused to take a deep breath and then continued. "I've come here today to talk to you about your house. A couple of colleagues and I are starting a theater school, and we may be interested in making an offer on your property to convert it into a building for the students. A common room and classrooms—that sort of thing."

"Well, you don't need my permission to do that. You'd have to get planning permission from the town council, I expect."

"Yes, exactly, but I just wondered how you would feel if your house was used for that purpose."

Mrs. Middleton raised one shoulder in a gesture of indifference. "It really doesn't matter to me what happens to it."

"Oh, I see. Well, that's fine. I just thought . . ."

"As long as you can meet the asking price, it's yours, as far as I'm concerned."

"Well, that's the thing, you see, we can't make the asking price. It's beyond our budget, I'm afraid."

"Well, then I guess we don't have much to talk about. I'm sorry your trip here has been wasted."

"Oh, I wouldn't say that. I got to meet you. My own mother lives in England, and I haven't seen her for some years. I miss her terribly. Do you have any children?"

As Mrs. Middleton looked down at her hands, Charlotte almost wished she hadn't asked the question.

"I'm so sorry, Mrs. Middleton. I didn't mean to . . ."

"It's all right. I had a daughter, but she died."

"I'm terribly sorry."

Mrs. Middleton's mood instantly changed from one of sadness to anger.

"It's all right. Talking about her keeps her memory alive. They said it was a hiking accident, but I know it wasn't. They said she fell, but she was too good for that. She'd climbed that cliff dozens of times. I didn't believe for a moment that she fell."

"She fell? Are you talking about the accident at Devil's Path?"

"I am. It happened in March."

"And are you saying that the woman who died was your daughter?"

"Yes, she was. My Joanna."

"But that was Hugh Hedley's mother! Oh, Mrs. Middleton, I'm so sorry. Your daughter and then grandson. Those are terrible losses and so close together."

Mrs. Middleton acknowledged her words silently.

"But if you don't think your daughter's death an accident, did you mention this to the authorities?"

"I know it wasn't an accident," Mrs. Middleton said, emphasizing "know." "And of course I told the police. I told anyone who would listen." Her lips narrowed in an expression of disgust.

"Well, I'm listening, Mrs. Middleton. What do you think happened that day?"

Mrs. Middleton hesitated. "I can't name names, mind you, because I don't know for certain, but I do have my suspicions. I think she met someone on the path who had it in for her, and that person pushed her or did something to make her fall. It's a steep climb, apparently, almost vertical. You have to hold on to roots or vines or something. Not for the fainthearted. Experienced hikers only, which Joanna was. She'd walked the route many times. Yes, it was difficult, she said, but so well worth it when you get to the top. You can see for miles and you feel exhilarated. And then you continue on your way and come down by a different path—it's a circuit, you see."

"Was she alone that day?"

"No, she was climbing with her husband, but he wasn't as experienced or as brave as she was, so he went by a different route and was waiting for her farther along the path."

"And he didn't see anyone?"

"Just a few more hikers who were there that day. The police asked for any witnesses to come forward, but nobody did. That's understandable. A lot of tourists hike there, so the other people could have come from, well, anywhere, really, and gone back to where they came from, not knowing anything about the incident. I refuse to call it an accident, because that's not what it was."

Charlotte thought this over for a minute.

"The Walkers Ridge police chief is a friend of mine. I'll have a word with him, if you like. See if he would take another look at the case."

Mrs. Middleton brightened and she leaned forward in her chair.

"Oh, would you? That would be wonderful."

"There's something else I wanted to ask you today," Charlotte said. "When I toured the house, in one of the bedrooms, there was a photo on the dresser of a woman with two little girls. I wondered if perhaps it had been left behind, and if it's important to you, I'd be happy to bring it to you."

A dark frown creased Mrs. Middleton's face. Her eyes narrowed and she licked her lips.

"I don't know what you're talking about. There's no such photograph on my dresser."

Charlotte knew there was no point in arguing, so she handed Mrs. Middleton her card and asked her to contact her if she needed anything before saying good-bye.

She and Aaron drove home in silence.

"You're very quiet," he said. "Is anything the matter?"

"She's Hugh Hedley's grandmother, would you believe? I was so shocked when she told me that. And then when I mentioned a photo to her, one I saw on her dresser, she said, 'There is no such photograph on my dresser.' But there is. I saw it."

"She's old. You know what old people are like. They can't remember anything."

"Aaron! Not all old people are forgetful, and Mrs. Middleton certainly isn't. Quite the opposite, in fact. She seemed very with it, if you ask me."

"Well she forgot about the photo, didn't she?"

"Maybe not. Maybe she didn't know it was there. Maybe somebody put that photo there for some reason. I thought I saw someone in the house when Ray and I drove by earlier." After a moment she added, "You know that feeling when something's just not right, when things just aren't adding up? It's like that. Something's not right."

*

They arrived back at the hotel to find Lynda Flegg and Brian Prentice seated on the Adirondack chairs. The chairs had been pulled close together, and their heads leaned toward each other. At the sound of approaching footsteps, Brian got to his feet.

"Ah, Charlotte, hello." He nodded a greeting at Aaron and waited.

"Well, Charlotte, I'll be off," said Aaron, picking up on Brian's cue. "Talk to you later."

"I'd best be off, too," said Lynda, and after saying goodbye, she walked off with Aaron, she to her car and Aaron toward the hotel.

"Would you like to sit down, Charlotte?" Brian asked.

"What is it, Brian? Has something happened? You're making me nervous."

"Well, as you may have gathered, I haven't been happy here for some time. Not ever, really, but it wasn't until I talked it through with Lynda that I realized what I have to do." His eyes searched her face. "The thing is, I've decided to return to England."

"So you're leaving. Have you told Simon yet?"

"No, I wanted to tell you first."

"Right. Well, now you have, but I think you should have told Simon first. He's the one who hired you. You'll have to sort out all the contract details with him, of course, and what about the theater school?"

"Well, that's part of what was making me unhappy. I don't want to go to meetings or worry about budgets and money. I don't even really want to teach. I just want to act. I'll leave my money in the project as an investment, but I don't want an official role."

"I see. Well, thanks for telling me. I'm sure you and Simon can sort something out." The light had almost come back into Brian's brown eyes.

"Oh, I'm sure we can." He stood up. "In fact, there's another reason why I've got to go home. I've got a medical condition that's going to require treatment, and I'd rather get it seen to in the UK."

"Oh, Brian, I'm sorry to hear that. I hope it's not serious."

"Thanks, Charlotte. I'm off to talk to Simon now. I hope he'll be as understanding as you were."

"I'll walk over to the hotel with you. I have some work to catch up on."

And as she'd expected, it wasn't long before Simon arrived in her office, a coffee in each hand.

"So he told you," she said, accepting the coffee he held out to her.

"He did."

"What do you think?"

"It's probably the right thing for him to do. If he isn't happy, he won't be performing as well as he should be, and if he needs medical treatment, he needs to get it."

"What about his contract?" Charlotte asked.

"He can get out of it on health grounds. There's a medical exclusion clause. He wants to leave as soon as he can, so we'll have to bring in a new headliner for the fall season. And that means we're not going to be ready to open the theater school this fall, if I have to find and prepare a new lead. So I'm suggesting we put off the school for a year so we can be properly prepared, with everything in place. We still have time to do that, as we haven't accepted any students."

"I agree."

"We'll talk more later." He gathered up his coffee cup, and as he was about to leave, her phone rang. Lynda Flegg was letting her know Joseph Lamb was available for a showing in the morning and wondered if she and Simon could make it. She checked with Simon and let Lynda know they could. With the school's opening now postponed, they could take their time deciding what to do about the Middleton property.

# Chapter 27

"Aaron, we're going to view the Middleton house this morning. Would you like to come with us? You could look at it from a student's point of view and tell us what you think."

"Yeah, sure."

"Have you thought any more about going back to Parsons?"

"Haven't decided anything yet."

"Good, because Ray and I have come up with a solution that will get you into your own place, if that makes a difference to your staying here."

"Tell me!"

"Not yet. Still some details to be worked out. But you'll know soon." He gave her a wide grin, and they set off for the Middleton house.

"I'll be back in twenty minutes," said Joseph Lamb as he unlocked the front door. "And I hope you can make up your mind. I can't keep wasting my time like this. You either want to make an offer or you don't."

"It's only my second viewing," grumbled Charlotte, "and these other two haven't seen it at all."

"Don't pay any attention to him," said Lynda, taking a seat in the living room. "I'll give you a few moments to look around on your own, and then I'll see you up there."

"Let's start upstairs," said Charlotte, leading the way. They looked into each bedroom, Simon commenting that they could easily knock two rooms together to make a decent-sized classroom and Aaron commenting that it would be nice if the windows could be enlarged to let in more light. When they came to the master bedroom, Charlotte noted the photograph on the dresser and stood by it while Simon and Aaron gazed around. When they had moved on, she picked up the photo, tilting it toward the window to catch the light. As she pulled her phone out of her pocket to photograph it, Lynda entered the room, paused, then wordlessly and gently took the photo from her and replaced it on the dresser.

"Ten minutes left," Lynda said.

Charlotte followed Lynda downstairs, trailing her hand along the oak handrail, and entered the kitchen. The first visit had been so hurried, she hadn't had time to view the kitchen, but now she took in the faded curtains of a brown-and-mustard-yellow pattern of circles covering the window above a glass pane in the back door. She half expected to see a fondue set on the counter and had no doubt there'd be one in the cupboard.

She tried the handle on the back door, but it was locked. She took a step closer to the counter and peered into the deep porcelain double sink. The smaller, shallower side was empty, but a badly rinsed cup with some brownish water in it sat at the bottom of the larger, deeper basin.

Off the kitchen was a small half bathroom that contained a pink toilet and square, pink sink. A small window above the toilet was open about two inches. She reached over to close it, expecting it to be stiff, but it moved easily in its frame. She left it as it was, turned the tap on and off, and then returned to the living room.

"I'm just going to poke around outside," Charlotte told Lynda.

She left by the front door and walked around to the back of the house. A patch of land that might once have been a vegetable garden, now overgrown with weeds, with a dark-green wooden shed beside it, took up most of the backyard.

She pulled the shed's rusty bolt latch back, and the door swung crazily open on loose hinges. The gloomy semidarkness of the interior was relieved only by slim bands of sunlight that managed to filter in between the vertical boards. The air was dank, with a deep, earthy smell. A few tools, including a shovel and rake, hung from pegs on one wall, and a shelf littered with newspapers, clay pots, and spoons took up the other wall. On a nail hung an old dog leash, its leather now cracked and its clip rusted. She turned it toward her so she could read the name on the tag. Bella. Her eyes misted as she held the tag. *A dearly loved pet now long gone*, she thought. *How little they leave behind.* As love for her own Rupert flooded her heart, she released the tag, lifted the sagging door back in place, and shot the bolt home.

As she prepared to leave the backyard to rejoin the others, a pile of weeds and dead leaves under the window caught her eye. She took a few steps closer, leaned over, and discovered a clumsy, almost half-hearted attempt to camouflage an upturned, antique galvanized washtub under a small window.

As she turned away, the sole of her shoe sank into something soft and squishy, and as a dog owner, she knew immediately what it was. She let out a little exclamation of disgust and scraped as much of it off her shoe as she could on the nearest patch of grass. She then hurried around to the front of the building to meet up with the others.

Wreathed in his usual curt impatience, Joseph Lamb was waiting for them on the porch.

"We're interested in buying this property for our theater school," Charlotte said, "and someone suggested that you might be able to help us with the legal aspects of that."

"Yes, I can," Mr. Lamb said, locking the door and dropping the key in his briefcase. "If you call my office, we can set up an appointment to go over everything. There are state laws and regulations you must conform to."

"Thank you." And although she found it difficult to talk to him through his professional coldness, she charged ahead and repeated the question she had asked him last time. "Did you know Hugh Hedley well? In the photo in the *Hudson Valley Echo* taken the night of the performance at Paula Van Dusen's estate, you were talking to him."

This time, he was more responsive.

"That's right. In fact, we were sitting together."

"You were?"

"Well, for the first half. At the intermission, he said he was meeting someone, and then he never returned to his seat. His lawn chair, I should say."

"And did he say who he was meeting?"

Lamb scowled at her. "No, he did not."

He gave her a curt nod and then strode off to his car. After thanking Lynda, Simon, Aaron, and Charlotte walked back to the hotel.

"I think the building is doable," Simon said. "But not at the asking price. The renovation will just cost too much. We'll have to see if we can get it for less, much less."

Aaron looked around and finally focused on Charlotte. "What's that smell?" he asked.

*

"I need you to help me with something tonight," Charlotte said later that afternoon.

"That's fine," said Aaron. "It's not like I have any kind of life. What do you need me to do?"

"I need you to climb in through a window."

"Whose window? Why?"

"The ground-floor bathroom window at the Middleton house."

"Why?" he repeated.

"Because I want you to go upstairs and get a photograph from Mrs. Middleton's bedroom. It's in a frame sitting on her dresser. Won't take you a minute. You'll be in and out in no time."

"If you want that photo, why didn't you take it when we were in the house? You could have done it then. Or at least taken a photo of it."

"Take something from the house on Lynda's watch? Absolutely not. That just wouldn't be right. And I did try to take a photo of it, but she caught me with it in my hand. She didn't say anything, but when you're viewing a property, you're not supposed to touch any of the owners' possessions."

Aaron's mouth dropped open. "Are you kidding me? It's not okay to take something from the house on Lynda's watch, but it's okay for me to go breaking and entering to get it?"

"Well, technically, I don't think it is breaking because the window's open, so all you have to do is climb in. Oh, and there's a toilet right under the window, so you'll have to be careful of that, but I made sure the seat's down."

"Well, that makes it all right, I guess."

"Here's the thing, Aaron. An aluminum washtub's been conveniently placed under the window, which leads me to believe somebody else is going in and out of that house, possibly even squatting there. And I think that somebody else, whoever they are and for whatever reason, placed the photo we want to look at in Mrs. Middleton's bedroom. She was very emphatic that it wasn't there."

"I've already told you what I think. She forgot about it, that's all."

Charlotte shook her head. "I don't think so."

"Anyway," said Aaron, "you know this is illegal, and if you think somebody's been in the house, then you should just tell Lynda Flegg. Or your policeman fiancé."

"He's not really my fiancé yet."

"Well, your boyfriend then."

"We don't need to tell him about this because we're just going to borrow the photograph for half an hour or so."

"We are? Why?"

"So I can photograph it."

"Why can't I just take a picture of it in the house?"

"Because it'll take time to remove it from the frame, there won't be enough light to photograph it properly, and because I want to take a closer look at it. When we've done that, we'll replace it."

"You mean I'll put it back."

"Exactly. Because you are so much younger than I am, and climbing through the window will be easy for you." She thought for a moment. "Which leads me to believe that whoever else is going through that window must also be young and as fit as a butcher's dog."

"Oh, the things I must do," moaned Aaron. "When?"

"After dark. I'll meet you outside the hotel at ten. Oh, and wear black. That's what they do in the movies. And bring a flashlight."

*

Darkness had fallen when Charlotte and Rupert left their bungalow and walked the short distance to the hotel.

Aaron was waiting for her beside an overgrown spirea bush, almost invisible in its untrimmed branches.

"I don't like this," he said. "We shouldn't be doing this."

Charlotte didn't reply, and the three kept walking. The road was deserted, and they slipped along the side of the house and into the backyard without seeing anyone.

"See?" said Charlotte. "No problem."

At the bathroom window, Aaron climbed onto the overturned washtub, slowly raised the window, put one leg through the window, then followed it with the rest of his body. He let out a few groans and exclamations as he twisted himself through, then silence. A moment later, the beam of a flashlight came on, then disappeared. Charlotte walked over to the fence to wait. Knowing he wouldn't leave her, she dropped Rupert's leash so he could have a good sniff around.

As the minutes ticked by, she was beginning to think something might have happened to Aaron, when the back door was flung open, and a black-hooded figure raced out.

Startled by the sudden movement and barking furiously, Rupert flew toward the figure, and just as it was about to sprint around the side of the house, he caught up with it, his trailing lead tangled in its feet. Swearing and shouting, the figure crashed to the ground, and as it fell, the hood came off, revealing long blonde curls tied back in a ponytail.

Charlotte rushed up to her. "Alex! What are you doing here?"

Beforc Alex could answer, Aaron emerged from the house, rubbing his head as he thrust the photo into Charlotte's hand. "He came up behind me and hit me with something. Oh, God, it hurts."

"Not he, Aaron. She." Charlotte gestured to Alex, who was sitting up, rubbing her ankle, glaring at them.

"There's something else," said Aaron. At his coaxing, the pointed face of a dog emerged, followed by a body covered in curly white hair. It placed one front paw and then the other on the step and then hopped daintily down onto the grass.

Dropping to her knees, Charlotte reached out for the dog.

"Oh, God. Mandy." She turned to Aaron. "Take Rupert's lead and tie up Alex while I call Ray."

"Why did you take the dog?" Aaron demanded of Alex.

"I didn't take the dog myself. Some friends did. But yes, I arranged it. As a gift for my mother."

# Chapter 28

"We're in big trouble," whispered Aaron after securing Alex's hands behind her back.

"I know," said Charlotte. "But if we hadn't been here, we wouldn't have found Mandy."

"Is she okay?"

"She really should be vet checked." Charlotte ran her hands down the sides of the dog, feeling her rib cage. "At least she's been fed." She straightened up.

"How are we going to explain what we were doing here?" Without waiting for an answer, Aaron continued. "Maybe you could say we were here this afternoon and you dropped something and we came back to look for it."

"The thing is, Aaron, I can't lie to him. That'll just make things worse when he finds out the truth. And he will. People lie to him all the time, and he knows when they're doing it. And besides, that's not the kind of relationship we have."

Aaron let out a little groan.

"Are you all right? Is your head hurting?"

"No, it's not that. It's, well, you don't think he'll arrest us, do you? If he does, my aunt will kill me."

"I don't think he will, but he's not going to be too happy with me, either." They sat on the upturned washtub, and Charlotte put her arm around Mandy while Aaron kept a close eye on Alex.

And then, unable to sit any longer, Charlotte stood up. "You stay with Alex. I'm going round to the front of the house to wait for Ray. And if you need a leash for Mandy, there's one in the shed."

A few minutes later, a vehicle slowed in front of the house and shone blinding headlights in her eyes as it turned into the driveway.

"So what's happening?" Ray asked, putting on his hat as he stepped out of the car.

Explaining how they'd found Alex in the house with the dog, Charlotte led him around to the back of the property.

"I'm surprised the property hasn't been broken into before now," Ray said, helping Alex to her feet. After asking her if she was all right, he untied her, handed Rupert's leash to Aaron, and holding her arms behind her back, snapped a pair of handcuffs on her. "Everybody knows the place is empty, and the locks are practically useless. Still, I'm surprised at you two breaking in." He looked from Charlotte to Aaron. "Well, maybe not that surprised."

He gestured at Alex. "We're going to need Phil's help. Let's all go around to the front while we wait for him." He took Alex by the arm and led her away as Charlotte and Aaron followed with the dogs.

It wasn't long before another set of slowing headlights signaled Phil's arrival. Ray walked Alex over to the car, put her in the back seat, and gave Phil his instructions.

"Now," said Ray, "let's get Mandy home."

"Are you going to arrest me? Us?" Aaron blurted out.

"No, I'm not," said Ray. "Since I believe you to be of good character, I'm letting you off with a stern warning. Consider yourself sternly warned." He opened the car door. "Let's have Charlotte in the back with the dogs, and you can ride up front with me. Unless you'd rather just go home."

"Oh, no," said Aaron. "I wouldn't miss this for anything."

"Have you called Lynda yet?" Ray asked.

"No, I didn't know if we'd have to take her to an emergency vet to get the microchip checked before we return her."

"We'll assume for now she's Lynda's dog, and the microchip can be checked in the morning when Lynda takes her to her own vet. Anyway, we'll know from the way they greet each other if this is Mandy. I'll ask Phil to get her address for us."

"Mandy will let us know before we get there if she's on the way home," said Charlotte.

They waited in silence, and when Phil came back on the radio with Lynda's address, they set off.

As they turned off the main road onto a quiet street, just as Charlotte had predicted, Mandy sat up, stiffened, and looked out the window into the darkness. Her tail started to wag and she made little whimpering noises. A moment later, she let out a couple of excited, joyful barks, and everyone in the car laughed.

As Ray slowed the car, the barking got louder. When the vehicle stopped, Charlotte jumped out, ran up to the front porch, and rang the doorbell. The downstairs lights were still on, and a moment later Lynda appeared, wearing lounging pajama bottoms and a red T-shirt. At the sound of the excited barking coming from the car, the curious, expectant look on Lynda's face that wordlessly asked, 'Who is it at this time of night, and what do you want?' melted into pure elation. She let out a little whoop, hugged Charlotte, then danced down the sidewalk to the car. As Ray opened the rear door, Lynda crouched, and Mandy bounded out and dove into Lynda's outstretched arms. Sobbing, Lynda held her tight until Mandy wriggled free, then ran up the sidewalk and through the open front door.

As she hugged Ray and Charlotte, Lynda asked, "How did you find her? Where was she?"

"We found her at the Middleton house, would you believe?" Charlotte said.

"The Middleton house! But how can that be? I've been there so often. I'm stunned. I really don't know what to say."

"We think someone was squatting or spending time in the house," said Ray, "and this person had her. When we know more, we'll let you know."

"And what about charges?" asked Lynda. "I hope this person will be punished for what they've done."

Ray nodded. "We'll let you know," he repeated.

"I'd better get back to her," said Lynda, looking longingly at the door to her home. "I can't thank you enough, but thank you. Oh, this is the best outcome possible. I can't believe my darling girl is really home."

"You'll need to take her to the vet in the morning," said Ray, "to get the microchip confirmation for my report. Call me after you've done that to let me know how she is."

When Mandy's head appeared in the doorway, Lynda called out a hasty "Thank you again" and raced up the sidewalk toward her dog. She paused for a moment in the doorway to wave and then followed Mandy into the house.

"There's no doubt in my mind that's her dog, but the microchip confirmation will make for a stronger case when it goes to court," said Ray, putting his arm around Charlotte. He checked his watch. "I'm going off duty now. Let's go home." Charlotte brushed away her happy tears and climbed into the back seat.

"Since we're all here, I thought we'd take a little detour," said Ray as he put the car in gear. A few minutes later, they pulled up in front of his place. "Charlotte will probably want to wait in the car," said Ray, "but why don't you come in, Aaron? Just going to pick up a few things." He unlocked the door, and they entered. "Feel free to have a look around," said Ray as he disappeared into the bedroom. A few moments later, Aaron followed him in. "This is such a cool place, Ray."

"That's what I thought," said Ray. "Until Charlotte came along and hated it. Have a seat." Aaron perched on the edge of the old, gray sofa, and Ray sat in a facing armchair. "Charlotte tells me you're unhappy where you are, so we thought you might like to move in here. I'm hardly ever here, so you'd have it all to yourself, and I'll keep paying the rent on it until I've worked out something more permanent with Charlotte. But you could move in as soon as you like. Anyway, it would be better if someone was living here. Do I have to remind you what happens to empty houses? People who should know better climb in and out of bathroom windows at all hours of the day and night." He paused while Aaron winced, and then Ray smiled at him. "This arrangement would probably be just for a few months while Charlotte and I figure out what we're going to do. So what do you think? You could bring your stuff over tomorrow, if you like." He looked around the room. "You'll have to clean it up, but I'm sure in no time you'll have it looking much better than I ever did."

Aaron grinned his thanks.

"Good," said Ray. "That's settled. Let's go home, and you can talk to your aunt and uncle."

Charlotte looked up from her phone as the two men got in the car.

"Well?" she said.

"This has been quite an interesting evening," said Ray. "One good dog returned home, thanks to you two and your criminal activities. Hopefully Phil will find out the rest of the story when he interviews her. So that makes two cases we've wrapped up today."

"Two?"

"With all the dog business, I haven't had a chance to tell you. Adrian Archer and Gino Bartucci have been arrested for the murder of Hugh Hedley."

# Chapter 29

Waiting for Ray to join her, Charlotte lay in bed examining the black-and-white photograph taken from the Middleton house. It was a formal studio shot of a woman seated on a backless seat, like a piano bench, with two little girls in old-fashioned smocked dresses. The woman, whose eyeglasses in plastic frames covered half her cheeks, was turned slightly to the side, with one arm around a fair-haired girl who stood in front of her and the other arm around the waist of a dark-haired girl who sat beside her on the bench. The dark-haired girl gazed up at the woman, but the woman's face was turned toward the fair-haired child who stared into the camera with a determined, confident look.

As Ray turned off the bathroom light, Charlotte turned over the photo. A faded, blue, oval-shaped stamp of a local photographer included the name, address, and telephone number of the studio and a number, presumably the number to quote if you wanted to order reprints. Underneath the stamp, someone had written in ink, "J & P, 1971."

Ray slid in beside her, and she showed him the stamp. "Ever heard of this photographer?" she asked. He shook his head and put his arm around her.

"Before my time, I guess," he said.

"I wonder what happens to all the old negatives when a photographic studio closes its doors," she mused. "All those occasions—weddings, graduations, anniversaries that people thought important enough to mark with a formal photograph—all those moments, gone."

"I guess they are." He yawned and turned toward her. "One of these days we're going to have a chat about your behavior. If we're going to have a future together, as the wife of the local chief of police, you'll have to stop breaking into people's houses and stealing stuff. With an accomplice. It just doesn't make me look good."

Charlotte laughed. "No, I guess it doesn't. Thank you for taking this so well."

"Well, we haven't had that chat yet."

Charlotte turned the photo over again to show him the two little girls. "This one," she said, pointing to the blonde girl. "I'm pretty sure this is Joanna Middleton. She died recently in what was reported as a fall, up on Devil's Path. But when I spoke to her mother, she said she didn't believe for one minute that Joanna fell. She said she was an experienced climber who had done that route dozens of times. She didn't want to name names, but she suspects someone pushed her."

"We hear that more often than we'd like to, unfortunately. Parents can't bring themselves to believe their child committed suicide and insist there must have been foul play."

"Mrs. Middleton isn't talking about suicide. This was ruled an accident, but she definitely thinks it was something more. That foul play was involved." When Ray did not reply, Charlotte pressed him. "Do you think it's worth asking your state colleagues to look into it? I told Mrs. Middleton I'd mention it to you."

"I don't know."

"How about this, then? Joanna Middleton is the mother of your murder victim, Hugh Hedley. Do you think that'll get their attention?"

"It's always possible. I'll mention it to them in case they're not aware. And as long as Mrs. Middleton agrees to be interviewed." He took the photo from her, placed it on the bedside table, switched off the light, and pulled her closer to him.

"Ray?"

"Hmmm."

"I've been thinking. About becoming the wife of the chief of police."

"You haven't really let me ask you yet, remember?"

"Well, that's the thing. I was thinking . . . when you do ask me, how about asking me in England? We could visit my mum; she could meet you and be part of this. I was thinking we could go in the autumn for a couple of weeks once the fall theater season is up and running, if Simon can spare me. What do you think?"

"I think it sounds like exactly the right thing to do."

Charlotte snuggled up against him.

"I wonder who P is. The other girl in the photograph."

But the only reply was his soft, rhythmic breathing, and soon Charlotte, too, was asleep.

# Chapter 30

"I wonder who P is. The other girl in the photograph," Charlotte repeated at breakfast the next morning. Ray took a sip of coffee.

"It shouldn't be too hard to find out," he said. "If the Middletons had two daughters, someone will know."

At the sound of knocking on the door, Ray shot Charlotte a quizzical look, then walked across the kitchen and opened it.

"Morning, Aaron."

"Morning. I just wondered if I could get the keys to your place. Wanted to drop off some stuff this morning." Ray threw Charlotte a grin over his shoulder and then pulled a key off his key ring and handed it to Aaron. "Why don't you get a copy made while you're out today, and you can drop mine off at the police station when you're driving by or leave it with Charlotte?"

"Perfect." Aaron turned to go, but Charlotte invited him in. "Come in, Aaron, and have a cup of coffee with me."

Ray picked up his hat, kissed Charlotte, and let himself out.

"I don't really want coffee, thanks, Charlotte," said Aaron. "I want to drop this stuff off at Ray's, and then Simon needs me."

"Tell you what. You can take the stuff to Ray's later, and I'll sort out things with Simon. I need you to drive me to Saugerties now. I need to speak to Mrs. Middleton this morning."

"Oh, not her again."

"Yes. I thought Ray would take the photo with him, but he didn't, so this is our only chance. I'll meet you at the car in a minute." She hurried into the bedroom, gathered up the photo and frame from the bedside table, and rushed out to Aaron's car.

"Right, off we go."

"I'll get the key cut while you're in the nursing home."

"Good idea." She spent the rest of the journey thinking about what she wanted to say to Mrs. Middleton and how to say it. By the time they arrived at the home, she'd replaced the photo in the frame and tucked it in her purse.

*

"Oh, it's you again," said June Middleton. She was seated in a burgundy-and-white-striped wing chair in a tastefully appointed lounge. A foursome of bridge was being played quietly in the corner. As on Charlotte's earlier visit, Mrs. Middleton's hair had been combed perfectly, and she wore a light touch of makeup. Today, she had on a summery dress in a cheerful pattern of watermelon slices and a pale-green cardigan. "I haven't lowered the price, if that's why you're here."

"I'm sorry to hear that, but that's not why I've come. I wanted to show you the photograph I mentioned last time that was found on a dresser in your house," Charlotte said, removing it from her handbag. She held it out to Mrs. Middleton, who reluctantly took it, glanced at it, and turned it facedown on her lap.

"Is your daughter Joanna the little blonde girl?" Charlotte began. Mrs. Middleton nodded.

"And the other girl. The dark-haired one. Was she your daughter, too?"

Mrs. Middleton nodded again.

"Did her name start with the letter *P*?" Mrs. Middleton did not reply and made no sign of having heard.

"Is that your daughter?" Charlotte repeated.

"Yes, that's my daughter." She let out the longest, saddest sigh Charlotte had ever heard and then said, in a voice drenched in resignation, "Phyllis. Phyllis was—is, I guess I should say—my daughter. We haven't spoken in many years. Not since, well, since it happened."

"Phyllis? What happened?"

"She got pregnant. Only sixteen she was. You think times have changed, but thirty-odd years ago in a small town, there was still a lot of talk when the daughter of a prominent lawyer gets pregnant. Especially when he's running for political office. And everyone gossiping about who the father was, and then when the child was born, there was no doubt. There was no hiding it."

And then it all fell into place. Alex, the young woman with the lovely head of springy blonde curls, who acted as a server at Paula Van Dusen's parties, is Phyllis's daughter. The same woman they'd discovered in the Middleton house just last night.

"And her father is . . ."

"A young lawyer who had then recently joined my husband's law firm. And my husband blamed his own daughter instead of his new employee."

"Joseph Lamb?"

"Yes."

"Did he know about the baby?"

"Of course he did. But he denied it was his."

"But he's looking after your house!"

"That was all laid out in my husband's will. He made all the decisions. He decided what was going to happen because he always knew what was best for us. And when he found out Phyllis was in the family way, he threw her out and told us we weren't to speak of her again or have anything to do with her. She named her child Alex after her father. Maybe she hoped that would soften him a little toward her, but of course it didn't." She dabbed at her watery blue eyes with a crumpled-up tissue. "Appalling when you think of it."

"But she didn't go far."

"No, old Mrs. Van Dusen, that's Paula's mother-in-law, she very kindly took her in and gave her a job."

"But that's all in the past now, Mrs. Middleton. Everything happened such a long time ago. Couldn't you reach out to Phyllis now, and your granddaughter, and try to put things right?"

"No," replied Mrs. Middleton. "Not now. I don't think I could now."

"But why?"

"Let's just say I have my reasons."

"This is all such a lot to take in," said Charlotte. "You've had to live with some terrible memories." They sat for several minutes, saying nothing. And then, as an idea slowly dawned, Charlotte asked, "Did Phyllis have a dog?"

"She did. Oh, how she loved that dog. Meant everything to her. And then when she got pregnant, her father got rid of the dog to punish her. She was devastated. Heartbroken." She shook her head slightly and looked away, unable to meet Charlotte's eyes. "I was never sure what happened. He said he gave it away, and I hope he did, but . . ."

Not permitting herself to go where that train of thought wanted to lead her, Charlotte asked, "And this dog. Was it a white poodle called Bella, by any chance?"

Mrs. Middleton gave her a bemused look. "How did you know?"

Wanting to take Mrs. Middleton's hand, but afraid the gesture would seem too familiar, Charlotte leaned forward.

"Mrs. Middleton, you've been very open with me about things in your past that are very painful to you. Why are you telling me all this? You barely know me."

"Because I've wanted to talk about them for a very long time. Who could I talk to? My husband?" She made a little *pfft* of disgust. "He managed our household by fear and intimidation. One of those strict, God-fearing men that terrorize everyone they come in contact with. My greatest regret is that I didn't stand up to him. He was such a tyrant. In a way, I'm glad Phyllis got out when she did. Joanna left home as soon as she could, and I had another twenty years of him."

"Couldn't you have left him?"

"Women like us didn't do that in those days. We were expected to stick it out."

"About the photograph," Charlotte said. "Alex has been sneaking into the house. I think she left it on a dresser in your bedroom."

"Why would she do that?"

"Maybe to validate her and her mother's place in the household that disowned them. Maybe it was her way of trying to repair the pain that's hurt two generations. Maybe to send you a message." She paused as if she was about to say something else and then thought better of it, so she ended by simply saying, "I don't know. Something for you to think about, maybe." She held out her hand. "Do you want me to take the photo away?"

Mrs. Middleton's hands closed around it. "No, you can leave it with me."

"We've both got a lot to think about. You look tired. I should go. But one thing before I leave. I did speak to the police about Joanna's death, and if they reopen the case, they will likely want to talk to you again. Would you be willing to tell them what you suspect?"

Mrs. Middleton closed her eyes. "Talk to me again?" she said. "They never talked to me at all. Why should they? I'm only her mother. Nobody listens to old people. What do we know?"

Charlotte stood up, and Mrs. Middleton's eyes fluttered open.

"I hope you'll come back and see me again soon. We could have a cup of tea. We could talk about other, nicer things. You could tell me all about the theater. I wanted to take the girls, but he wouldn't let us. It would have been so nice for them."

Charlotte touched her blue-veined hand. "I'd like that."

# Chapter 31

"Paula told me to pick up the dress boxes anytime, so I'd like to go to Oakland now and get them," said Charlotte when she got back in the car. "One more thing off the to-do list. But you've waited around for me long enough today, so why don't you drop me off and I'll make my own way home?"

"Okay," said Aaron. "How did the visit go? Did you find out what you wanted to know?"

"She gave me a lot to think about. So much, I hardly know where to start." They rode in silence, each lost in thought, until Aaron dropped her off at the now-familiar front door of Oakland. As he drove off, she walked to the side of the house and surveyed the garden. The tenting that had covered the spot where Hugh Hedley's body had been found was gone, and a figure kneeled on the grass close to where it had been. *Ned*, she thought, *restoring order to his garden now that the police have finished trampling all over it.*

She returned to the front of the house and rang the doorbell.

After what seemed a longer wait than usual, the door opened slowly, and Phyllis peered cautiously out; seeing who it was, she opened the door wider and invited her in.

"Sorry to bother you, but I've just come to pick up the boxes I forgot to take home last time," Charlotte said.

"If you wouldn't mind just waiting in the hall here, I'll get them for you. We're having a very busy day, but I shouldn't be long. I just have to deliver an urgent message to the kitchen."

Charlotte crossed the black-and-white marble floor and admired an arrangement of showy roses on an inlaid round table. Something Phyllis had just said was ricocheting around in her brain. *Message. What message?*

Suddenly, a memory came to her. She struggled to retrieve it.

*"He said to give you his apologies, but he had to leave just before the play ended."*

That's what Phyllis had said to Paula as they'd made their way into the house after the play, but she must have been lying, because Joseph Lamb said Hugh did not return to his seat after the intermission, and the police hadn't been able to find anyone, in that whole crowd, who had seen him during the second half of the play.

At the sound of approaching footsteps, she turned, and, expecting to see Phyllis with the garment boxes, was dismayed to see Alex, carrying a small cardboard box.

"What are you doing here?" Alex demanded. "Haven't you caused enough trouble for us?" She set the box down and stood in front of Charlotte, arms folded and eyes blazing.

Charlotte's mouth went dry. "I didn't expect to see you here. I thought they'd have held you . . ."

"Why would they hold me? I've only been charged with theft," Alex sneered.

"Look, I'm just here to pick up a couple of dresses, and then I'll ring for a ride into town," Charlotte said. "In fact, I'll ring now. By the time he gets here . . ." Her voice trailed off as Phyllis arrived carrying the dress boxes. "Oh, good, here they are." And then, instead of just walking away, she heard herself blurting out, "Phyllis, I just want to ask you something."

"Ask me what?" said Phyllis in a flat, even tone. Charlotte scanned her face, and in her eyes she saw nothing. No interest, no concern, no hope.

"Did you tell the police you'd seen Hugh Hedley during the second half of the performance? Because you implied in your message to Mrs. Van Dusen that you had. And if you did see him, you need to tell the police."

Phyllis's eyes darted to her daughter, as if looking for an answer.

"She knows," Alex hissed to her mother, reaching into her box and pulling out a roll of duct tape. "Look what I just happen to have. Today's my lucky day, but it might not be yours."

Charlotte ran toward the door, but Alex got there first, blocking it.

"Now it's my turn to tie you up," she snarled. "Hold out your hands and let's see how you like it." With her heart pounding and brain racing, Charlotte looked around wildly. "Give me your hands," repeated Alex, grabbing them. Charlotte winced as Alex wound duct tape several times around her wrists and then used her thumb and forefinger to rip it off the roll. Satisfied that Charlotte was tightly bound, she ordered her mother to open the door.

"You don't want to do this," Charlotte protested as they pushed her out the front door. "It won't work, and it won't get you anywhere."

"How much do you know? And when did you figure it out?"

Charlotte stopped and faced them. "Well, I'm not so stupid that I'd come here on my own to face two murderers," she said, "but when you said 'message' just then, Phyllis, everything came together. I connected your message with what Joseph Lamb told me."

Phyllis flinched at the mention of his name, but Charlotte continued.

"He said Hugh Hedley never returned after the intermission, but you told Mrs. Van Dusen that Hugh asked you to give her a message saying he had to leave just before the play ended. Yet nobody saw him for the second half of the play. And I think that's because you and Alex had already killed him. I know that you're June Middleton's daughter. If Hugh was out of the way, you hoped you and

Alex would inherit your mother's house and estate. Which I imagine is quite sizeable."

Alex and Phyllis exchanged glances.

"I think you lured Hugh away from the party on some pretext or other, killed him, then carried his body into the garden." She turned to Alex. "It was you I saw running across the garden that night, wasn't it Alex? You stole the donkey head and placed it on Hugh to humiliate him. And then you changed into your fairy costume and served the champagne as if nothing had happened." She shifted her gaze to Phyllis. "Both of you. That must have taken nerves of steel."

Out of the corner of her eye, she detected a small movement farther down the garden. *Keep talking*, she thought.

But Alex had other ideas. She grabbed Charlotte roughly by her arm and pulled her forward. "Come on," she said. "Let's go." With one woman on each side of her, they steered her to the edge of the house and around the corner into the garden.

Ned, who had been working his way up the flower bed, was much closer now and trundled toward them with his wheelbarrow.

Charlotte called his name.

Ned caught on and advanced toward the women, brandishing his shears. "Step away from her!" he shouted. Charlotte raised her hands above her head and, keeping her elbows together, swung them down below her hips as hard as she could. The duct tape ripped apart, freeing her hands.

"Oh, Ned, am I ever glad to see you!" she said. As Phyllis and Alex tried to run to the front of the building, Ray Nicholson appeared.

"What's going on?" He grabbed Phyllis, and when he had her, Alex stopped running.

"How did the police get here so quickly?" Ned asked in amazement. "Holy moley, that's good work."

"Aaron happened to mention when he dropped off my key that Charlotte was picking up a couple of boxes here and needed a ride home, so I came to get her."

"How did you get in?" Ned asked. "Who opened the gates?"

"I did," said Paula Van Dusen, joining the group. "Would someone like to tell me what on earth's going on?"

"Ray's here to arrest Phyllis and Alex for the murder of Hugh Hedley," said Charlotte. "And I just came to pick up those dress boxes."

"Oh, dear God," said Paula Van Dusen. "Is there no end to this?"

"Not yet," said Ray. "There'll be more police arriving for these two."

*

Ray loaded the boxes into the back seat of the police car, and Charlotte climbed into the passenger side.

"Really," he said, "tell me the truth. Are you okay?"

"I'm fine," she said. "It was scary enough, but I didn't think for a minute they were going to kill me."

"Why not?"

"In broad daylight, with Paula Van Dusen likely to show up any minute? And I don't think Phyllis has it in her. She's so defeated. I don't know what they were thinking. It was just the last desperate act of two women who never stood much of a chance."

Ray looked at Charlotte's wrists, still red from the duct tape. "Criminals love tying up victims with duct tape. It's fast and easy, not to mention cheap. You'd be surprised how many dead bodies we find with duct tape on them. I don't understand how you managed to get out of it."

"Oh, it was just some self-defense video I saw online," she grinned. "You hold your hands high above your head and swing them down, and the tape comes off." She turned her hands palm up. "It works, apparently. I'll show you when we get home. It might come in handy for you one day, too."

*

Ray set the dress boxes on the bed and turned to Charlotte, taking her in his arms. "I'd never forgive myself if anything ever happened to you," he said. She nodded into his chest, and a moment later, he released her.

"Drink?" he asked.

"Glass of wine, I think. But first, I'm going to take a shower."

Half an hour later, wrapped in a terry robe and seated on the sofa, Charlotte took a grateful sip of wine.

"So you gave June Middleton the photograph?" Ray asked. "Why would you do that?"

"Because it was hers, and she wanted it," Charlotte replied, licking her lips.

"Well, there goes our B&E case against you and Aaron," said Ray.

"So I guess Bartucci and Adrian Archer are in the clear."

"Their alibis were sketchy, to say the least. They were both trying to hide something. Archer did spend the night with another woman, and Bartucci was at a jewelry store, picking out a surprise for his wife's birthday, which naturally he didn't want her to know about."

"I thought he said he was at an event."

"He was. He slipped out for an hour or so. No one noticed except his wife, and she wasn't going to say anything, was she? And anyway, he wasn't gone nearly long enough to get up here, kill Hedley, then get back to the city. The state police have been investigating Bartucci pretty thoroughly, though, and although they've cleared him for this murder, they've turned up lots of interesting stuff about his business operations."

"I can believe that. Manhattan real estate is a crazy world of insane amounts of money." Charlotte finished her wine. "I'll get dressed while you make dinner."

*

Charlotte lifted the two dress boxes onto the bed and opened the first one. It contained the torn dress Belinda had worn to the after party. She fingered the light material, unsure what she could do with it but certain that she'd find a good use for it sooner or later.

And then she folded back the tissue paper on the second one and gasped. A compliments card, with Oakland engraved on the top, tucked inside read, "I know you loved this, and it would look beautiful on you. Belinda x."

She gently lifted out the tea-length wedding dress she had fitted for Belinda. Smiling, she held it in front of herself and pirouetted in front of the mirror.

"Dinner will be ready in ten minutes," Ray called.

Charlotte carefully folded the dress, tucked it back in the box, folded the tissue paper around it, and placed the box on the top shelf of her closet.

# Chapter 32

It was a perfect summer evening. Bright sunshine had warmed Paula Van Dusen's elegant garden, and now as a light breeze caressed the fragrant floribunda pink-and-red roses, guests were arriving for her annual Fourth of July barbecue.

Under a red, white, and blue marquee with open sides, bartenders in cheerful straw boaters dispensed glasses of beer and wine, along with cold lemonade and soft drinks. Alongside the tent, stretching toward the back of the garden, hamburgers and hot dogs were being cooked to order on long metal barbecues. Tables groaning with salads and corn on the cob had been set up, along with tables and chairs, in front of a small stage where a Dixieland jazz band was performing. The atmosphere was festive and fun. Charlotte, Ray, and Aaron found a table and sat down.

Paula Van Dusen wafted across the lawn, waving and smiling at friends to the strains of "Bill Bailey, Won't You Please Come Home." Charlotte broke into a broad smile.

As Paula reached their table, Charlotte jumped out of her chair and bent down to pet the pretty red-and-white corgi puppy Paula had on a red leather leash.

Paula greeted Charlotte warmly. "I didn't want to tell you about her," she said, smiling at the dog. "Wanted you to meet her in person. I just got her last week. Her name's Coco."

"She's adorable," smiled Charlotte. "I'm so happy for both of you. This is such a wonderful place for a dog to live—all this beautiful garden to explore. And you look very good together, I must say."

"Shall we walk?" Paula asked. Charlotte exchanged a quick look with Ray and strolled off with Paula. "Coco's been wonderful company, since all that awful business happened with Phyllis and her daughter. We were all so shocked, but I guess when you think about it, this unhappiness has been building up inside her for years. All that anger and resentment against her father. I gather her mother was powerless to do anything to help her. I hope the law will go easy on her."

"I think you told me once that your mother-in-law hired her?" Charlotte said.

"Yes. She heard about the trouble Phyllis was in—Mrs. Middleton, I think, must have appealed to her when her father threw her out—and offered her a job here at Oakland. Then she found her a little place in town to live after the baby was born. It's awful to think how girls and young women were treated in the not-so-distant past."

"That's almost word for word what her mother said. Speaking of which, I see the Middleton house has been taken off the market."

"Yes," said Paula. "I noticed that too. I wonder what the new owners will do with it. Anyway, I've got more news, and I'm going to need your help. Belinda and Adrian."

Charlotte laughed. "Oh, I'm sorry. I shouldn't laugh. But it isn't on again, is it?"

Paula gave a sheepish grin. "Yes, it's on again, despite everything. I've tried to tell her, but what do I know? I'm just her mother."

"Oh, well. 'The course of true love never did run smooth.' And the wedding . . . will it be here at Oakland? Going to give them another chance, are you?"

"Certainly not. They can make their own arrangements in Manhattan or wherever they like. I'll go, of course, but I'm not putting it on for them. Well, I say that now. The thing is, they're thinking about December. A Christmas wedding. So we're going to need new dresses for the bridesmaids, and of course Belinda needs a winter wedding dress, so I wondered if you'd ask Aaron if he'd be kind enough to . . ." Charlotte hesitated. Aaron hadn't been paid yet, and she wasn't sure how to broach the subject. But she didn't have to. Paula handed her an envelope. "Give him this and ask him to think about another commission and let me know. I think he'll find it's quite generous."

"Right."

"I was very sorry to hear Brian's had to go back to the UK."

"Yes, I feel rather guilty. With all that rapid weight loss, we should have recognized it was something more serious, but I thought it was just because he'd given up drinking. Anyway, he's in the best place now to get treatment."

"Must be leaving you in the lurch."

"Well, his understudy is happy to take over for now, and Brian suggested that a friend of his might be interested in joining us for the fall season. I can't say who she is yet, because details aren't finalized, but if she does join us, it will be something, I can tell you. She's very well known and will be a huge boost for the company. And the area, too."

"Oh, please tell me! I won't breathe a word."

"Well, actually, if she does come, we're going to need your help with a project. The current star accommodation—the shabby, old bungalow—just won't suit, so something else will have to be done for her. She's a major star."

"Oh, who is she? Let me guess!" Paula Van Dusen rattled off a few names of prominent British actresses who had made big names for themselves in the theater.

Charlotte laughed and shook her head. "No, good guesses, but none of those. It's . . ." She moved a little closer to Paula, lowered her head, and whispered the name of an actress whose career had soared to stratospheric heights over the past few years with a period drama that had earned huge international success.

Paula gasped and covered her mouth with her hand.

"Really! Oh, my God! That's incredible. We must roll out the red carpet for her. When does she arrive?"

"Paula! It isn't final yet, so you have to promise me you won't say anything! When you hear officially, you must act surprised—just like you did then."

They made their way back to the table, and Paula moved on to mingle with the rest of her guests.

The garden was filling up, and among the crowd, Belinda and Adrian strolled by, hand in hand.

Aaron tracked their progression, turned to his friends at the table, and laughingly said, "'Lord, what fools these mortals be!'"

# *Acknowledgments*

Thank you to Rupert, the loveable corgi who turned out to be the star of this series, to his mom, Deb Reid, for lending his name, and to the greater corgi community for their support. I couldn't have chosen a better dog for Charlotte.

At Crooked Lane Books, my thanks to Matthew Martz, Heather Boak, and especially Sarah Poppe for her thoughtful edits. In Toronto, Sheila Fletcher's editing and proofreading contributions were brilliant.

I'm grateful to my agent, Dominick Abel, for his wise counsel, and finally I thank my son, Lucas Walker, and his partner, Riley Wallbank, for their love and encouragement.

Read an excerpt from

# *MUCH ADO ABOUT MURDER*

the next

# *SHAKESPEARE IN THE CATSKILLS MYSTERY*

***by Elizabeth J. Duncan***

available soon in hardcover from
Crooked Lane Books

# Chapter 1

*Car arriving now.* Charlotte Fairfax read the text out loud to her companion and added, "They're here. Show time."

Paula Van Dusen adjusted the curtains one last time, allowing a wider band of late afternoon sunlight to spill into the sitting room and illuminate the vase of exuberant pink-and-white roses cut from her own garden that she had carefully positioned on the mahogany side table. After ensuring the silver spoons on the tea tray were lined up precisely, she took a deep breath, stepped back, and surveyed the room.

"I hope they like it."

"They'd better," Charlotte replied. "And I can't see why they wouldn't."

The two women, who had spent the afternoon arranging furniture and putting the finishing touches on their redecoration project, closed the door of the star bungalow and fell into step on the path that led to the front entrance of Jacobs Grand Hotel.

"Do you think it was wise to bring Rupert?" Paula Van Dusen asked, referring to the tricolor corgi trotting along between them. "What if she doesn't like dogs?"

"Of course she likes dogs," Charlotte replied. "She's English."

"Well, being English yourself, you should know," replied Paula.

They reached the graveled drop-off area in front of the hotel to find Harvey Jacobs, the hotel's third-generation owner, standing at the top of the white-stuccoed steps. Wearing an old-fashioned three-piece suit, his thumbs tucked in the pockets of the pinstripe vest that strained across his well-upholstered stomach, he shifted his weight from one small foot to the other.

He acknowledged the two women as they took their places on a lower step, and a moment later, a gleaming burgundy Rolls-Royce glided to a slow stop in front of them. The little welcoming party waited while the chauffeur emerged from the driver's seat, opened the rear door closest to them, and stood to one side, touching the visor of his gray cap. A long leg clad in a black stocking and a sleek black pump emerged from the back seat, followed by the other leg and then the rest of an elegant woman. When she was out of the car, the chauffeur ambled around the back of the vehicle and opened the other passenger door for the last occupant, a short woman who wore her gray hair in a trim pageboy style. Her mouth drooped at the corners, accentuated by a sagging jawline, giving her a stern, unintended contemptuous look. She wore dark shapeless trousers and a pale-blue cardigan, with a beige raincoat draped over her left arm. In her right hand, she held a battered brown leather briefcase.

When the new arrivals were standing together beside the car, Paula Van Dusen stepped forward and extended her hand to the first woman. In her early fifties, Paula wore her dark hair pulled back in a tidy chignon. Her complexion was smooth and unlined, and she looked like the kind of woman who could wear red lipstick until the end of her days. She carried herself with an air of confident authority, as if she was used to asking for what she wanted in a way that was polite but firm and always got the result she expected.

"Miss Ashley. Hello. I'm Paula Van Dusen, chairperson of the board of directors of the Catskills Shakespeare Theater Company, and it's my very great pleasure to welcome you. Our cast and crew are so looking forward to working with you."

"Thank you," Audrey Ashley replied in a clipped, precise English accent. "And may I introduce my sister and manager, Maxine Kaminski."

Paula held out her hand to the other woman. "I hope you had a good journey from London. It's a long flight. You must both be exhausted."

"It has been a long day," Audrey Ashley acknowledged, "especially when you factor in the five-hour time difference."

"Of course." Paula Van Dusen gestured to her companion, who took a step forward. "And now I'd like you to meet Charlotte Fairfax, our company's costume designer."

When the women had greeted one another, Paula Van Dusen indicated to the man on the steps that it was his turn to be introduced. "And this is Harvey Jacobs, owner of the hotel."

"Miss Ashley," gushed Harvey, descending the stairs nimbly, considering his weight. "Welcome to Jacobs Grand Hotel. We hope you'll be very happy during your stay here with us." He nodded at her companion. "And you too, of course, Miss, er . . ." His words trailed off and ended in an embarrassed little cough.

"Thank you. That's very kind," Audrey Ashley replied, turning her gaze to the white-frame building behind him. Her head tilted back slightly as her eyes roamed upward over the three stories.

She then directed her wide-set blue-violet eyes to Charlotte's corgi.

"And who's this?" She bent over and gave the dog a friendly pat. Over Audrey's head of frosty-blonde curls, Charlotte threw Paula Van Dusen a rather smug I-told-you-so glance.

"That's Rupert," she said. Rupert waggled his bottom in his usual friendly fashion.

"Oh, what a lovely little fellow." Audrey straightened up. "And now, if you wouldn't mind showing us to our suite, please. I must admit, I am rather starting to fade."

"You'll be staying in our star bungalow," Harvey said. "We'll have your bags delivered in just a few minutes. These ladies will be happy to take you there now and help you get settled in."

"Oh, a bungalow! How charming. Like at the Beverly Hills Hotel, you mean?" she asked, referring to the famous Los Angeles hotel where the grounds were dotted with hill-side and poolside bungalows, and the likes of Marilyn Monroe, Elizabeth Taylor, and Richard Burton had partied.

"Yes, well, sort of." Harvey ran a pudgy finger around his sweaty collar. "I guess you could say that."

As Paula, Maxine, and Audrey set off for the bungalow, he hissed to Charlotte, "Have you seen Aaron? He was meant to be here to help with the arrival of the star actress."

"He must be nearby," Charlotte said. "He sent me a text letting me know they'd arrived, and since you're here, you must have got the text from him as well."

"When I get my hands on that boy . . ."

"Never mind that now. You've got to calm down," said Charlotte. "Look, here he comes," she added, tipping her head in the direction of the wooded parkland adjacent to the hotel. "There's no problem, so don't make this into one. Paula's more than capable of looking after Audrey and Maxine for a few minutes."

Slightly out of breath, Aaron lurched to a stop beside Charlotte and his uncle. Aaron was in his early twenties and had a head of dark curly hair and unremarkable but pleasant features. He had studied fashion design at Parsons in New York City but, after interning with Charlotte, had decided to pursue a career in costume design.

"Did you want me to carry the bags to the bungalow?" he asked.

"Yes," said his uncle. "That's the general idea." The chauffeur, who was staring into the trunk of his vehicle, breathed a sigh of relief when Aaron materialized and easily lifted four pieces of matching luggage in a timeless brown pattern and two plain black suitcases out of the car and set them on the gravel.

"Well, if there's nothing else, I'd best get back inside," Harvey said. "No point in hanging 'round here. Nancy's got plenty of things lined up to keep me busy for the rest of the day." He disappeared into the hotel, and Charlotte turned her attention to Paula Van Dusen's chauffeur, Barnes.

Tall and thin, he carried himself with a shoulders-back, no-nonsense posture that hinted at a military background. Although his employer had told him several times he could wear a plain dark suit, he proudly opted to remain in the traditional gray chauffeur's uniform with the double row of gold buttons that started wide at the shoulders and tapered as they descended toward the bottom of the jacket. A small gray mustache clung to his upper lip with the tenacity of an elderly centipede. His eyes were hidden behind dark-green aviator sunglasses.

"Barnes, I don't know how much longer Mrs. Van Dusen will be. So it might be best if you parked around the side of the hotel, and if you go inside to the staff cafeteria, they'll be happy to give you a cup of coffee while you wait for her," Charlotte said.

"A piece of pie wouldn't go amiss. This hotel used to serve the best homemade pies in the Catskills. People came from all over to have a piece of pie and a cup of coffee in the little coffee shop they had." Barnes let out a resigned sigh. "Long gone, of course. But then nothing nowadays is as good as it used to be."

"I'm sure they'll be happy to give you a piece of pie or cake, or whatever they've got," Charlotte assured him.

Barnes climbed back in the car, and as he drove slowly off, Aaron set the two black suitcases beside the stairs, picked up the two brown ones, and with Charlotte in charge of the matching carryall and beauty case, they set off down the path to the star bungalow.

In the hotel's heyday, the three bungalows in the grounds were occupied by vacationing families, but two were now home to members of the Catskills Shakespeare Theater Company: Charlotte and her partner, Ray, lived in one, and the second was included in the contract of the director, currently Simon Dyer. The third, known as the star bungalow, provided on-site accommodation for the season's star performer.

The star performer position was filled by a British actor or actress who still had several seasons of good performances ahead of them but was no longer the box office draw in the United Kingdom they had once been. On this side of the Atlantic, however, with the cachet of a polished British accent, they had box office clout. The previous star, who had been forced to return home to England for medical treatment, had suggested as his replacement an actress whose long and distinguished career had undergone a huge boost over the past few years when she portrayed a crusty dowager in a popular television costume drama. But concerned about the travel and time away from home, she had declined, recommending a colleague who had played a scheming servant in the same series.

The Catskills Shakespeare Theater Company normally performed three plays per season: two comedies and one tragedy. The spring and summer seasons had seen *Romeo and Juliet*, *King Lear*, and *A Midsummer Night's Dream* in repertoire. However, with the departure of the lead actor, it had been decided that the company would drop all three plays from the fall schedule and replace them with an exclusive run of *Much Ado About Nothing*.

And so, Audrey Ashley had agreed to play the part of Beatrice in *Much Ado*. A seasoned performer in her midforties who had enjoyed great popularity as a child actress, she had transitioned successfully into adult roles, and although she had timed out of playing some of the more youthful of Shakespeare's female roles and was at the outer edge of others, with soft lighting and a well-designed costume, she could still take on many of the best parts. Theater audiences, after all, agree at every performance to suspend disbelief and to believe the unbelievable.

Charlotte knocked on the door of the star bungalow, and a moment later, Paula Van Dusen answered it.

"You can leave the bags just there," Paula Van Dusen instructed Aaron as he and Charlotte entered the kitchen. "Thank you. Charlotte and I can manage from here." Aaron set the suitcases down, and Charlotte indicated he should return to the hotel to fetch the remaining luggage.

Charlotte picked up two large suitcases, carried them through the sitting room, and deposited them in the larger of the two bedrooms. Over the past three weeks, the bungalow had undergone a complete but somewhat unintentional refurbishment, as a bit of freshening up had led to a complete makeover.

Paula Van Dusen had sent workers from Oakland, her magnificent estate located a few miles outside town, to smarten everything up. Old flooring had been ripped up and new carpets and hardwood flooring laid, and a new kitchen and bathroom installed. The property had been painted inside and out, and clean, bright rooms were now filled with new, comfortable furniture.

Fortunately, Paula Van Dusen knew a lot of tradesmen and had called in so many favors that almost all the goods and services had been donated. And she herself had loaned one or two pieces of fine furniture and artwork to dress the sitting room.

Although the work had been done under pressure to ensure the rooms were ready for Audrey's arrival, Paula Van Dusen had seen to it that the work had been done right.

"You did a great job overseeing this project, Paula," Charlotte said when Paula appeared in the bedroom doorway with the lighter bags. She set them down and crossed to the window.

"It would have been better if we'd had a couple of days to air everything out," Paula said. "The smell of the paint and new carpet is almost overpowering." She unlocked the newly installed window and opened it. It slid easily along in its track, and a warm blast of late summer air drifted in. Charlotte ran a smoothing hand over the new coverlet on the queen-sized bed, and the two women returned to the sitting room.

Having slipped off her shoes, Audrey had settled herself in the sitting room, and thanks to the restorative properties of Earl Grey tea, had perked up a little. The plate of Scottish shortbread biscuits on the tea table remained untouched. Maxine hovered near her, ready to relieve her of the cup and saucer.

"I hope you aren't allergic to paint or carpeting," Paula commented. "That awful chemical smell they give off when they're new really bothers some people. Unfortunately, we were working to a very tight deadline, and there wasn't time to get the place aired out properly." Audrey handed her empty cup to Maxine and sank back into the comfort of the new dove-gray sofa. After lifting her stockinged feet onto the ottoman, she reclined fully, motionless, with her eyes closed.

"The smell is rather noticeable," she said, "but I can live with it. I expect we'll get used to it, and besides, it should go away soon." Her eyes remained closed. They had been expertly made up, with a light touch of blended mauve eye shadow, brown eyeliner, and mascara so finely applied it was difficult to tell whether she was wearing false eyelashes. Her brows were beautifully shaped. *She's older than she looks,* Charlotte thought. *And she's definitely had a little work done around the eyes, and maybe the jawline.* But it was well done, subtle, and whoever had done it had known when to stop. The result took ten years off her.

"Well, we'll leave you to settle in," Charlotte said. "There's a house phone on the end table, and my number is right beside it. Just dial the four digits if you need me. I'm in the bungalow nearest the hotel. It's the first one we passed on the way here. Oh, and we've got in a few groceries for you . . . milk, butter, coffee, cheese, eggs, strawberries, bread . . . that sort of thing, so you can make yourself a light supper. Or, if you prefer, you can ring the hotel and they'll send something over."

Audrey's eyelids fluttered open. "Thank you. I'd like a bath and then a quiet evening and early night. I expect I'll be meeting the director tomorrow, and we can start discussing how he envisions my role."

"Oh, I'm sorry," said Charlotte. "I should have explained that to you. Our director, Simon Dyer, asked me to pass on his apologies. He wanted to be here to greet you and he would have been, but he had to leave suddenly for a family bereavement in Colorado. We're expecting him back within the next day or two. In the meantime, he's asked that we schedule costume fittings for you. And in case he's delayed longer, he's left notes for Aaron, our stage manager, so we can get a rehearsal or two under way."

Audrey shifted her position so she could see her sister. The corners of Maxine's mouth sagged into a formidable scowl, but she said nothing.

"It's a bereavement, Maxine. He had no choice. He had to go. We'll just have to make the best of it."

"Exactly," said Charlotte. "Well, we'll leave you to it. And as I said, call me if you need anything."

*

Charlotte and Paula Van Dusen strolled the short distance to Charlotte's bungalow. "Drink?" Charlotte asked.

"I don't know about you, but I need one."

Although Charlotte had known about the influential and wealthy Van Dusen family for years, and Paula had been involved with the board of directors and fundraising activities of the theater, the two women had got to know each other just a few months earlier when a body had been found in the garden of Oakland, following the theater company's outdoor performance of *A Midsummer Night's Dream*.

With a new British star joining the company, Paula had offered to take on the refurbishing of the bungalow. She'd been on site almost every day, giving orders and checking that deliveries arrived on time, and during the course of the project, she and Charlotte became friends. Paula was lonely, and in Charlotte she had found someone who didn't want or need anything from her. Not her name to lend to a cause, not her time, and above all, not her money. Charlotte had no agenda and wasn't interested in what Paula could do for her. Paula had found that hugely refreshing and had been drawn to Charlotte for her honesty, sophistication, sense of humor, and common sense.

While Paula fetched a bottle of gin from the drinks table in Charlotte's sitting room, Charlotte placed two highball glasses on the counter, opened the fridge, and pulled out a can of tonic. She stepped aside while Paula added a few ice cubes from the door dispenser to the glasses and assembled the drinks.

"I don't suppose you've got any limes?" Paula asked. "For a wedge to add to the drinks."

"Sorry, no. But I'll get some in for next time. There's a lemon, though. Will that do?"

"Certainly." When she'd added a lemon wedge to each drink, Paula asked, "Where would you like to sit?"

"How about outside? It's such a lovely afternoon."

When they were settled in Adirondack chairs positioned at the front of the bungalow to overlook the river, Charlotte asked Paula what she thought of Audrey.

"She seemed nice enough, but it's hard to tell. I would imagine there's a lot of stress involved in starting a new job where you don't know anybody. She's joining a company that's already jelled. And then there was the disappointment of the director not being here to meet her, and she's just got in from a long flight."

"Speaking of the flight, it was awfully good of you to send Barnes to meet them at the airport. I'm sure Maxine thought driving from JFK to the Catskills in a vintage Roller is exactly the way Audrey should be treated."

Paula smiled. "Well, I thought it would get things off to a good start. Her joining our little company was all very last minute, and it was fortunate, I thought, that she was available and agreed to come here." She paused for a moment to consider what she'd just said. "I'm sorry, maybe that didn't come out right. I didn't mean . . ."

Charlotte laughed good-naturedly. "I know what you meant, and I thought the same thing. She's been a big star in the UK since she was a child—what on earth does she want with a small Shakespeare theater company affiliated with a Catskills hotel in upstate New York? She'd play Broadway in a heartbeat, of course, but the likes of us here in Walkers Ridge? Still, we might seem like a small, underfunded company, but we are professional and we've got a solid reputation. We're proud of the work we do. We manage to create a little more magic with a lot less budget than most companies have to work with."

She paused for a moment, then continued. "And many young actors who are serious about getting into traditional theater want to start their careers with us for the training and discipline. We get far more applications than we have room for.

"As for Audrey, we'll find out in due course what really brought her here. In my experience, most of the older actors are either running away from something or have nothing left to lose. But there's a third group, and these are the ones who bring joy. For them, the opportunities may have dried up, but they still want to perform. They want to continue to practice their craft in front of an audience, and they aren't bothered by how much it pays, how big the audience is, or how grand the theater."

"There're some curtains in the barn. Let's put on a show!" said Paula.

"Exactly. But the thing is, they're all in it for something. So we'll see what brings Audrey here. She'll have a good reason." Charlotte took a sip and smacked her lips with a satisfied *Ah* as the crisp lemony drink caught the back of her throat and infused her senses. "I wonder why gin is considered a summery drink when it tastes the way a Christmas tree smells," she remarked.

"No idea," said Paula as she drained the last of her drink and stood up. "To me it tastes all-year-round-ish. I'm going to fix myself another one. How about you? Are you ready for another?"

Charlotte shook her head. "No, just the one for me, thanks."

"I'll just have a small one, and then I'd better see what Barnes is up to. It's been a long day for him, at his age. Normally, he hates turnpike driving. He just likes meandering along our little two-lane blacktop highways, but he seemed quite keen at the prospect of picking up Audrey from the airport."

With a small sigh, Paula disappeared around the side of the bungalow and through the door that opened into the kitchen.

Charlotte leaned back in her chair and closed her eyes. Normally careful about sun exposure, she was enjoying the sensation of the late afternoon sun warming her face when her phone rang. She answered and listened for a few seconds, then, her body stiffening, she straightened up in her chair and asked a series of pointed questions. As she ended the call, Paula returned and slid into the chair beside her.

"We've got a problem," Charlotte said. "A big one. I'll have that drink after all."